Beach Bags
and
Burglaries

DOROTHY
HOWELL

KENSINGTON BOOKS
http://www.kensingtonbooks.com

KENSINGTON BOOKS are published by

Kensington Publishing Corp.
119 West 40th Street
New York, NY 10018

All Kensington titles, imprints, and distributed lines are available at special quantity discounts for bulk purchases for sales promotion, premiums, fund-raising, educational, or institutional use. Special book excerpts or customized printings can also be created to fit specific needs. For details, write or phone the office of the Kensington Special Sales Manager: Attn. Special Sales Department. Kensington Publishing Corp., 119 West 40th Street, New York, NY 10018. Phone: 1-800-221-2647.

Kensington and the K logo Reg. U.S. Pat. & TM Off.

ISBN-13: 978-0-7582-9496-8
ISBN-10: 0-7582-9496-4
First Kensington Hardcover Edition: August 2014
First Kensington Mass Market Edition: September 2015

eISBN-13: 978-0-7582-9497-5
eISBN-10: 0-7582-9497-2
Kensington Electronic Edition: September 2015

10 9 8 7 6 5 4 3 2 1

Printed in the United States of America

With love to David, Stacy, Judy, Brian, and Seth

Acknowledgments

The author is extremely grateful for the love, support, and encouragement of many people. Some of them are: David Howell, Stacy Howell, Judith Branstetter, Brian Branstetter, Seth Branstetter, Martha Cooper, and William F. Wu, Ph.D.

Many thanks to Evan Marshall of the Evan Marshall Agency, and John Scognamiglio and the talented team at Kensington Books for all their hard work.

CHAPTER 1

"You booked us on Alcatraz," Bella said.

I gazed across the ocean at the island shrouded in fog—or maybe it was cloud cover, or haze, or smog. I don't know. This was the California coast. It could have been anything.

"I didn't book us on Alcatraz," I told her.

"Is it Skull Island?" Bella asked.

I looked again at the outline of the stone hotel and the thick vegetation on the hills rising behind it. Yeah, okay, it did kind of look like Skull Island.

Bella and I were standing in the valet line outside the Rowan Resort welcome center. We'd just caravanned from Los Angeles, our friends Marcie and Sandy following us.

Two cars had been required for the trip because each of us had brought multiple suitcases, garment bags, totes, and duffels, all of which were absolutely necessary—I mean, jeez, we were staying a whole week.

We were all dressed in the latest resort wear. I had maxed out an impressive number of credit cards for the occasion.

I was willing to do more, of course. *Vogue* magazine had declared the Sea Vixen—a gorgeous polka dot beach tote—the *it* bag of the season, and I absolutely had to have one. In the last few days I'd scoured every high-end shop in L.A. and hadn't located one. It was majorly disappointing, but no way was I giving up the search.

Sandy jumped out of Marcie's car, while Marcie sat behind the wheel fiddling with her cell phone.

"Wow, Haley, this is totally awesome," Sandy said. "I can't wait to get there!"

According to the itinerary provided by the travel agent, we would relax in the comfort of the VIP lounge until we were picked up by a limo and driven to a helicopter for the flight to our all-expense-paid vacation at one of the world's most exclusive locations. The Rowan Resort catered to the every whim of A-list celebrities, royalty, and millionaires, offering privacy and seclusion amid ultra-luxurious accommodations.

So you might be wondering why I, Haley Randolph, a part-time salesclerk at the I-don't-tell-anyone-I-work-there Holt's Department Store—although I'm quick to mention my way-cool job as an event planner at L.A. Affairs—could afford such a fantastic vacation for not only myself but my three BFFs. Honestly, the whole thing was a bit hazy to me, too.

Not long ago I won a contest at Holt's—long story—and the grand prize was a seven-day cruise. I'd also won yet another contest at Holt's—again, long story—but the so-called prize required that I work at the Holt's corporate office, something I had no interest in doing, so I'd put that whole thing on ignore.

Anyway, when I called the travel agency to ask about booking the cruise, I was told the prize had been upgraded to a week at the Rowan Resort, which was cooler than cool, of course, and that absolutely anything and everything was mine for the asking.

I had no idea why the prize had been changed, but I rolled with it.

Seeing no reason not to take advantage of the situation, I immediately asked my three BFFs to come with me. I mean, really, who else would I invite?

Marcie and I had been friends forever. We're both twenty-four years old, but that's where any resemblance ended. She was short and a blonde. I was a five-foot-nine brunette.

We could pass for a ventriloquist act.

I'd met Bella—standing side by side we looked like piano keys—and Sandy—a redhead whose mother had, apparently, identified a little too closely with Olivia Newton-John in *Grease*—about a year ago when I took the salesclerk job at Holt's.

So you also might be wondering why I didn't have a boyfriend to take with me on this fabulous vacation. Actually, I had a boyfriend. His name was Ty Cameron. Ty was the fifth generation in his family to run the chain of Holt's Department Stores. He was handsome, smart, and generous, and he looked great in an Armani suit.

We broke up.

I'm not thinking about that now. I'm on vacation.

An army of valets swarmed around our cars—even though Marcie's Toyota and my Honda weren't the

Jaguars, Porsches, and Mercedes they were used to seeing here at the welcome center—as a woman in a burgundy suit greeted us. A gold name tag that read MILLICENT, HOSTESS was pinned to her lapel.

"Welcome," she cooed. "How was your drive, Miss Randolph?"

I had no idea how she knew who I was. Maybe searching guest info on the Internet was part of the service.

"Is Brad Pitt here? I saw online that he was here," Sandy said. "Oh my God, I'd die if I saw Brad Pitt."

Millicent gave Sandy an indulgent smile, then ignored her comment and gestured toward the doors of the welcome center. "Your lounge is waiting."

Bella cast another glance at the island. "We've got to fly to that place?"

"The Rowan Resort is a quick flight—"

Millicent stopped midsentence and did a doubletake at Bella's hair.

That happens a lot.

Bella's goal was to be a hairdresser to the stars—she worked at Holt's to save for beauty school—and she practiced on her own hair. Today, in keeping with the tropical theme of our vacation, she'd styled a dolphin atop her head.

Millicent recovered and said, "It's a quick flight in one of our luxury helicopters."

"There's no bridge?" Bella asked.

Millicent displayed yet another indulgent smile. "The island is miles from the mainland. A bridge across that expanse of the Pacific Ocean is an engineering impossibility."

"What about one of those ferry boats?" Bella asked.

"A ferry once took guests and family members back

and forth, but that was many years ago," Millicent explained. "Now our guests fly in using one of our helicopters."

"That's the only way to get on and off that island?" Bella asked.

Millicent gave her an I-give-excellent-customer-service-no-matter-what smile, then said, "A dock is located on the north side of the island where supply boats come in. But you needn't concern yourself with them. Our security personnel are on duty at the dock and helipad, ensuring complete privacy during your stay."

Millicent didn't hang around to answer more questions. She headed inside, leaving us to follow.

"Haley, this is so cool. We're going to see all kinds of celebrities, I just know it," Sandy said as she hurried past me.

Bella threw another look at the island, then followed Sandy inside.

Marcie finally got out of her car, her gaze still glued to her cell phone.

"Did he text you?" I asked.

She looked up. "What? Oh. Oh, no. It's—it's something else."

We walked inside the welcome center, a large room that looked as if somebody's great-grandmother had decorated it. It was filled with statues, paintings, and if-you-weigh-more-than-eighty-pounds-don't-sit-here furniture.

My Sea Vixen beach bag would have definitely brightened up the place.

Millicent held open a door on our right and said, "Your lounge."

We filed inside. The dimly lit room was cool and quiet. Accent lighting beamed down on black-and-white photos mounted on the walls. Several seating groups were scattered around. A guy in a burgundy vest and tie stood behind a bar, and a cart filled with food was nearby.

A man and woman had claimed the comfy chairs closest to the bar. They were gray-haired, a little thick around the middle. Definitely not celebrities. More like a couple whose kids had treated them to the trip of a lifetime for their wedding anniversary.

Marcie, Sandy, Bella, and I sat down, and the bartender was on us immediately. He rolled the food cart over and took our drink orders.

"That's him," Marcie said, nodding toward one of the photos on the wall. "That's Sidney Rowan. I saw his picture on the Internet. He bought the mansion and the island back in the day, and later it was turned into a hotel and resort."

In the photo, which from the depicted clothing, hair, and makeup looked like it had been taken a few decades ago, Sidney Rowan had on a tuxedo and stood between two young women decked out in evening attire. He was tall, thin, and handsome in an old-school way, and kind of looked like that guy who danced all the time in those black-and-white movies.

"Yes, that's right," Millicent said, suddenly popping up in front of us. "Mr. Rowan amassed an empire that reached every corner of the globe, then purchased his home on the island for occasions when he needed to get away from it all."

The bartender served our drinks, and we loaded our plates with delicacies from the buffet cart.

"Looks like he knew all the big stars back then," Sandy said, pointing to the photographs.

"That's Elizabeth Taylor," Bella said. "How old is that guy?"

"He's a recluse," said the woman seated near the bar. "He hasn't been seen in decades. Nobody knows if he's even alive now."

Millicent smiled her I'm-ignoring-that-comment smile and said, "The main structure was built in the thirties. After Mr. Rowan purchased it in the sixties, additions were made to accommodate his growing family, and guest bungalows were built for his many friends and business associates. Receiving an invitation to the island was highly prized."

Millicent's comments started to sound like a history lesson. I drifted off.

That happens a lot.

I got yanked back into reality when Marcie nudged me with her elbow.

"It's been all over the Internet," she whispered.

Something was all over the Internet?

"They're trying to keep it quiet," she said, "but bloggers and celebrity sites are making a big deal out of it."

I've been kind of out of the loop for a while.

"It's nothing," Millicent said. She was definitely in backpedal mode. "Speculation and conjecture, unfortunately, broadcast by people who have no actual knowledge of the event or the facts."

"That girl might be dead," insisted the woman near the bar. "Nobody just disappears—not off of an island. The whole thing is suspicious and very mysterious. She might even have been murdered."

"Was she a celebrity?" Sandy asked.

"Murdered?" Bella demanded. "A girl on that island was murdered?"

"Thank goodness it wasn't Jennifer Aniston," Sandy said. "I love Jennifer Aniston."

"She was an employee," Millicent said, as if that somehow made her possible death okay. "And nothing definite has been determined. She's missing. That's all. There's no reason to suspect foul play."

"The police were called in. The island was searched. They can't find her," the woman declared.

"There's no reason to worry," Millicent insisted. "This happened only yesterday."

"Yesterday?" Bella echoed. She waved to the bartender. "Bring me a bourbon on the rocks—make it a double."

"Does JLo know about this?" Sandy asked. "I read in *People* that she comes to the resort a lot."

"There's absolutely nothing to be alarmed about," Millicent said.

"Nothing to be alarmed about?" the woman exclaimed. "Somebody may have died!"

"Enough!" Her husband pushed to his feet. "It's nothing but gossip. I'm not listening to another word of this."

"But, Harvey—"

"Get our limo," he barked at Millicent. "Come along, Geraldine. We're going to the island, and I don't want to hear any more of this nonsense."

Millicent scurried to a door at the rear of the room and flung it open. Sunlight poured inside.

"You ladies can remain here as long as you'd like," she said. "Your limo will take you to the helicopter at your convenience."

The couple disappeared out the door. Millicent followed.

"Is that true?" Bella asked. "Did somebody really go missing, maybe get murdered out there?"

"Nobody knows for sure," Marcie said. "Right now it's just a lot of speculation."

"And it wasn't a celebrity," Sandy added. "Wow, I wonder if that old guy who owns the resort knows about this? I mean, if he's not dead, too."

I kept up on celebrity news, and nearly everybody on the planet knew there had been all kinds of rumors for years about Sidney Rowan. He'd been labeled an eccentric recluse who wielded power over his global, multi-billion-dollar empire from a chalet in Switzerland, a Buddhist temple in Nepal, a penthouse in Las Vegas—all sorts of places. There had been reported sightings of him in Paris, Belize, Moscow, most everywhere. But none of them had been confirmed by a legitimate news source—nor had anyone proved whether the old geezer was really alive or dead.

"I don't like hearing about dead people when I'm on vacay. Gives me the heebie-jeebies," Bella said. "Plus, I'm not loving that whole stuck-on-an-island thing, especially with all those bushes and trees and snakes and big bugs, and who knows what else."

"Are you sure you want to go to the resort?" I asked.

Bella stewed for a minute, then stood up.

"Yeah, I'll go," she said. "But if we get captured by

some psycho jungle tribe like you see in the movies and they demand a virgin sacrifice, we're in big trouble."

Nobody disagreed.

Millicent came into the lounge, and I told her we were ready to leave. She darted outside again.

"Hang on a second," I said as we headed for the door. "Remember our pact?"

The four of us formed a circle, and I could see that we were all thinking over the decision we'd made when we undertook this trip.

Things hadn't been great for any of us, dating wise. Marcie had a first date with a guy who seemed great but hadn't bothered to tweet, text, call, e-mail, or Facebook her since that night. Sandy's tattoo artist boyfriend had left on sabbatical without her. Bella wasn't all that anxious to get involved with a man, fearing he'd distract her from saving for beauty school. I, of course, had just broken up with my official boyfriend, Ty.

"No men, and no men-talk," I said. "No complaining, no whining, no moaning about the men in our lives. This is a girl trip. We're going to relax, have fun, enjoy ourselves, and not waste our emotion, time, and effort on them. Agreed?"

"You bet," Marcie said.

"Sounds good to me," Sandy said.

"I got no problem with it," Bella said. "But I brought my lucky panties, just in case."

Bella and Sandy headed out the door, but Marcie stayed put.

"Have you seen the latest news?" she asked.

I got a weird feeling.

"It's all over the Internet," she repeated.

My weird feeling got weirder.

"That girl who's gone missing at the resort?" Marcie gestured to her phone. "They found her driver's license and cell phone at the top of the cliffs on the back side of the island. Bloggers are speculating that she either jumped—or was pushed. She really might have been murdered."

Oh, crap.

CHAPTER 2

"So who is she?" I asked.

"Her name is Jaslyn Gordon," Marcie said. "According to the news reports, she's a maid at the hotel."

We'd just completed our surprisingly smooth helicopter flight to the island and were now riding in the air-conditioned comfort of a tram—sort of like the ones in *Jurassic Park*, except there were no dinosaurs—traveling along a narrow, paved road that wound through what the resort's Web site had termed "lush foliage."

I'm still thinking *Jurassic Park*—or maybe Skull Island.

Marcie handed me her cell phone. "That's her."

I looked at the photo posted online with the news story about how Jaslyn Gordon had disappeared from the Rowan Resort.

"She doesn't look like a maid, does she?" Marcie said. "More like a beauty pageant contestant than a—"

"No beauty pageant talk," I said.

My mom was a former pageant queen. Actually, she thought she was still a pageant queen. She and my dad lived in the house I'd grown up in with my brother and sister, a small mansion in La Cañada Flintridge that overlooked the L.A. basin. The house had been left to Mom—along with a trust fund—by her grandmother, allowing Mom to take what she saw as her rightful place among the wealthy and privileged of Los Angeles, which was all well and good—unless you're her daughter and can't quite live up to her look-at-me-I'm-a-beauty-queen expectations.

But I'm not thinking about that now. I'm on vacation.

Jaslyn Gordon looked more like someone who'd be a guest at the resort rather than an employee. She had long, pale blond hair and huge blue eyes, and was exceptionally attractive—movie star attractive. According to the news story, she was a twenty-one-year-old college student working at the resort during semester breaks.

"How do you go missing on an island?" Marcie said. "How many places could there be to look for someone?"

"Probably a lot," I said.

According to the info provided by the travel agent, Rowan Island—as the old geezer himself had named it—was average size, as islands go. The eastern portion of the island was gently sloping land on which the hotel was situated. Sandy beaches suitable for swimming and water sports swept around to the south side of the island. To the west behind the hotel grounds, the hills grew higher and more rugged, reaching impressive peaks with sheer cliffs that dropped off into the ocean.

"She must have left the island and nobody realized it," Marcie said. "You know, like a family emergency or something."

Marcie could have been right—she's almost always right—but I doubted it this time.

"The security personnel are bound to keep track of who comes and goes from the island. Probably an employee ID card they have to swipe. How else would they know for sure that she's missing?" I said.

"Maybe she really did commit suicide by jumping off the cliffs," Marcie said.

"Maybe. Or maybe whoever pushed her over the edge left her things there so it would look like she jumped," I said.

"Oh, dear," Marcie mumbled.

I didn't like that picture in my head either, so I pushed it out.

"It sounds like the police aren't sure what happened," Marcie said. "The online news reports are still calling her disappearance mysterious."

The tram turned onto another narrow road, and the Rowan Hotel came into view. The gray stone building was three stories tall, topped with an additional story of crenellated towers on the corners that made it look like one of those old castles in Europe. Zillions of flowers, shrubs, and palm trees were everywhere. People dressed in comfy casual attire—that surely cost thousands—strolled around, while others climbed into and exited trams.

"Look!" Sandy shouted, bouncing up and down on the seat in front of us. "It's Brad Pitt!"

I spotted a woman carrying a Sea Vixen beach tote.

"It's him! It's him!" Sandy declared.

Oh my God, the Sea Vixen looked even better than I had imagined. I absolutely *had* to get one.

"Where?" Bella asked, bobbing and weaving to get a better look out the window.

"In that tram! I just saw him!" Sandy said.

"That's not Brad Pitt," Bella insisted.

"Yes, it is," Sandy said. "It's Brad Pitt, isn't it, Haley?"

Brad Pitt? Who said anything about Brad Pitt?

"I'm not so sure," Marcie said.

"It was him," Sandy said. "I know it was him. Oh my God. Angelina must be here, too. And the kids."

The tram glided to a silent stop at the foot of the wide stone steps leading to the hotel entrance. The driver hopped out and opened the doors for us as a woman approached. I figured her for a few years older than me. She was tall and slender, with dark hair and that I'm-superconfident look some people naturally have. Her uniform was a little more casual than Millicent's—burgundy capris and a white polo shirt with the Rowan Resort emblem on it.

"Welcome. I'm Avery, your personal hostess," she said, and greeted each of us by name as we piled out of the tram.

"Oh my God," Sandy said, throwing her hands in the air. "We just saw Brad Pitt."

"It wasn't Brad Pitt," Bella insisted. "And if it was, what was he doing going some place by himself? He ought to be with Angelina helping her with all those kids."

"The hotel is beautiful," Marcie said. She gestured to the fourth-floor towers. "The view must be spectacular from up there. I'd love to stay in one of those rooms."

"Sorry, but the towers are off-limits to guests, as is the third floor. Family only," Avery said. "If you're ready, I can show you to your rooms."

We followed her inside. The lobby was a gigantic room with lots of dark wood, huge chandeliers, sconces, and a fireplace big enough for eight people to stand in. Heavy pieces of furniture were grouped together, some covered in leather, others in what looked like old tapestries. Oil paintings, statues, and sculptures were everywhere. A few people were sitting around the room, most of them reading.

No sign of another Sea Vixen beach bag.

"Where are all the celebrities?" Sandy asked.

"I'm pretty sure they're not out looking for that missing girl," Bella said. She turned to Avery. "What's up with that, anyway?"

Avery's nothing-can-rattle-me expression disappeared for a split second, then she straightened her shoulders and said, "Everyone here is deeply concerned about the missing member of our Rowan Resort family, and we're working closely with the authorities to ascertain her whereabouts as quickly as possible."

I was pretty sure that statement had been written by the resort's PR staff, but this didn't seem like the time to say so.

Apparently, guests at the Rowan Resort didn't have to stand in line to check in at the registration desk because Avery led the way up a wide, sweeping staircase to the second floor. We turned right down a carpeted corridor decorated with more sculptures, statues, and paintings.

"You're staying in the main structure, our most desirable location," Avery said. "It's the original mansion purchased by Mr. Rowan. Two wings were added to the rear of the house to accommodate his family as it grew. Bungalows were built over the years for visitors."

"Two wings, plus this big house?" Bella asked, gazing around. "How many kids did he have?"

Avery smiled. "Mr. Rowan was married six times, producing nine children."

"One of his daughters was a model," Sandy said. "I read all about the family in *People* magazine."

"Many of Mr. Rowan's children are very accomplished," Avery said.

"Another of his daughters was in jail, another one married a European king, and one of his sons died in a skiing accident," Sandy said.

"Maybe we should have you conduct tours for us?" Avery said with an easy smile.

"Wow, that would be so cool," Sandy said. "But my boyfriend wouldn't like me to be away from him. He's an artist."

"He does tattoos," I said.

"It's art, Haley," Sandy said. "That's why he's on sabbatical right now. It's what artists do."

"No boyfriend talk," Marcie said. "Remember our pact?"

Avery stopped outside of room 212 and presented us with packets from the organizer she carried.

"Inside is your resort pass. Please present it when you dine or make a selection from one of our shops. It's also your room key," Avery said. "My cell phone number is in the packet, also. If you need anything, simply call or text me. I'm available day and night, throughout your stay."

Marcie opened the door—we'd decided she and I would share—as Avery gestured for Bella and Sandy to move down the corridor to room 214, which adjoined ours.

Avery hung back and said, "This is a girl trip?"

"We decided we needed a break," I said.

"So it's just the four of you?" she asked. "All week?"

"Yeah, just us," I told her.

She looked at me for a few seconds, then headed down the corridor. I went inside our room.

The place was huge—two queen-size beds, dressers, chests, desks, chairs, a sofa, and an armoire with a TV—decorated in varying tones of dark green, gold, and brown. Everything looked as if it had come from a museum. Large windows let in the gorgeous California sunshine.

"Would you look at this closet?" Marcie said, opening bifold doors. "Oh my gosh, look—robes."

I gazed out the window overlooking the rear of the hotel. Below was a large courtyard bordered by the two hotel wings and the bungalows. It was hard to make out much of anything because of all the trees and landscaping, but I saw several people walking on the paths that meandered through the gardens, fountains, and sculptures.

Still no sign of anyone with a Sea Vixen beach tote.

"Somebody unpacked our bags and put everything away," Marcie said. "Now that's what I call service."

A knock sounded on the door to the adjoining room. Marcie opened it, and Bella and Sandy came in.

"Wow, this place is fabulous," Sandy said.

"Except for that missing girl who might be dead," Bella said.

Sandy held up a brochure with a photo of the Rowan Hotel on the cover and said, "There are a million things to do here. They've got a movie theater, an outdoor hammock terrace, fresh and salt water pools, horseback riding, a spa, bars, grottos—"

"What's a grotto?" Bella asked.

"According to the brochure, they're secluded, private pools hidden away in the hills amid lush vegetation," Sandy said. "Very romantic."

Bella rolled her eyes. "I can imagine what goes on in those grottos. No way am I getting in that water."

I was with Bella on this one.

"And the whole place is eco-friendly," Sandy said. "They use solar heating, deep ocean water cooling, and coconut oil biofuel."

For no real reason, the Sea Vixen beach bag popped into my head.

I gazed out the window again and—oh my God, I spotted a woman carrying a Sea Vixen. That's the second time I'd seen it on the island.

Immediately, my senses jumped to high alert. I had to get one. I couldn't be the only one here who didn't have one. If I caught up with her, I could ask where she got it and have Avery get me one, too. She said to let her know if we needed anything. That included beach bags, didn't it?

"I'm going for a walk," I announced as I sprinted for the door.

No way was I letting that woman get away from me.

I hurried down the stairs to the lobby, then turned right figuring there had to be an exit that opened into the courtyard. I went down a long, wide corridor, past all kinds of rooms, then out into the lush gardens.

The woman with the Sea Vixen had disappeared, so I took off in the direction of the bungalows, where I'd seen her headed. I figured she wouldn't be walking very fast and I could catch up with her easily.

I followed the meandering path, my head swiveling so as not to miss her. I spotted a few women, but none of them carried the Sea Vixen. I kept going.

I walked past the bungalows and—yikes!—what if she'd gone inside one of them? An all-night stakeout flashed in my mind—which I had no problem doing, of course—but I decided I'd keep moving, just in case.

The sound of the surf grew louder as I pushed on. Vegetation here was thicker and wilder, with lots of rocks and boulders and swaying palm trees. Finally, the paved path gave way to a sandy beach and rolling ocean waves. I figured that, even though I couldn't see them, off to my left around the natural curve of the island was the helipad and the dock for the supply boats.

I stopped and looked around. No sign of the Sea Vixen. In fact, there was no sign of anything. This stretch of beach was deserted. The waves were rough, which I guess was the reason the swimming area was located on a different side of the island.

Jeez, where was that woman? Where could she have gone?

I jogged down the beach a short ways but didn't see her, so I jogged the other way. Still no sign of her.

And why the heck would she be out here in the first place?

Then I thought—ugh—maybe she was out here for a hookup with a man. Yeah, okay, no way did I want to walk in on that.

I figured I must have missed her somehow and that I was sure to run into her—or someone else with the bag—again; I'd seen it twice already and we'd only just arrived. Plus, I could ask Avery if she would help me locate one.

I headed back toward the path. A flash of color caught my eye. I spotted a swatch of yellow fabric near a big boulder that was almost hidden amid a stand of palm trees.

I got a weird feeling.

I walked over.

My weird feeling got weirder.

I circled the boulder and spotted a young woman lying on the ground.

It was Jaslyn Gordon.

She wasn't missing anymore.

She was dead.

CHAPTER 3

So far, sticking to our no-men pact hadn't been a problem for me. I had yet to spot one young, good-looking guy at the Rowan Resort—just a lot of old, gray-haired, pot-bellied geezers who were, I guess, mostly the kind of men who could afford this place.

But that suited me fine, because I didn't want anything to do with men during my vacation. In fact, I much preferred it if I didn't see one single, handsome guy anywhere near my target age range.

Luckily, the two detectives across from me were firmly in the undesirable-old-guy category, both of them easily a minus ten on my own personal luscious-o-meter.

I was sitting in yet another this-place-looks-like-a-boring-museum room on the hotel's first floor, in front of a huge desk that was probably way older than me and all my friends put together. After finding Jaslyn Gordon's body, I'd come back to the hotel, spotted

Avery in the lobby, and given her the news. She hadn't seemed all that surprised—I guess Rowan Resort employees are trained to roll with anything. She'd made some phone calls, and I'd ended up in this room with these two homicide detectives who wanted to talk to me, which didn't really suit me.

I'm not supposed to be dealing with this kind of thing. I'm on vacation.

They'd introduced themselves as Detectives Vance and Pearce. They looked like a set of really unattractive bookends. Both had gray hair, spreading middles, and questionable taste in their coat-tie-shirt combos.

"So, Miss Randolph, do you want to tell us how this happened?" Detective Vance asked.

Homicide detectives always spoke in a way that made you feel guilty—even if you hadn't done anything. But I was wise to their ways. I'd been in this situation before—long story, no, actually, lots of long stories—and I wasn't about to fall for their tactics.

"I went for a walk, and I spotted Jaslyn Gordon's body on the rocks near the beach," I said.

"So you knew the victim?" Detective Pearce asked, as if he'd just made a major breakthrough in the case.

"I didn't know her," I said. "But who else could it have been? I mean, jeez, how many people are missing on this island?"

Both of them frowned like two pug dogs in the same litter.

I don't think they appreciated my commentary.

I could have pointed out that I'd had experience solving murders—with help from L.A. homicide detective Shuman and private detective Jack Bishop, both of whom looked way hotter than these two guys—but this didn't seem like a good time to mention it.

"Why were you in that area of the island?" Detective Pearce wanted to know.

Why was I still being questioned? It's not like I was wearing a T-shirt that read I'VE SOLVED MURDERS, LET'S TALK ABOUT IT.

"It's isolated," Detective Vance said. "There was no reason for you to be out there."

"Or was there?" Detective Pearce asked, leaning toward me with a you-can-confess-now look on his face.

As alibis go, I doubted that my I-was-trailing-a-fabulous-beach-tote was a good one so, really, what could I do but ignore their question?

"Look," I said. "I was out for a walk. That's it. I wanted to see the island, so I—"

The door opened behind me, and the two detectives jerked their heads up to see who had interrupted their interrogation. Seeing this as a possible opening to escape, I turned too and caught a glimpse of a guy ducking out of the room, as if he entered by mistake.

Hang on a minute.

Was that—?

My senses jumped to high alert. My heart started to pound. My thoughts raced trying to match the glimpse I'd gotten to a person I knew.

Tall, rugged build, maybe thirty, dark brown hair, green eyes, really handsome.

Then it hit me. Oh my God. *Oh my God*. Luke Warner.

Luke was an FBI agent. He'd been working undercover on a case in the L.A. Garment District a few months ago. I was there too, looking for the same murderer. Something had definitely sparked between us—long story—but I'd put an end to it after he—

I'm not thinking about that now. I'm on vacation.

But was that really Luke I'd seen coming into the room? Or had my no-men thoughts conjured up a hot guy from my past?

And if it was Luke, what was he doing here? Why would the FBI be involved?

"Miss Randolph," Detective Pearce said, "if you're not willing to cooperate with us during this interview, we can always go to the station."

Okay, now I was a little ticked off. I didn't like being threatened—and I didn't like thinking about Luke Warner.

"Look," I said. "I went for a walk. I found a body—something that, apparently, you police hadn't been able to do after searching for two days."

They both drew back a little, which was kind of nice.

Then it hit me that I'd be better off just answering their questions so I could get this so-called interview over with quickly. If I gave them too many problems they might decide to investigate *me*—which would lead them to L.A. homicide detective Madison, Shuman's partner, who had tried, and failed, numerous times to find me guilty of *something*. Plus, I didn't want to be stuck in this room so long that my BFFs started to wonder where I was and ask questions. I really didn't want anyone to know I'd discovered a murder victim.

It might spoil our vacation.

I mean that in the nicest way.

And, of course, I needed to get back to my search for the Sea Vixen—plus, a Snickers bar or two would go a long way toward boosting my day right now.

"So, that's it. I went for a walk, spotted the body, and reported it. That's the sum total of my involvement," I said, and rose from my chair. "If you have any more questions, you can contact my lawyer."

I gave them my pageant queen mom's I'm-better-than-you glare—which wasn't easy for me to pull off, especially since I didn't actually have a lawyer—then whipped around and left the room.

In the hallway I saw no sign of Luke—if it really was Luke—which annoyed me. And I was annoyed further that I'd thought about him and maybe it wasn't even *him*, which made no sense either, but there it was.

I drew a deep breath, forcing my thoughts onto my no-thinking-about-men policy for this vacation. It was proving harder than I imagined. Maybe I needed a distraction.

The image of massive amounts of chocolate floated through my brain. Jeez, what was I waiting for?

I headed down the corridor, sure that a gift shop or snack bar had to be here somewhere, and heard someone call my name.

Immediately, my own personal interpretation of the Holt's Department Store customer service training kicked in and I walked faster—too bad that outdistancing customers who might want help wasn't an Olympic event; I'd have the gold for sure.

"Haley?" Avery jogged up beside me.

Wow, these Rowan employees must be really dedicated. She'd moved pretty fast.

Maybe she'd worked retail.

"Oh, hi, Avery," I said, as if I hadn't heard her call my name six times.

"Could I speak with you for a moment?" she asked.

I followed her to a little alcove.

"Please allow me to apologize for the . . . unpleasantness you've endured since your arrival," Avery said.

I guess *unpleasantness* was code for *finding-a-dead-body* here at the Rowan Resort.

Avery seemed kind of nervous—and a heck of a lot more upset than I was.

"Let me assure you that this sort of thing never happens here." Avery drew a quick breath and straightened her shoulders. "It's understandable if you and your friends want to leave, but I hope you'll stay. Rowan Resort will do everything possible to ensure that the remainder of your stay exceeds your wildest expectations."

I figured that someone up the management chain had decided it would be Avery's fault if four guests departed prematurely—a story bloggers and tabloids would pick up on and spin into something bigger than it actually was. If that happened, the resort's reputation would take a major hit—not to mention the celebrity cancellations they might get.

I didn't like the way detectives Vance and Pearce had been giving me stink-eye. While I had no intention of leaving because of them, I figured the quicker the investigation was wrapped up, the better it would be— for me, of course—so I saw no reason not to take advantage of the situation.

"Do the detectives think Jaslyn was murdered?" I asked, and managed to use my gee-I'm-worried-a-killer-is-on-the-loose voice.

Avery glanced up and down the corridor, then leaned closer and lowered her voice. "I overheard the detectives say that it didn't appear Jaslyn had been attacked. They think she'd been climbing on the rocks, then fell and struck her head."

The detectives thought it was an accident? An accident? How could that be?

"What about her cell phone and driver's license that was found on the opposite side of the island, up on the cliffs?" I asked.

"They believe she accidentally left them," Avery said. "The detectives don't know how long they were lying there."

Okay, well, that made sense. Kind of.

"So, you see," Avery said, "the whole incident, while very upsetting, was probably just an accident."

A few seconds passed, then I asked, "Do you really think that?"

I guess my words sounded sincere, because Avery's shoulders slumped a little and she said, "I don't know what to believe."

"Why wasn't Jaslyn found sooner?" I asked.

"I don't understand it. The entire island had been thoroughly searched immediately upon realizing she was missing." Avery shook her head. "I can't imagine why she was out there in the first place."

A great reason zapped me immediately.

"Maybe she was hooking up with someone," I said.

I didn't think that end of the island was a good spot for a hookup. The hills behind the hotel offered much more seclusion and privacy.

Not that I'd ever do that, of course.

"Many of our employees are college students who work here during their school breaks. Dating is frowned upon," Avery said.

Just because a fling was against the rules didn't mean it never happened.

Not that I'd know anything about that.

"In fact, it's cause for termination," Avery said.

Ignore a corporate directive? *Who* would do such a thing?

"Jaslyn wasn't the type to get romantically involved," Avery said.

But if the guy was really hot?

No comment.

"She was more interested in finishing college and starting her career," Avery said. "I saw her studying to get a jump on her upcoming classes."

Okay, that was weird.

It was weird too that Avery seemed to know so much about one of the hotel maids.

"Were you two friends?" I asked.

"We work in teams here at the resort, to maximize guest satisfaction," Avery said. "Housekeeping and room service report any special needs to me so I'm aware of guest preferences. Jaslyn was one of my team members."

"You monitor what every guest orders and how they use their rooms?" I asked.

"That's the level of service we provide our clientele," Avery said. "It's one of the reasons they return to our resort."

So, as a maid, Jaslyn knew the intimate details of the lives of the rich and famous. And so did Avery.

Huh. Something to think about.

"Please, Haley, let me know if there's anything you need," Avery said, switching back to I-really-want-to-keep-my-job mode. "Anything at all, any time of the day or night."

Avery left, and I headed down the corridor again in a desperate search for something chocolate. As I passed the room the detectives had used for my interview, I saw the door was open and inside a half-dozen men wearing off-the-rack suits were standing in a circle, talking. Detective Pearce cut his gaze to me. I shot him serious stink-eye and kept walking.

At the end of the corridor I found a snack shop, a small place with refrigerated cases of sodas and water, a coffee bar, baked goods, and all sorts of treats. French doors led outside to tables and chairs.

The place smelled great, and immediately I was hit with a major craving for my all-time favorite drink, a mocha Frappuccino, from my all-time favorite spot, Starbucks. I didn't know how I'd get through this entire week without one—or more.

But thanks to the Rowan Resort's all-inclusive policy I could have anything I wanted—including mass quantities of chocolate—so I figured I could manage. I grabbed a Snickers bar and two bags of M&M's, swiped my resort pass, and I headed outside.

I had the maze of walkways between the hotel and bungalows mostly to myself, so I wandered through the fountains, trees, flowers, and shrubs enjoying the fantastic California weather and, of course, the candy. By the time I'd finished off the Snickers and one bag of the M&M's, the chocolate had given my brain a huge boost and Jaslyn Gordon loomed large in my head.

If Jaslyn wasn't the type of girl to hook up for the romantic fling, as Avery had claimed, and if she really was interested in studying to get a jump on her upcoming classes—which still seemed really weird to me, since I wasn't exactly thrilled by my own slow plod toward a college degree—then maybe she was on that secluded end of the island thinking that the view from atop the rocks might jazz up whatever totally boring subject she was reading about. But when I'd discovered her body I hadn't seen a backpack, notebook, laptop, iPad, or even a textbook.

According to the info I'd read on the Internet about Jaslyn's disappearance, she'd gone missing yesterday. Security personnel from the resort had searched the island and, finding nothing, had called for backup. Still nothing.

I couldn't understand how the search parties had missed her. I mean, jeez, I hadn't even been looking and I'd stumbled over her body. And why had her cell phone and driver's license been found just today? Surely they'd looked on the cliffs yesterday. How could they have missed them?

I finished off the last bag of M&M's as I wandered past the line of vine-covered bungalows, and the Sea Vixen beach bag flashed in my head. Where the heck was that woman I'd seen earlier with the bag? I'd trailed her through the courtyard, then lost her. I wondered again if she was staying in one of the bungalows.

I could stake them out and wait for the woman to appear with the bag—a sacrifice I was willing to make, of course, though under normal circumstances I didn't really have the patience for long-term waiting—or I could start knocking on doors.

My choice was easy.

Just as I approached the first bungalow, movement off to my right caught my eye. I turned and spotted Marcie barreling toward me, her jaw set, her brow furrowed, her gaze transmitting an urgent run-for-it message.

Oh my God, what now?

CHAPTER 4

Marcie blasted past me. I fell in behind her. Wow, she was really moving, so I knew something major had happened. I could barely keep up with her and I've got pageant legs, the only beauty queen gene my mom passed on to me.

We whipped through the palms, shrubs, flowers, and fountains, and finally Marcie ducked behind a huge fern plant and stopped.

"It's that girl," she blurted out in a hushed voice. "Yasmin."

I gasped. "Yasmin? The one who's dating Tate-Tate-Tate?"

"Yes."

"I hate her."

Marcie peeked through the greenery. "I just saw her."

"Here?" I demanded.

"Yes."

"Now?"

"Yes."

"I hate her."

"I think she's getting married here," Marcie said.

"Crap."

Between Marcie and me, we knew a lot of people. We'd see friends and acquaintances at bars, clubs, out shopping, and at the purse parties Marcie and I gave, which is how we'd met Yasmin. She'd somehow rotated into our circle of friends.

Marcie got along with Yasmin okay—Marcie can get along with most anyone—but I absolutely couldn't stand her. All she ever talked about was her boyfriend, Tate. No matter what kind of conversation we were having, she always turned it around to focus on him. She was so obsessed with the guy we'd started referring to him as Tate-Tate-Tate—behind her back, of course.

I pulled back a fern branch and peeked out. "She didn't see you, did she?"

"No," Marcie said. "I took off as soon as I spotted her."

"No way am I dealing with her on this vacation," I said. "I don't want to see her, or talk to her, or even be in the same room with her."

"I know," Marcie said.

"I hate her."

"She had on one of those T-shirts that had the word 'bride' spelled out in rhinestones," Marcie said.

"Hang on a minute," I said, now irritated in a whole new way. "Yasmin is getting married? And she didn't invite us?"

"That's what it looks like," Marcie said.

"We're supposed to be her friends," I said, totally outraged now.

"I know," Marcie agreed.

"And she didn't even invite us to her wedding?" I demanded.

"Nope."

Yeah, okay, I couldn't stand her—which I'm sure she didn't realize because she was always so focused on Tate-Tate-Tate—but I was majorly miffed because she hadn't invited me to her wedding, which made no sense but there it was.

"We'll avoid her. It'll be easy, really," Marcie said. "She'll be so caught up in her wedding, she probably wouldn't notice us even if we walked right past her."

Marcie was almost always right. I hoped she was this time, too. Not only was this supposed to be my no-men vacation, but I'd recently broken up with my fabulous boyfriend Ty, so the last thing—the very last thing—I wanted to be around was a couple who were blissfully happy, totally in love, and actually getting married.

"Bella and Sandy are at the beach," Marcie said. "Let's go, too. It'll be fun."

My mood instantly improved. Surely I would spot a Sea Vixen if I was at the beach.

We made our way through the courtyard, took a couple of wrong turns, and finally found the rear hotel entrance.

Thanks to my extraordinary peripheral vision—enhanced significantly by months of avoiding eye contact with Holt's customers desperate for help—I saw that lots of men were still in the room where Detectives Vance and Pearce had interviewed me.

Luke Warner popped into my mind again.

I pushed him out.

Upstairs in our room, Marcie and I changed into bikinis—mine was blue, Marcie's black—gathered our things, and went downstairs. A tram pulled up just as we walked outside, so we climbed onboard. I immediately turned my attention out the window, hoping to spot a Sea Vixen.

"You'll find one," Marcie said, reading my mind as only a BFF could.

"Darn right I will," I said.

The tram glided silently and effortlessly along the paved road, and stopped a few minutes later beneath tall, swaying palms. The sandy beach stretched to the edge of the blue, rolling surf. A thatched roofed bar had attracted a crowd. Servers in white shorts and burgundy shirts brought drinks to the guests relaxing on lounge chairs. People splashed in the water and floated on the waves.

Immediately I scanned the area for the most sought-after bag of the season. Not a single one in sight.

"There they are," Marcie said, and pointed to Bella and Sandy as we left the tram.

They were lying on chaises near the bar, sipping drinks from tall, umbrella-topped glasses. Sandy had on a red one-piece and a floppy hat. Bella wore a bright yellow bikini and huge sunglasses; no way would she put on a hat and ruin her carefully sculpted hair.

An attendant brought us towels and spread them over our chairs, and we settled in. The waiter came over, and Marcie and I ordered frothy, beach-vacation-worthy drinks.

"Oh my God," Sandy said. "You'll never guess what just happened."

"Did you see Brad Pitt?" Marcie asked.

"No, something even better," Sandy declared. "Two little girls came up to us and asked for Bella's autograph. They thought she was Beyoncé."

"No kidding," Marcie said.

"So what did you do?" I asked.

Bella shrugged. "I gave them an autograph."

"And then," Sandy said, "they took her picture."

"I smiled and waved," Bella said.

I figured that photo would make one heck of a vacation memory for someone—Bella in her bright yellow bikini and a hair-sculptured dolphin atop her head.

I sat back ready to enjoy the ocean view, the breeze, and the late-afternoon sun. This was great. Just what I needed. Nothing—except maybe spotting another murder victim—could spoil the moment.

Then it was spoiled.

"Haley! Marcie! I can't believe you're here!"

Oh my God. Yasmin.

She walked toward us through the sand smiling and waving—just as if she actually thought we were glad to see her. She had on a pink bathing suit, pink sandals, pink hat, pink-framed sunglasses—really—and a pink cover-up that had BRIDE written across the front in dark pink hearts.

Where was that waiter with my drink?

"It's really you!" Yasmin declared as she sat down totally uninvited on the foot of Marcie's lounge chair.

Yasmin was about my age with dark hair and a great figure that her dad had paid one of L.A.'s highest profile personal trainers serious bucks for to keep his little girl happy—or at least quiet.

Her dad was a hotshot lawyer. He brought down seven figures a year representing celebrities who ran afoul of the law. Honestly, I didn't know how he put up with some of those people. I wouldn't have the patience to deal with them. I pictured finding myself in his position captured in a YouTube clip with a celebrity who'd just been sentenced to jail for violating the terms of her probation *again*, as she sobbed and threw herself on the defendant's table, and me in her face screaming, "What did you think was going to happen, you crazy bitch?"

Anyway, Yasmin's parents had money, which she seemed to think was *her* money, so she got pretty much everything she wanted.

"I'm Yasmin," she said to Sandy and Bella, and they introduced themselves. "Haley and Marcie have been my friends for—well, forever. Since I started dating Tate. Oh my God, I can't wait for you to meet Tate. We're getting married!"

Nobody said anything.

"So, let me tell you all about the wedding," Yasmin announced. "Oh my God, Tate insisted I pick pink for my color. He's so sweet about giving me absolutely everything I want. Somehow, he just knows!"

Nobody said anything.

"When Tate first asked me out, I wasn't sure if I should go out with him," Yasmin said, and made a little frowny face I'm sure she'd perfected early in her teen years. "He was nice, but he didn't compliment me much—not as much as I thought he should."

"I can see why you wanted to break up with him," I said.

Yasmin, deep in Tate-Tate-Tate mode, didn't hear me.

"But then he started sending me flowers, and calling me, and texting me, all the time," she said. "That's Tate. He's just so thoughtful."

"Are you honeymooning here?" Sandy asked.

"Tate's a lawyer, you know," Yasmin said. "He works at my daddy's firm, and he's so smart. Everybody at the firm loves him, and they all think he's brilliant."

"How many bridesmaids do you have?" Sandy asked.

"Tate picked out the most gorgeous tuxedo for the ceremony," Yasmin said. "He has perfect taste in absolutely everything."

Bella caught my gaze and mouthed, "What the hell?"

I mouthed back, "I hate her."

Bella just nodded.

I sat up in my chair and looked around. Where the heck was that waiter? I desperately needed a drink.

"You won't believe my flowers," Yasmin declared, and clapped for no apparent reason. "Lilies, shipped all the way from Holland. And tucked inside my bouquet will be a special pendant called the Heart of Amour. It's an antique, or something. It has a huge jewel in it that Tate's cousin bought in Paris, which is, oh my God, the most romantic city in the world."

Nobody said anything.

"The necklace has been inside the bouquet at four weddings in Tate's family," Yasmin said, "and whoever caught the bouquet got married within a few months— all of them! So Tate said we absolutely have to use the Heart of Amour in our wedding."

Nobody said anything.

"And then—*then*—Tate insisted I go to New York to buy my wedding gown. He planned the whole trip. Me, my mom, all my bridesmaids. Limos, champagne, a personal escort, everything," Yasmin said. "He's always thinking about new ways to make me happy."

It sounded to me as if Tate-Tate-Tate was always thinking of new ways to make partner in her daddy's firm.

"Tate insisted I try on every gown in every shop so I would get the one I really wanted, so I did." Yasmin pulled her cell phone from the pocket of her cover-up. "Let me show you the pictures."

I sprang out of the lounge chair as if I were lunging for the last Michael Kors satchel on a Macy's sale table.

"I have to go," I said.

Bella hopped up, too. "Yeah, so do I."

"But you just got here," Sandy said.

"And I haven't told you Tate's ideas for the reception," Yasmin said.

"I'm—I'm expecting a call," I said.

"Yeah, and I have to be careful not to get too much sun," Bella said.

We grabbed our things and took off. Marcie and Sandy—who were clearly nicer than Bella and me—stayed.

"Why didn't you tell me you were going to a wedding here?" Bella asked as we trudged across the beach.

"I'm not," I told her. "I wasn't invited."

Bella frowned. "She's your friend?"

"Yeah, sort of."

"And she didn't invite you to her wedding?" Bella asked. "That's b.s. You ask me, that's b.s."

"Really, I'm okay with it," I said.

Bella nodded. "I can see why."

We caught the next tram, rode back to the hotel, and went upstairs.

"Want to go get something to eat?" Bella asked as we walked down the corridor.

"Sure," I said, digging in my tote for my resort pass room key.

"I'll meet you in the lobby in a few minutes," she said, and let herself into her room.

I scrounged through my tote—I was positive the Sea Vixen had better pocket organizers—and finally came up with my key.

"Excuse me?" someone called.

From the corner of my eye I glimpsed a young woman hurrying toward me. My initial reaction—thanks to my Holt's training—was to ignore her, but then I saw that she had on a burgundy uniform and figured she was one of the hotel maids.

"You're Miss Randolph, aren't you?" she asked, stopping in front of me.

Wow, even the maids knew me by name. The Rowan Resort gave top-notch service, all right.

"I'm Tabitha," she said, pointing to the name tag pinned to the lapel of her uniform.

She was blond with bright blue eyes, probably just out of her teens. I figured she was one of the college students who worked here.

Tabitha was really small, and I wondered how someone so tiny could push those heavy housekeeping carts up and down the halls. I glanced around but saw no cart.

She gestured to my room. "I just wanted to see if you needed anything, Miss Randolph."

Was my picture up in the employee lounge above the caption "Be extra nice to this person, she discovered a dead body"?

"Everything's great," I told her.

She nodded and twisted her fingers together for a few seconds, then said, "I heard you're the one who found Jaslyn."

I wasn't all that anxious to talk about Jaslyn—I should have gone with my Holt's instincts and bolted when I saw her coming—but there was nothing I could do about that now.

I shouldn't have to be constantly on my toes. I'm on vacation.

"That's right," I said.

Tabitha glanced around and leaned a little closer. "Is it true what everybody is saying? You know, that the detectives think it was just an accident?"

Okay, now I felt kind of bad. Obviously, Tabitha was concerned for her safety.

"That's what somebody told me," I said. "But, really, I don't know anything for sure."

"What did the detectives say?" she asked. "Exactly?"

"They mostly just asked me questions," I said.

"Do they have any evidence?" Tabitha asked.

Of course, workers at the resort would be interested in the details of Jaslyn's death. Word must have gotten around that the detectives thought it was an accident and Tabitha wanted to confirm the news. I guess it would give a little more peace of mind to everyone working here. Tabitha seemed anxious for details, but if I were in her shoes, maybe I would be, too.

"I don't know anything about their evidence," I said, then decided to move the conversation in another direction. "You and Jaslyn were friends?"

"Kind of," she said. "We live here, all the employees. Well, not here at the hotel. There's a dorm near the docks for us. We stay there for our shifts, then we can leave the island on our days off, if we want to."

I eased closer to my door, more than ready to end this little talk, but Tabitha was having none of it.

"Where did you . . . find her?" she asked. "It wasn't on the cliffs, was it?"

"No," I said, thinking it better I didn't go into too much detail.

"Jaslyn wouldn't have gone up there unless . . ."

She stopped.

I hate it when that happens.

"Unless what?" I asked.

Tabitha shook her head as if dismissing the thought she'd had, then a few seconds later she seemed to change her mind again.

"Unless her boyfriend made her," she said. "He was always trying to get her to go up there. But if you didn't find her there, I guess it's okay."

So Avery was wrong about employees dating each other. Surprise, surprise.

"She had a boyfriend?" I asked.

"Just some guy," Tabitha said.

She looked at me for a few seconds, then backed away.

"Okay, well, thanks," she said.

Tabitha looked only marginally more relieved than when we'd started talking. But I didn't know anything else I could tell her.

I went into my room, took a quick shower, and dressed in white capris, a yellow T-shirt, and flip-flops. I didn't hear Bella moving around in her adjoining room, so I knocked. I got no answer, so I figured she was already in the lobby. I slid my resort pass into my pocket and headed downstairs.

Just as I stepped into the lobby I spotted a guy heading my way. Kind of tall, late twenties, shaggy brown hair, good-looking. He had on rumpled khaki pants and a stretched-out blue polo shirt.

Hang on a minute.

I'd seen those clothes before.

He saw me in the same second and froze. I froze too because, oh my God, I knew him. It was Ben Oliver, a reporter for the *L.A. Daily Courier*. We had history—sort of. What the heck was he doing here?

He didn't give me a chance to ask. Ben spun around and took off, heading for the door.

No way was I letting that happen. I took off after him.

I dashed across the lobby and out the hotel's front entrance, and caught a glimpse of something blue disappear behind a planter of ferns. I followed, weaving my way down the path and around all the plants, then skidded to a stop beside a fountain with a sea horse shooting water from its nose. No sign of Ben. I'd lost him.

Still, I wasn't giving up. I was about to bolt to the right when a hand touched my arm. I whirled around, ready to grill Ben on why he was here.

Only it wasn't Ben.

It was Luke Warner.

CHAPTER 5

"Haley."

Luke said my name in a mellow voice that made my stomach feel gooey and my toes curl. But I didn't want a gooey stomach or curling toes. This was a no-men vacation, and if I felt those things while I was here I sure as heck didn't want Luke to be the one who caused them—not after what he'd done the last time we were together.

"Luke," I said, and, darn it, my voice sounded all gooey and toe-curly.

He had on khaki cargo shorts and a shirt with palm trees on it, standard resort wear that somehow made him look more rugged and masculine. The breeze ruffled his dark hair.

"How have you been?" he asked.

Luke had the most awesome green eyes. They seemed to look straight through me, somehow, and see my inner thoughts—or maybe that was his FBI training.

"Great. I've been great," I said.

It wasn't really true, but I certainly wasn't going to tell Luke what my life had been like lately.

"How about you?" I asked.

He nodded thoughtfully and said, "Okay. Just okay."

His gaze drilled me as if he were trying to convey some deeper meaning. I figured he was thinking about how, the last time we saw each other, he'd tried to make things up to me and had asked for a second chance, but I was having none of it—*that's* how upset I'd been with him.

Luke angled closer and asked, "What brings you here?"

Oh my God, he smelled great.

"Vacation," I said, and it came out sounding kind of squeaky.

"Are you . . . with someone?" he asked.

"Friends," I said.

He looked relieved that I wasn't here with a boyfriend—or maybe that was just my imagination.

"I'm here for a wedding. A buddy from college," he said.

Was that a weird coincidence or what?

We just stood there for a few seconds looking at each other and not talking—this wasn't my first junior high moment with Luke—then we both seemed to realize it at the same time.

"Maybe I'll see you around," Luke said.

"Maybe," I said.

We gazed into each other's eyes for another couple of seconds, then Luke stepped back.

"See you," he said.

"Yeah," I replied, and walked away.

Oh my God, where was Marcie at a time like this? I absolutely *had* to tell her what had just happened. She had to help me interpret every word, every look, every gesture.

I took off down the pathway, not sure where I was going as thoughts of Luke raged in my mind.

He was here to attend a wedding? At the same time I was here on vacation? Now Luke and I were linked together. We'd found each other on this remote island. Did that mean we were destined to be together? Was it just a crazy coincidence? Was this some sort of sign?

Was I getting carried away?

I slowed my steps, drew in a couple of deep breaths, and tried to calm myself—something I'm not really good at.

Oh my God, I desperately needed a mocha Frappuccino from Starbucks.

I was going to have to ask Avery to have one flown in from the mainland—it was the only way I could deal with this Luke thing.

I whipped around and headed back toward the hotel entrance, and noticed a flash of blue through a trellis of bright red blooms. I circled back and spotted Ben Oliver in a little alcove of flowers, parked on a bench, pounding away on his laptop.

So it was him I'd seen inside the hotel earlier. I knew it.

But what was a reporter for the *L.A. Daily Courier* doing here? Could he simply be vacationing on the island? I doubted it. Ben didn't give the impression that he was flush and could afford a place like this, where a day's stay could cost more than an average family's mortgage payment, not judging from the clothes he wore, anyway—I was pretty sure he had on the same khaki pants and blue polo shirt I'd seen him wearing several months ago.

If Ben wasn't vacationing, he must be here investigating a story. But that didn't make sense, either. The Rowan Resort would never—*never*—allow a reporter on their property. The privacy of their guests was their top priority.

So why was he here?

I decided to ask him.

I walked closer and said, "Hi, Ben."

His head jerked up, his eyes widened, and he shouted, "Get away from me!"

Wow, was that a different reception than I'd gotten from Luke or what?

"I just want to talk—"

"Stay back!"

Ben slammed the lid on his laptop and sprang to his feet. He lurched right. I jumped in front of him. He cut left, cradling his laptop to his chest and holding out his other hand like a running back going down field for a touchdown. I went with him, blocking his escape.

"Why are you being such an idiot?" I asked.

"Because I don't want you to ruin my life—again!" he told me.

"I didn't ruin you life," I insisted.

"Yes, you did!"

Okay, he was right. Kind of. But it wasn't all my fault. Really.

A few months ago I'd given Ben some hot tips on breaking news—long story—that should have propelled him to the top of the newspaper journalist world—whatever that was—but things hadn't worked out exactly as

I'd thought they would. In fact, they'd gone sideways big-time and, to put it mildly, Ben's editor hadn't been pleased. Ben had ended up covering chili cook-offs, community Little Miss pageants, and craft projects at retirement homes.

Ben hadn't seemed to appreciate the effort I'd put into feeding him those potential career-making stories, for some reason, and had blamed me for all the bad things that had happened to him. Seems he was still holding a grudge.

"Look," Ben said, "just stay away from me."

He circled around me and disappeared.

Yeah, okay, I guess it made sense that Ben would be a little miffed at me, but jeez, he seemed to be holding on to his anger a little too tightly.

Or maybe something else was going on. Was he here investigating the disappearance and death of Jaslyn Gordon?

The idea zinged around in my head for a few minutes—and I hadn't even had a mocha Frappuccino— until I finally decided that even if that was the reason for Ben's presence at the resort, it had nothing to do with me. I didn't know Jaslyn, I wasn't involved, and I didn't have reason to become involved. In fact, if the rumors I'd heard were correct, the whole thing was an unfortunate accident. End of story—except that I still needed a mocha Frappuccino.

I found my way back to the hotel's front entrance, went into the lobby, and stopped dead in my tracks. Oh my God—a Sea Vixen.

My heart rate picked up. My breathing got shallow.

There it sat on the floor beside a chair in all its polka dot glory. The blue, orange, yellow, and green mesmerized me, drawing me across the lobby as if in a trance. I drew closer, arms extended, my fingertips tingling. Within seconds, it would be mine.

"Oh, hi there," somebody said.

My world shattered. I blinked back to reality and saw a woman sitting in the chair. Oh my God, the Sea Vixen belonged to her.

Her? How could that be? She was old—like fifty, or something. She had on—yikes!—those were shorts I'd seen on the rack at Holt's, and Holt's sold the most hideous clothing known to mankind. How could she have a Sea Vixen? She didn't deserve it. Not like I did.

Maybe I could just take it. I glanced at the hotel's entrance and considered making a break for it. She was old. She couldn't possibly move very fast. I could lose her in a heartbeat. Except this was an island. Where would I run to? She'd find me sooner or later.

I hate it when that happens.

"I'm Geraldine," she said with a big smile. "From the welcome center. Harvey and I met you and your friends there. Remember?"

"Oh, yeah, sure," I said, forcing myself to calm down. I pointed to the Sea Vixen. "I love your bag."

"Isn't it just the cutest thing?" Geraldine said. "I saw it and just had to have it, even though it cost a small fortune. But Harvey said I should get it. It's my one impulse buy here."

If I'd had floppy, pointed Scooby-Doo ears, they would have shot straight up.

"Here?" I asked. I might have said that a little too loud.

"Why, yes," Geraldine said.

"At the resort?" I think I shouted that.

"Yes," she said, and pointed toward the rear of the hotel. "At one of the shops."

"Which one?" I screamed that.

Geraldine drew back a little. I forced myself to calm down.

"Sorry," I said.

She waved away my apology and said, "Don't give it a thought. Everyone is on edge, what with that poor girl getting murdered."

The death of Jaslyn Gordon rushed into my brain crowding out the vision of the Sea Vixen.

"I thought it was an accident," I said.

"Oh, no," Geraldine said, and gestured to her smart-phone lying on her lap. "I just read it online. The police announced that she was murdered. Hit on the head with something, probably a rock."

Wow, news—particularly bad news—really traveled fast these days. Only a few hours ago the police were saying it was an accident—or that's what Avery had told me. It made me wonder if she actually knew the real story, or if that was what the resort management had instructed their employees to report.

"They have a suspect," Geraldine said.

Oh, crap. I hope it wasn't *me*.

"And they're working on leads," she said. "That's what the report said online, anyway."

Luke Warner flashed in my head. He was an FBI agent. He'd worked undercover—which was what had caused our whole problem a few months ago. Was the story he'd told me about being here for a wedding the truth? Or was he really here undercover?

And what about Ben Oliver? No way was he here

for vacation, so he must be undercover too, following a story.

Both Luke and Ben were working undercover? How come I couldn't do something cool like that? I wanted to be undercover somewhere, too.

Maybe I need to reevaluate my life.

"Shh," Geraldine said, and lowered her voice. "Here comes Harvey,"

I followed her line of vision and saw her husband approach. Harvey looked a lot like Geraldine, both graying, both with thick middles, both wearing ho-hum resort wear.

"Don't say anything to him about that girl being murdered," Geraldine whispered. "Harvey doesn't want to hear anything bad on vacation."

Can't say that I blame him.

Harvey joined us, and I introduced myself. If he remembered me from the welcome center, he gave no indication.

"Great place, great place," he said, gesturing to the hotel in general. "Have you seen the library?"

This place had a library?

"The Rowan estate has an impressive book collection," he said.

Somebody wanted to spend their vacation reading?

"Several pieces of art are in there, too," he added.

And looking at art?

Maybe I should go to Disneyland next time.

"There's an art curator on the premises at all times," Geraldine said. "I read it in the resort brochure. One of the members of the Rowan family."

"The art collection on display here at the resort is extensive," Harvey said.

"Sidney Rowan was an avid collector," Geraldine added.

"Do you enjoy art, Haley?" Harvey asked.

Did doodling on an Etch-A-Sketch count?

"You can take lessons right here at the resort," Geraldine said, then paused for a few seconds and said, "Maybe I'll do that. You should too, Haley. It's very relaxing."

I thought about it for a second. Sitting in front of an easel dabbing paint onto a canvas always made a person look superintellectual—almost as much as sitting in Starbucks, wearing a scarf, and typing on a laptop.

"I'll check it out," I said.

"Let's have a look at the restaurants," Harvey said. "I want to see them all so we can decide where to have dinner."

"Will you join us, Haley?" Geraldine asked.

"No, thanks, I'm meeting friends," I said, and glanced around the lobby. Where the heck was Bella, anyway?

Geraldine rose, picked up the Sea Vixen, and left with Harvey.

My senses jumped to high alert. Geraldine had said she'd found a Sea Vixen at one of the resort's shops. I had to find it.

I was about to take off when I saw Sandy and Marcie walk into the lobby from outside. They were still dressed in their beachwear, and seemed to be involved in a deep discussion.

"We'll let Haley decide," Sandy said as they walked up.

Marcie gave her a have-at-it wave.

"I met this guy on the beach," Sandy said. "His

name is Sebastian and he works here. I didn't want to talk to him, and Marcie thinks I should have."

"It was only a conversation," Marcie said. "Besides, he was really good-looking."

"Vacation flings never work out," Sandy said.

How had I gotten into the middle of this?

"He liked you," Marcie said.

I had to find a Sea Vixen tote.

"I already have a boyfriend," Sandy insisted. "Besides, this is our no-men vacation. Right, Haley?"

The vision of the very last tote being snatched from the shelf while I stood here zapped my brain.

"Right, Haley?" Sandy asked again.

I had to get this discussion over with so I could find that shop.

"Right," I said.

"See?" Sandy said. "Haley is committed to our pact, and so am I. She didn't run after a good-looking man today, did you, Haley?"

Jeez, did hunting down Ben count?

"Or get all crazy and girlie because a good-looking man talked to her," Sandy said. "Right, Haley?"

Had I gotten all crazy and girlie talking to Luke Warner?

"Haley?" Sandy asked.

Yikes! I had.

They both stared at me, waiting for an answer. But I couldn't tell them the truth.

Thankfully, I didn't have to respond, because Bella appeared out of nowhere and pushed her way into our group.

"This is b.s.," Bella announced, scowling and planting her hands on her hips.

I'd seen Bella angry only one time—and it wasn't pretty.

Sandy gasped. "What happened?"

"I was robbed," Bella declared. "Somebody stole my lucky panties."

We all just stared at her.

"Stole them right out of my room," Bella said.

"Somebody stole your panties?" Marcie asked.

"My *lucky* panties," Bella declared. "What kind of place is this, anyway?"

"Maybe you just forgot to pack them," Marcie said.

"I'd never forget my lucky panties on vacation," she told us.

"The hotel staff unpacked for us," Sandy said. "Maybe whoever put your things away put them in the wrong drawer or something."

"I looked everywhere," Bella said, still fuming. "I already talked to that woman—what's her name, Avery?—and told her all about it. She said she was sure they hadn't been stolen. But if they're not in my room—and I'm sure as heck not wearing them—what else could have happened to them? Nothing, that's what. Somebody stole my lucky panties."

"Haley!"

A gut-wrenching scream caused us all to jump. I turned and saw Yasmin, still dressed in her bride-to-be pink beach ensemble, rushing toward our little group. Tears streamed down her cheeks. Her fists were clinched, and her mouth hung open as she sobbed.

It wasn't a good look for her.

"Haley, you have to help me," she said as she pushed her way between Bella and Sandy. "You all have to help me. You have to!"

Nobody said anything.

"My guests have cancelled! Almost all of them!" Yasmin leaned her head back and cried harder.

Around us, other people in the lobby stared.

Yasmin shook her fists in the air. "All because that stupid girl got herself murdered!"

I didn't need the Hubble to see where this was going.

I backed away, but Yasmin lunged and grabbed my arm.

"You all have to come to my wedding!" she screamed. *"You have to!"*

Oh, crap.

CHAPTER 6

"No way," I said. "Forget it. I'm not going to that wedding."

"But if guests aren't there, her wedding will be ruined," Marcie said.

"No," I told her.

"Where's your compassion?" Marcie asked. "Just look at her."

Yasmin had collapsed into a chair. Her arms hung at her sides, her head was thrown back, and she was bawling so loud that the other lobby guests had gotten up and moved.

"I'm not doing it," I told Marcie. "Look, when I said earlier that I hated her, I meant it."

"Oh my God," Yasmin wailed. "My wedding! My wedding! What's going to happen to my *wedding!*"

Sandy looked at me. "She's really upset."

"What is Tate going to think?" Yasmin screamed.

"She can't have a wedding with just family and a couple of guests," Sandy said.

"Yes, she can," I insisted. "She'll still be married, no matter how many people are there."

"And, oh my God, what will happen if there's no one to catch my bouquet? What if I'm the one who breaks the Heart of Amour chain of weddings?" Yasmin panted for a few seconds, then let out another sob. "Tate's family will talk about me *forever!*"

Sandy shrugged. "I guess it wouldn't hurt to go to the wedding."

Bella rolled her eyes at Yasmin and said to me, "I'm with you."

"It's no big deal, really," Sandy said. "All we have to do is show up for the ceremony, which won't take long. Then we can go to the reception. It might be fun."

"And it isn't for a few more days," Marcie said. "There's a good chance the police will solve the murder by then, and if that happens, her guests will come after all."

Yasmin's caterwauling was giving me a headache, and I was annoyed beyond belief.

This wasn't supposed to happen—I'm on vacation.

"Okay, fine," I told them. "We'll go—if she'll just shut up."

"Yasmin," Marcie said.

She kept crying.

"Yasmin!" Marcie shook her arm. "We'll go to your wedding."

She sniffed and blinked up at Marcie, then looked at all of us. "You will? You'll all go?"

"Sure," Marcie said, and gave her an everything-will-be-fine smile.

Yasmin burst out crying again.

Good grief.

"I'm out of here," I said.

I guess everyone's good intentions had played out.

Marcie headed for the stairs, pulling Sandy along with her, and said, "We'll change and meet you and Bella back here for dinner."

"I'm going to find that head security guy and see what he's doing to find my lucky panties," Bella said, and walked away.

I headed across the lobby, then heard sniffing and panting behind me. Yasmin jumped in front of me. She drew in a really long breath and swiped at her face with her palms.

"You're saving my wedding, Haley," she whispered, then gulped a few times. "And to thank you, to *really* thank you, I'm going to throw my bouquet directly at you."

Oh, crap.

She sniffed. "Tate will be so proud of me."

I hate my life—but I'm not supposed to. I'm on vacation.

Yasmin headed up the lobby staircase and I shot eye-daggers at her—which she didn't see, but still.

No way was I going to that wedding. No way was I waiting around for the cops to solve Jaslyn's murder so the guests would show up and get me off the hook. I would find the killer myself.

Right after I found the Sea Vixen.

Everybody has their priorities.

I headed down the long corridor at the rear of the hotel, searching for the shop where Geraldine had bought her she-doesn't-deserve-it-but-I-do tote. I followed the signs, turned down a corridor, then another.

Jeez, how big was this place?

Finally, I came upon a row of shops, their windows displaying high-end clothing and accessories for men, women, and children. My senses perked up. The Sea Vixen was here, only steps away. I could feel it.

I have a sixth sense about handbags. It's a gift, really.

Immediately, I was drawn into one of the shops. There, at the entrance, stood a shelving unit filled with all sorts of bags: satchels, clutches, shoulder bags, cross-bodies, and—oh my God, totes—all in buttery leather, fabulous textiles, patterns, solids, a rainbow of colors.

This was where Geraldine had found her Sea Vixen— it had to be. My heart began to beat faster. The Sea Vixen was here. *Here.* I was mere seconds away from claiming one for myself.

"Can I help you?" someone asked.

I spotted a salesclerk in a Rowan Resort burgundy uniform standing nearby. I noted she hadn't come too close. Apparently, I was giving off an I'm-a-crazed-shopper vibe.

I forced myself to calm down and channeled my pageant queen mom's I'm-better-than-you attitude.

"I'm looking for a Sea Vixen tote bag," I said.

"Oh, dear," the clerk said and frowned. "I just sold the last one."

"What?" I'm pretty sure I said that too loud.

She didn't back off, as I expected her to. This place catered to celebrities, so I guessed she was used to dealing with lunatics.

"Yes, I sold it just a few minutes ago," she said. "I'm so sorry."

Sorry? She was sorry? I was within minutes of buying the most fabulous tote of the season and she was *sorry?*

She glanced at the telephone behind the counter. Oh my God, was she thinking about calling security?

I drew in a breath, and steadied myself. "No problem. I'll check with the other shops."

I got her oh-dear frown again. "All the shops have sold out. It's such a popular bag."

Like that was supposed to be a comfort? Of course it was popular. Would anyone vacationing *here* want it if it weren't?

"We're expecting another shipment," the clerk told me with a see-how-helpful-I-am smile.

"When?" I demanded. "Exactly."

"It could be at any time. The supply ships come in several times a day," she said. "Would you like me to hold one for you?"

I resisted the urge to turn a cartwheel and said, "Yes, please."

She moved behind the counter and wrote my name, room number, and cell phone number in a little book.

"Call me as soon as it comes in," I said. "Day or night."

"Of course," she said.

"No matter where I am on the island, I'll come immediately," I told her.

"If there's a delay reaching you, I'll call your personal hostess," she assured me. "I'll contact Avery and alert her to the situation."

I had no idea how this salesclerk knew that Avery was my personal hostess, but I rolled with it.

"Thanks," I said.

She looked relieved when I left.

This had taken longer than I'd anticipated, I realized as I left the shop. I had to get moving on my investigation. I had a wedding to avoid and a murder to solve, and I knew just where to start.

Regardless of what Ben claimed, I knew there was no way he'd be at this resort unless he was investigating a story—and what story could he possibly be checking into but the death of Jaslyn Gordon?

If I used the hotel's house phone to call his room, I knew he wouldn't answer. I had his cell phone number from a few months ago, but if I called he'd see my name on the caller ID screen and wouldn't pick up, so I didn't bother trying. That meant I was going to have to do what women had been doing since the dawn of time to find a man—hunt him down on foot.

Immediately, my I'd-really-like-to-be-a-cool-private-investigator skills sprang up—they usually worked better with a mocha Frappuccino, but I was willing to tough it out.

I remembered that Ben liked to do his writing outside. I also knew he was avoiding me like the plague—not a great feeling, but oh well. Since I'd seen him earlier near the front of the hotel I figured he'd think that if I looked for him again, I'd head to the back of the hotel. Thus, being the crafty sort-of kind-of private investigator that I was, I headed once again for the front of the hotel.

Outside, the sun was sliding into the Pacific, lighting the low clouds with stunning shades of orange. A number of trams unloaded weary beachgoers. I strolled through the walkways and, sure enough, spotted Ben sitting on a bench beside a fountain decorated with ceramic frogs. He was in his writing trance, staring at his laptop screen, pounding on the keys. I crept up, then slipped around the bench and plopped down beside him.

Ben cut his eyes to me and growled—yes, actually growled. It was kind of hot.

"Why do you keep showing up?" Ben demanded.

"Maybe because you need help dressing," I said, and tugged on the sleeve of his tired-looking, stretched-out polo shirt.

Wow, there was a good muscle under there. I hadn't expected that.

"There's nothing wrong with my clothes," Ben insisted.

"This is the same shirt and pants you were wearing when I saw you ages ago," I told him. "How about if I give you a makeover?"

"Go away," he said, and turned back to his laptop.

"Don't you want to look your best so you can hook up with some hot-looking chick?" I asked. "I mean, why wouldn't you—if you're really not here investigating a story?"

Ben turned to me again, his eyes narrowed, his jaw set. His nose flared a little and his chest expanded. Wow, that was way hot. If he'd only growl again.

I gave myself a mental shake.

"Because you're here investigating Jaslyn Gordon's murder, aren't you," I said. "Admit it. You are."

Ben drew a breath and closed the lid of his laptop.

"I can tell you without a moment's hesitation," he said, "that I am absolutely not here to investigate a murder—although I'd gladly investigate yours, if the situation presented itself."

This, I hadn't expected—which didn't suit me, of course.

"I know why you're here," I insisted. "You're on a story. You have to be. A reporter like you wouldn't be at an expensive resort like this unless there was some huge story—"

"Quiet," he told me, glancing around to make sure we weren't being overheard.

I glanced around, too. It made me feel very covert.

"Nobody can know—or even suspect—that I'm a reporter," Ben said quietly.

"So maybe you'd better tell me what I want to know," I said, thinking a little blackmail might work.

Ben glared at me and clamped his mouth shut. My attempt at blackmail definitely hadn't worked. I had to try something different.

"Okay, look," I said. "I can help you and you can help me. I happen to have inside information about Jaslyn Gordon's murder."

"Why are you so interested in that girl's murder?" Ben asked, then shook his head. "No. Never mind. I don't want to know."

"You don't?" I asked, stunned. "What kind of reporter are you?"

"The kind who's not investigating that story," Ben told me.

He tucked his laptop under his arm and walked away.

Huh. Well, that didn't go exactly as I'd planned.

I sat on the bench as the sunlight faded and shadows crept across the fountain. So far, my murder investigation had gotten nowhere. I had no suspects and no mo-

tive. Nothing. And my one potential source of info—
Ben—wasn't even interested in the story, which made
me believe that he was telling the truth. His presence
here at the resort was in no way connected to Jaslyn's
murder.

Still, I couldn't believe that Ben was here simply on
vacation. Something else was definitely going on with
him.

But I couldn't worry about that now. I had to come
up with some way to find Jaslyn's killer—and quick.

People didn't get murdered for no reason. There had
to be something going on with Jaslyn Gordon that had
resulted in this horrible crime.

Mentally, I reviewed all the people at the resort who
I needed to talk to—which would have been a heck of
a lot easier if I had a mocha Frappuccino available.

I decided I'd start with Tabitha, the maid I'd seen in
the hall outside my room earlier. She'd asked about
Jaslyn and seemed to know her pretty well. I figured
that Tabitha could probably give me some good info
about what was going on in Jaslyn's life or at least
point me toward someone who could.

My cell phone in my pocket vibrated. I checked the
caller ID screen and saw Avery's name. Oh my God,
was she calling because that salesclerk had gotten a
Sea Vixen into the shop already?

My day could really use a boost.

I leaped off of the bench and pushed the green button on my phone in one smooth, well-practiced motion.

"Haley, could you meet me in the lobby?" Avery
asked.

This *had* to be about the Sea Vixen. There was no other reason for Avery to call me.

Maybe she wanted to escort me to the shop herself. Maybe there was some sort of presentation planned.

"Sure," I said, already heading toward the hotel. "I'll be there in a few minutes."

I hurried through the gardens to the hotel entrance and dashed up the stairs and into the lobby. Immediately, I spotted Avery standing by the staircase. I rushed over.

"I'm sorry to disturb you," she said.

"No, it's no problem," I assured her, bouncing on my toes.

"This can wait, if you'd rather," she told me, and gestured down the corridor. "Are your friends expecting you for dinner? I don't want to keep them waiting."

"They're fine," I told her, in my get-on-with-it voice.

"All right, if you're sure," she said.

Avery led the way toward the rear of the hotel and down the long corridor, past the room in which— ugh—the homicide detectives had interviewed me earlier. But instead of turning right toward the shops, Avery opened a small door on the left bearing a tiny sign that read EMPLOYEES ONLY and gestured me in ahead of her.

Okay, this was weird.

There was a short hallway in front of me that led to a room with a partially closed door. I glimpsed several people inside and heard the hum of their conversation.

My weird feeling got weirder.

A man stepped out of a small office off to my right.

He was tall with square shoulders and a trim waist, dressed in a shirt and tie. He had a full head of gray hair, cut short. I guessed his age at fifty, maybe.

"Miss Randolph, thank you for coming," he said. "I'm Walt Pemberton, chief of security here at the Rowan Resort."

My really weird feeling got even weirder.

"I'd like to speak with you about a telephone conversation I just had with an acquaintance of yours," he said. "A homicide detective with the Los Angeles Police Department named Madison."

Oh, crap.

CHAPTER 7

APD's Detective Madison had been trying for ages to find me guilty of somebody's murder. He continually twisted evidence and circumstances around so that I looked guilty—in his mind, anyway. I'd never done anything wrong. Really. Well, okay, maybe a few things—but I sure as heck had never murdered anybody. It helped that Madison's partner, Detective Shuman, had always been on my side. Most always—which wasn't my fault, either. Okay, yeah, maybe it was.

Anyway, Detective Madison didn't like me, which was okay because I didn't like him either, except that he had—and still could—make my life miserable. And now it looked as if he'd done it again by ratting me out to the head of security at the Rowan Resort.

"Please, Miss Randolph, have a seat," Walt Pemberton said, gesturing to the chair in front of his desk.

He spoke as if we were old friends and he just wanted to have a nice chat and catch up on things. No way would I fall for that. I'd been questioned too many times by the police—none of which was my fault—to believe him.

Then it hit me—oh my God, what if Detective Madison is here? In the next room? Waiting to come in and arrest me? Had Avery lured me into a trap?

I glanced around. Avery was nowhere to be seen.

"Miss Randolph?" Pemberton said, a little louder this time.

I knew I had to play it cool.

I'm good at that. Kind of.

I waited another few seconds, then lowered myself into the chair, as if *now* it suited me to do so. Pemberton took a seat behind his desk.

The office was small but well appointed. The walls were beige, the furniture a dark wood, and the photos on the wall were black-and-white, back-in-the-day shots of the resort when it was still Sidney Rowan's home. A computer sat on the corner of his desk. I figured the room down the hall was where the other members of the security team worked.

"Thank you for coming in," Pemberton said, and gestured to a credenza on the far wall that held a coffee service. "Would you like something?"

If he'd offered a mocha Frappuccino, I'd have jumped at it.

"What's this about Detective Madison?" I asked.

Pemberton shrugged. "Professional courtesy. We like to make sure all our bases are covered."

I wasn't sure just what that meant, but I decided it was better—for me, of course—not to dwell on anything to do with Madison.

I glanced at my wristwatch. "Will this take long? I have friends waiting."

I had no idea if Marcie, Bella, and Sandy were standing around somewhere waiting so we could all have dinner together, but I wanted Pemberton to know that friends were expecting me and would notice if I didn't show up.

"I won't keep you for long," Pemberton said. "I'd like to talk to you about what happened today."

Okay, now I was annoyed. I'd already told Detectives Vance and Pearce everything I knew about Jaslyn's murder—which wasn't much, really—so I didn't want to have to go through the whole thing again with this guy. Then I was double-annoyed, thinking that maybe this was their way of checking my story to see if I'd been lying earlier. All law enforcement agencies worked together—including private security firms, it seemed—which caused Luke Warner to pop into my head and triple-annoy me.

"Your welcome to the Rowan Resort is most unfortunate," Pemberton said. "My apology, on all counts."

I guess he was apologizing for my finding a murder victim, then being questioned by homicide detectives, as if I were a suspect. I hadn't expected this, but I appreciated it.

My foul mood dropped back to double-annoyed.

"Avery told me about your involvement," he explained, and shook his head. "Believe me, this isn't the kind of thing that routinely happens here. I'm sorry you got caught up in all of it."

Okay, he was being really nice and sounded sincere, plus Avery, it seemed, had gone to the trouble to pass word up the chain of command that I deserved an official apology, so I relaxed a little and quit visualizing a

S.W.A.T. team storming the room and taking me into custody.

"If I may," he said, "could I ask if you have any information that might help in the investigation?"

I guess my irritation showed again, because when I opened my mouth to tell him that I wasn't involved, he cut me off.

"That's okay," he said. "I understand that these things are confidential."

Confidential? What's so confidential about a murder?

"But I want you to know we're taking this seriously," Pemberton said. "We take all of these matters seriously."

All of them? Jeez, how many people had been murdered here?

"Guest confidentiality is a top priority to us," Pemberton said. "We have electronic surveillance, but very little of it. Regardless of how tightly we control the video footage, there's still a chance it will be pirated and released to the public. We can't have that."

What the heck was he talking about?

"We rely primarily on our own security personnel. Boots on the ground." Pemberton paused for a moment then said, "Our guests often travel here under assumed names. They wear disguises. Their entourages maintain, as they should, their employers' right to privacy."

Why was he telling me this?

"But could you tell me, without putting yourself in a compromising situation, if there's anything you know?" Pemberton asked.

Did he have me mixed up with someone else?

I couldn't think of anything to say—because I had

no idea where this conversation was going—so I just sat there with my I'm-really-considering-your-question look on my face, something I'd perfected while nodding off at staff meetings at every job I'd worked.

I guess my I'm-thinking-hard look was correctly interpreted by Pemberton, because he continued.

"Anything you could tell us, anything at all, would be helpful," he said. "Do you recall anything about the theft?"

Theft? Who said anything about a theft?

Then it hit me. All this talk about disguises, assumed names, and entourages was about Bella's lucky panties. I'd been brought in here thinking I was going to be arrested, and all along the head of security was concerned about a pair of stolen panties?

What was up with him? He had a murder to solve. Who cared about panties—lucky or not?

"Did you see anyone near your rooms?" Pemberton asked. "Or perhaps someone who was paying undue attention to the arrival of you and your . . . your friends?"

The only people I'd seen upstairs near our rooms were Tabitha and Avery, and both of them had good reasons for being there, so no way was I going to waste any more of my time with this guy talking about this situation.

I hopped out of my chair. Pemberton rose with me.

"If I think of anything, I'll let you know," I said.

He must have interpreted my words as a blow-off—which was exactly how I meant them—because he nodded and said, "Thank you."

I left the office, went back down the hallway and through the door to the hotel corridor. I was reaching for my cell phone to call Marcie and hook up with them for dinner when something Pemberton had asked me shot through my head.

He'd asked if anyone was near our rooms and I hadn't told him about Tabitha approaching me earlier and asking for info about Jaslyn's murder. At the time I'd figured she was just nervous about a killer being on the loose, but now I wondered if something more was going on with her. She hadn't had one of those big housekeeping carts with her, which must mean that she wasn't there during her official duties and hadn't spotted me by chance.

Had Tabitha been in the hallway outside our rooms during her off-duty time? Was she waiting for me to show up? And if so, was it simply to ask about Jaslyn's death? Or had she talked to me and asked those questions to make it look like cover for letting herself into Bella's room and stealing her panties?

Jeez, this made no sense. Why would anybody—*anybody*—want to steal Bella's panties?

Of course, I could have gone back inside the security office and told Walt Pemberton about seeing Tabitha. But I wasn't going to rat her out and get her in trouble, especially since the whole thing was absurd.

Still, I couldn't let it go. I decided I should find Tabitha and ask her myself.

Then something else hit me—I'd never asked Pemberton what Detective Madison had told him about me. I figured it couldn't be good, given my history with Madison, but I wanted to know the extent of their conversation.

There was only one way to get that info. I was going to have to call Detective Shuman.

* * *

I found a quiet spot among some shrubbery just outside the rear exit of the hotel and pulled out my cell phone. A few people meandered through the gardens, most heading in the direction of the delicious smells wafting through the air from barbeque grills somewhere nearby. The aroma reminded me that I was hungry and needed to make this call so I could eat, but I couldn't quite bring myself to scroll through my phone contacts.

Not that there was a problem between Shuman and me. We'd met about a year ago when I'd started working at Holt's and Shuman and Madison had come to the store to investigate a murder—long story. The two of us had hit it off and, at times, I'd felt something spark between us; I'm pretty sure Shuman felt it, also.

But two things had kept us apart—my boyfriend and his girlfriend.

Shuman had always been there to help me out of a jam, and I'd assisted in some of his investigations. Everything had worked out well for us, professionally speaking. We kept our emotional distance. I had Ty, my official boyfriend—I'm a real stickler about things like that—and Shuman had a girlfriend he was crazy about.

Then everything changed. The girlfriend was gone—long story—and Shuman was devastated. He showed up at my apartment, an emotional train wreck, looking for . . . well, let's just say he was in need of comfort. I gave it to him, in the form of three beers—which wasn't exactly what he'd come there hoping for. When he passed out on my sofa, I went to bed; the next morning when I got up, Shuman was gone. I hadn't seen or talked to him since.

I didn't like that our friendship was suffering, but having been in his situation myself I knew that some time was needed to get normalcy back in his life. I didn't want to wait too long, though, because I didn't want to lose his friendship—or whatever it was that was going on between us—and what better way to break the ice than to call him about something that would benefit *me*.

I hit the button on my phone and heard it ring in my ear. My heart rate rose a little. His voice mail picked up. I left a message asking him to call me as soon as he could. I hung up.

I was about to call Marcie and see where she, Bella, and Sandy were when I spotted them walking out of the hotel. Marcie and Sandy had changed into sundresses, and Bella wore bright orange capris.

"There you are," Marcie called as they walked over. "Come on. We're heading to dinner."

"I'm starving," Sandy declared.

"Me too," Bella said, and adjusted the waistband of her capris. "That's why I'm wearing my buffet pants."

"We want to try the grand patio tonight," Sandy said. She waved the resort brochure. "I read all about it. The floor is the original stone selected by Sidney Rowan himself and imported from a quarry in Peru."

"Sounds great," I said.

We followed the path, and the fabulous aromas, through the gardens to a large outdoor dining area amid trees and shrubs alive with twinkle lights. Bright yellow cushions decorated white wicker chairs, and tables were set with fresh flowers and elegant china and crystal. Chefs in big white hats manned the grills and food stations.

The hostess—another college student, from the look of her—showed us to a table, then we headed for the serving line.

"Oh, girls, hello," someone called, and I spotted Geraldine and Harvey at a nearby table. We walked over.

"Are you enjoying the resort?" Geraldine asked, smiling up at us.

"My lucky panties got stolen," Bella told her.

Geraldine drew back a little. Clearly, she wasn't expecting to hear anything about panties, lucky or not.

"They're purple with zebra print trim and a hairdryer appliqué," Bella said. "Have you seen them?"

"Well, no. No, I haven't," Geraldine said, then rushed ahead, changing the subject—not that I blamed her.

"I signed up for that art class we talked about, Haley," Geraldine said. "Did you?"

I had, of course, totally forgotten about it.

Geraldine leaned in a bit and lowered her voice, indicating a choice bit of gossip was about to be delivered.

"The instructor is none other than Colby Rowan herself," she said.

Sandy gasped. "She's one of Sidney Rowan's daughters. I read about her in *People* magazine."

"She's the curator of the Rowan family art collection at the resort," Geraldine said. "She has an art studio and lives right here on the island."

"Wow, that is so cool," Sandy said. "I'm going to take a lesson just so I can meet her."

"She could use the support, I'm sure," Geraldine said, nodding wisely. "Especially after what happened—"

"You girls enjoy your meals," Harvey said, nailing his wife with a stern look.

We took the hint, mumbled something appropriate, and got in line for food.

"So what happened with Colby Rowan?" Marcie asked as we inched forward.

"It was so sad," Sandy said. "She got mixed up, somehow, with this bunch of criminals, or something, a few years ago."

"Did they go around stealing panties?" Bella grumbled.

Sandy thought for a few seconds, then said, "No, I don't think that was it. I can't remember, really."

Marcie pushed her way a little closer to the rest of us and whispered, "Look who's headed our way."

We all turned and looked, not nearly as slick as we usually were—but we were on vacation—and I spotted a guy wearing a Rowan Resort polo shirt and cargo shorts weaving between the tables, coming toward us.

He was probably one of the college students who worked here. Early twenties, brown hair, maybe an inch or two taller than me. He didn't look as if he spent much time in the gym, but he was kind of cute.

"Who's he?" Bella asked.

"That's Sebastian Lane," Marcie said. "We met him on the beach. He's the one who was trying to talk to Sandy."

"I have a boyfriend," she pointed out. "Besides, this is our no-men vacation. Aren't we going to honor our pact?"

"Won't be a problem for me," Bella said, "since I've got no lucky panties now."

"What does he do here?" I asked.

Sandy frowned, as if she were trying to recall. She shook her head and said, "I don't know."

That was weird. Men were always yammering on about their job.

I looked at Marcie, sure she'd have asked him at the beach and remembered what he'd said, but she shook her head.

"He didn't say," she realized.

Just as the line reached the salad station, my phone vibrated in my pocket. I pulled it out.

Shuman was calling.

CHAPTER 8

"Hey, how's it going?"
I answered my phone using my everything-is-strained-between-us-but-I'm-pretending-it's-not voice.

"Good. Everything's good," Shuman replied, using the same voice.

I'd left the buffet line and found a quiet spot away from the dining area to take the call, not knowing exactly what to expect from Shuman. Now I knew, and it wasn't great.

A minute dragged by with neither of us saying anything because we both knew what we were doing.

Finally, Shuman said, "So, what's up?"

I was relieved to have something concrete to talk to him about—even if it was Jaslyn's murder.

I mean that in the nicest way, of course.

"I was wondering if Madison had accused me of murdering somebody lately," I said.

Shuman chuckled. It was good to hear him laugh.

"You can't stay out of trouble, can you?" he asked.

"I didn't do anything," I told him.

"Then why would Madison accuse you of murder?" he asked.

"He was provoked, I guess," I said, and gave him a quick rundown on my vacation at the Rowan Resort, Jaslyn Gordon's murder, and how I'd found her body and then been questioned by two homicide detectives and Walt Pemberton.

"So Pemberton phoned Madison to get some sort of personal reference, I guess," I said.

"How did he know about your history with Madison?" Shuman asked.

"Good question," I said. "All I can figure is that this resort is wired-in big-time. Everybody here knows everything about the guests."

"The resort probably does routine background checks, since there are so many high-profile guests staying there," Shuman said.

I could tell he was in cop mode now. It was kind of hot.

"That's creepy," I said.

"Better than booking a room for a celebrity stalker," he said.

I couldn't argue with that.

"Okay, here's the weird part," I said. "All Pemberton asked me about was stolen panties."

Shuman was quiet for a moment, then said, "Were they *your* panties?"

A warm rush went through me, which I ignored.

"No," I said, and figured it was better not to get into too much detail.

Shuman didn't say anything and, honestly, I couldn't blame him.

"I'm not following you," he finally said.

"I don't get it either," I told him. "Why would Pemberton ask me about stolen panties when he has a murder to solve?"

"Maybe it was his way of bringing you in, getting a read on you without accusing you of anything," Shuman said. "Maybe he was using the panty theft as cover."

"Maybe," I agreed.

Shuman was quiet for a few seconds, then said, "I'm surprised the head of security would involve himself with a theft of this nature."

"Well, they were *lucky* panties," I told him.

Shuman got quiet, but I was pretty sure I heard him breathing heavier.

I decided it was a good time to move our conversation along.

"They take this sort of thing seriously here," I said.

"Yes, but they'd try to keep it quiet," Shuman said, shifting into cop mode again. "It's not the kind of thing they'd want the other guests to know about, and bringing you in to ask about it would only create an opportunity for word to spread."

"Makes sense," I said.

"Something else might be happening," he said. "Who knew you'd found the body and also knew about the stolen panties?"

Huh. Good question. Besides Bella, Sandy, Marcie, and me, I could think of only one person.

"Our hostess, Avery," I said.

Of course, everyone up the management chain probably knew I'd discovered Jaslyn's body. Avery could have told her supervisor that the theft of Bella's panties was connected to me too, but I kind of doubted it. She probably wouldn't have wanted to admit that the same guest—me—whose satisfaction she was responsible for had encountered yet another problem at the resort.

I'm pretty sure they note stuff like that in the staff members' personnel files.

"Avery told Pemberton about the theft," Shuman concluded. "Why?"

"I think she was worried that I was an unhappy guest, after finding a dead body, plus having my friend's panties stolen out of her room," I said. "It was her way of dealing with the problem without getting herself into trouble by reporting it to her direct supervisor."

That's what I would have done.

"Maybe," Shuman said. "Or maybe the panty theft was her way of getting you in front of the head of security."

I gasped. "You think she might have thrown me in front of him on purpose?"

"Possibly, if she wanted to make sure Pemberton considered you a murder suspect," he said. "I can think of only one reason she'd want to do that."

I could think of only one reason too—that Avery was involved in Jaslyn's death.

I remembered then that Avery had told me Jaslyn had been on her team, cleaning the rooms of guests assigned to Avery. That meant they'd known each other and had worked together. Definitely something I needed to check into.

"Madison hasn't mentioned you," Shuman said, "but I'll try to get some info."

"Thanks," I said.

A few awkward seconds dragged by. I felt I should say something more personal to Shuman, and I got the idea he felt the same, but neither of us seemed to know exactly what that would be.

"I'll call if I learn something," Shuman said.

"Great," I said, and we hung up.

"This place is so cool," Sandy said.

The four of us were sitting at a table near the bar on the beach. We'd stuffed ourselves at dinner but, of course, that was no reason not to have drinks and snacks afterward. Tiki torches and twinkle lights illuminated the darkness. A dozen people were on the dance floor swaying to the rhythm of the reggae band. A resort hostess had organized a limbo game in the sand nearby.

Sandy sprang up in her chair. "Oh my God, there's Vin Diesel."

We all whipped around, craning our necks to see through the crowd, in time to see what could—or could not—have been Vin Diesel disappear behind a stand of palm trees.

"Wow, that was so cool," Sandy said.

We all nodded and sank into our chairs again.

"I can't believe Holt's would give you something as fabulous as this resort vacation for a contest prize," Sandy said.

"I was surprised, too," I admitted.

"It's b.s. You ask me, it's b.s.," Bella said, and sipped her drink. "But I'll take it."

"It is kind of odd," Marcie said, and gave me her something-else-is-going-on look that only a BFF could pull off.

I knew she was questioning the prize upgrade, which

had occurred after I turned out to be the winner of the Holt's contest, and I knew she was thinking that my boyfriend—my *former* boyfriend—Ty was involved, since he owned the department store chain. But I didn't agree with Marcie. Ty and I had broken up, so he had no reason to bestow such a fantastic prize on me, especially since the breakup had been his idea—long story.

"Hey," Bella said, sitting up straighter in her chair. "Holt's ought to reimburse me for my lucky panties that got stolen. Maybe I can sue them for emotional distress, get disability or something."

"You should do that," Sandy agreed. "My boyfriend says that an inspiration piece is crucial to living a full, happy life. That's how he's able to produce such beautiful works of art."

"Do you mean those tattoos he does?" I asked.

"It's art, Haley," she said.

We'd had this conversation a couple of zillion times. I didn't like Sandy's boyfriend—even though I'd never actually met him, that was no reason not to dislike him. He treated her like crap and she definitely deserved better, which was all I needed to know.

Marcie suddenly leaned forward and bobbed her brows in the universal something's-going-down gesture. We all immediately leaned in with her.

"Look who just walked up," she whispered. "And it's not Vin Diesel."

We all leaned back, looking casual and unconcerned while our gazes darted around the bar like we'd just walked into Nordstrom on the morning of their after-Christmas sale, until we spotted Sebastian. He stood near the band looking at our table. I noted he wasn't wearing his Rowan Resort uniform.

"I'll bet he's here looking for you," Marcie said to Sandy. "Go talk to him."

Sandy shook her head. "I shouldn't."

None of us had a chance to disagree, because Sebastian walked over to our table.

"Good evening," he said, with an easy smile. "Sandy, would you like to dance?"

Sandy immediately had an I-don't-think-I-should look on her face, so what could I do but take over?

"She'd love to dance," I said, then drilled Sandy with a go-do-it glare.

She grinned, and Sebastian escorted her onto the dance floor.

We stared after her, all of us rethinking our no-men pact—at least, that's what I was thinking.

Marcie jumped to her feet. "Let's go do the limbo."

"Sounds good to me," Bella declared.

"I'll get a fresh drink first," I said.

They headed off to the limbo game, and I grabbed my drink and headed for the bar. It was a big rectangle covered with a thatched roof and decorated with fake fish and nets. About a half-dozen people were scattered around the bar. I found an open seat away from everyone.

The bartender came over. He was a little taller than me, around thirty, with neat brown hair and an I'm-really-too-competent-to-be-working-in-this-place aura about him. He looked a little old to be a college student, like so many of the other Rowan Resort employees I'd seen, so I figured he had something else going in life and this bartending gig wasn't permanent.

He took my empty glass, a tall, frothy thing with a chunk of pineapple stuck on the rim, one of those cool drinks that are fun to have at the beach, especially for people like me who weren't hard-core drinkers.

"Another one?" he asked.

"Sure," I said, and read his name tag pinned to his burgundy shirt. "Thanks, Shane."

He glanced at the dance floor and the limbo game. "Are you girls having fun, Haley?"

"Okay, look," I said. "You've got to tell me the truth. How does everybody here know who I am?"

Shane grinned as he mixed my drink. "It's a secret. Do you like secrets?"

"Of course," I said, "as long as I'm the one who knows them."

His grin bloomed into a smile—a naughty smile, which was kind of hot.

"In that case, I'll tell you," he said as he set my drink in front of me. "Resort employees are required to study guest photos and memorize who's who."

Jeez, and I thought waiting on customers at Holt's was tough.

"Not that we're supposed to talk to any of the guests, except to respond to their every need," Shane said.

I could see where employees fraternizing with guests could create a problem. Aspiring actors might hit up a visiting director for an audition, or a computer geek might badger a multimillionaire for a Silicon Valley job. No way would the resort want guests' vacations interrupted with personal requests from their employees.

I nodded toward Sebastian and Sandy on the dance floor, and asked, "What about him?"

Shane's expression soured. "He's golden."

"Why does he rate a pass?" I asked.

"You got me," Shane said, with more than a little disgust in his voice, and turned away to wait on another customer.

I sipped my drink and watched as the band struck up another song, and Sebastian and Sandy kept dancing. They were a nice-looking couple which made me think of Ty.

I pushed him out of my head.

Then Luke Warner popped in.

I pushed him out, too.

Ben Oliver appeared in my thoughts. Then he mentally disappeared and Ty took his place.

Ty. Tall, handsome Ty. Had he really engineered my contest win at this gorgeous place, thinking I'd ask him to join me?

The image of the two of us here together raced through my head. Walking the beach hand in hand, swimming, hiking up the cliffs, maybe horseback riding. It seemed so romantic, so perfect, my heart started to hurt a little.

"You found Jaslyn's body," Shane said, standing in front of me again.

Nothing like a dead body to jar you back to reality.

Since Shane already knew, I saw no reason to deny it.

"Yes, it was me, unfortunately," I said.

"She wasn't on the cliffs, was she," he said.

The only people I'd shared that information with— other than law enforcement—were Avery and Tabitha. One of them must have told Shane.

I shook my head. "It was near some big rocks on the north side of the island, close to the dock."

"She was murdered, and whoever did it put her

phone and driver's license on the cliffs to make it look like she'd killed herself," Shane said. His expression darkened. "Jas would never do that. Never."

My this-could-benefit-me mental alarm sounded in my head. Bartenders heard all kinds of things—drunk people had a tendency to blab on—so I figured Shane was in a good position to give me the inside scoop. Plus, since this place was an island and employees lived here much of the time, he probably had the inside track on his coworkers, too.

"You don't think so?" I asked.

"She had a lot to live for. All she talked about was getting her degree and touring Europe," Shane said.

"Sounds cool," I said.

"Jas was a lover of beautiful things. She was an art major." Shane frowned. "And she would never have gone up on those cliffs, no matter how great the view was. She didn't like high places."

I wondered if something had been going on between Jaslyn and Shane, since he knew so much personal info about her.

"Were you and Jaslyn dating?" I asked.

"No, she was just a cool girl," Shane said. "Her room was near mine in the employee dorm, so we'd see each other and talk."

Shane seemed to drift off into thought, probably remembering those good times he'd shared with Jaslyn. But I didn't have time for his stroll down memory lane. I had a murder to solve and, thus, a wedding to avoid.

"So who was Jaslyn dating?" I asked.

His expression hardened. "A real bastard. Gabe Braxton. Works maintenance."

Shane glanced behind him at two couples who'd just taken seats at the bar, then turned to me again.

"Tell your friend Sandy to watch out for that guy," he said, nodding toward the dance floor.

His comment totally threw me.

"Sebastian?" I asked. "Why?"

"He's trouble," Shane said.

Oh, crap.

CHAPTER 9

"So what happened last night?" Marcie asked.

The four of us were seated at yet another of the resort's outdoor patio dining areas, finishing breakfast. The day was gorgeous, of course, since this was Southern California; people from back East often claimed that we have no seasons here, but we do—just not the crappy ones.

We were all dressed in our resort wear shorts, capris, tees, and tanks, each outfit fully accessorized, of course. Bella had fashioned her hair into the shape of a starfish, continuing her tropical theme.

Sandy giggled. "You mean with Sebastian?"

"Hell, yeah," Bella said. "It's not like any of us are getting any action at this place."

"We had a great time," Sandy reported, her cheeks turning a light shade of pink. "We walked on the beach and talked for hours."

"Really?" Bella asked. "That's *it?*"

"He was a perfect gentleman," Sandy said.

"Damn . . ." Bella muttered.

"Tell us about him," Marcie said.

"He's so nice," Sandy said. "He asked about me. You know, where I was from, where I worked, what I liked. And he even asked about all of you. He wanted to know everything about me and my friends."

Okay, that was weird. A guy who was actually interested enough to ask questions and not just blab on about himself?

"Did he actually listen to what you said?" Marcie asked.

I could see that she and I were thinking the same thing.

"Oh, yes," Sandy told us. "He listened. He asked follow-up questions and everything."

My spirits lifted, thinking maybe Sandy had found a guy who was really nice and would treat her decently, and I was glad that I'd practically put the smack-down on her to dance with him last night.

"What does he do here at the resort?" I asked.

"He's a consultant," Sandy said.

"What kind of consultant?" I asked.

Her brows pulled together. "I don't think he said. But he's very successful. He owns his own firm."

Okay, now I wasn't feeling so great about insisting that Sandy get involved with Sebastian.

"He's from Connecticut, and he's rich," Sandy said. "His whole family is rich."

Now I *really* wasn't feeling great about sticking my nose in.

"He told you that?" Marcie asked.

"Well, kind of," Sandy said. "He told me his whole name. It's Sebastian Cannon Lane. Who would give their baby that kind of name if they weren't rich?"

She had a point.

I'd guessed Sebastian's age at early twenties, and that seemed young for him to own a consulting business. But Ty wasn't even thirty when he'd taken over the reins of the Holt's Department Store chain after his dad fell ill, so I guess it wasn't a big stretch to think that Sebastian headed up a consulting firm. Maybe his family really was rich and he'd used his trust fund to get the business started.

"I'm having an art lesson this morning. Sebastian called last night and got me scheduled," Sandy announced. "I've never had an art lesson before. I can't wait. I'm actually going to meet Colby Rowan."

"She's Sidney Rowan's daughter, right?" Marcie asked. "The one who got into legal trouble?"

"She's like a celebrity, almost," Sandy said.

"You think because she got involved with a bunch of lowlifes and turned criminal, that makes her a celebrity?" Bella asked.

"She was in *People* magazine," Sandy said.

"Are you going to make a coffee cup or something to take back home for a souvenir?" Marcie asked.

"Colby doesn't do ceramics, even though she has a kiln at her studio. Today's lesson is about painting with watercolors," Sandy said.

Avery walked up to our table.

"Good morning," she said, smiling her it's-early-but-I-can-pull-this-off smile. "Do you girls have something planned for today?"

"I'm having an art lesson," Sandy said, "with Colby Rowan herself."

Avery pulled a small catalogue from the organizer she carried and passed it to Sandy.

"Take a look at this," she said. "It's photos and descriptions of all the art in the resort's collection. The pieces are on display throughout the hotel."

"Cool," Sandy said, thumbing through the pages.

"Let's go horseback riding," Marcie said. "Or maybe play tennis."

Avery already had her phone out and was pecking away. "I can book you for both this afternoon."

"Bouncing around on a dumb animal and chasing a ball around doesn't sound like much of a vacay to me," Bella said.

"How about if we go to the beach this morning," Marcie said.

"That's more my speed," Bella said as we all rose from our chairs.

"I'll catch up with you later," Sandy said. She gave us a little wave and headed off for her art lesson.

"Haley, could I speak with you for a moment?" Avery asked. "Something's come up."

The Sea Vixen tote bag flashed in my head. Oh my God, was Avery about to tell me that it had arrived and was, at this very moment, waiting for me in the hotel shop? If so, I didn't want to keep Marcie and Bella standing around while I picked it up. Besides, I always needed some alone time with a new bag.

"I'll catch up with you at the beach," I said to them. They nodded and left.

"Our wedding planner would like to speak with you," Avery said.

My-handbag-dream-is-coming-true bubble burst.

"Joy is our wedding planner," she said, and gestured across the dining area.

Standing near the hostess stand was a tiny woman who appeared less than five feet tall, maybe in her forties, with a blond helmet of hair, tiny glasses, dressed in a burgundy business suit and wearing, for no known reason, pumps.

She waved and shot me an everything-is-terrific smile.

What the heck was going on? Why was I talking to a wedding planner? Had I drifted off during a crucial conversation somewhere and missed something?

That happens a lot.

I followed Avery through the tables of diners. She made introductions and took off.

"Now, don't you worry about a thing," Joy said to me, giving me a big smile and a fist pump. "The wedding is going to be super. Just super."

"What wedding?" I asked.

Joy threw back her head and laughed. "I love a maid of honor with a sense of humor."

"Maid of—what?"

She whipped open her iPad. "Now, first of all, there's the bachelorette party."

"Hang on a minute," I said. "What are you talking about?"

"Yasmin and Tate's wedding," Joy said.

Okay, I was totally lost.

Joy must have picked up on my what-the-heck expression, because she said, "Yasmin told me you're taking over for Gretchen, her maid of honor."

"Gretchen was her maid of honor?" I asked.

I knew Gretchen, one of the girls who rotated through our circles of friends. She was really smart, competent, and levelheaded. How had she gotten involved with somebody like Yasmin to the extent of agreeing to be her maid of honor?

"Gretchen cancelled," Joy said. "She's afraid to come here because of that poor girl getting killed."

It flashed in my mind that maybe Gretchen had second thoughts about being Yasmin's attendant and had murdered Jaslyn herself just to get out of the wedding—not that I blamed her, of course.

"I'm not Yasmin's maid of honor," I said. "I'm only a guest."

Joy frowned, then typed something into her iPad.

"I'll have to get back to you on that," she said. "What about the bachelorette party?"

My spirits lifted. A bachelorette party would be cool—some male strippers, a couple of kegs, and a cheese tray would be just the thing to perk up this vacation.

The entire party bloomed in my head, because I'd recently taken a job as an event planner at L.A. Affairs, a company that catered to celebrities, Hollywood insiders, and the rich and famous of Los Angeles. I could definitely use these elements if I was called upon to plan a bachelorette party, which I expected to happen since L.A. Affairs loved my work.

My first big assignment for them had been to organize a huge Beatles-themed bash for Hollywood's top movie director, and the whole thing had come off flawlessly—except for that girl getting murdered.

Anyway, L.A. Affairs had been so pleased with my work that they'd graciously given me time off for this vacation. I'd used the my-uncle-Bob-died-excuse, a personal favorite of mine, but I'm sure—pretty sure—they would have given me the time, regardless of the reason.

"Definitely count me in for the bachelorette party," I said.

"Super," Joy said. "Let's keep in touch."

We exchanged cell phone numbers, and she clacked away in her pumps.

My morning definitely needed a boost. I decided to check with the resort shop and find out if my Sea Vixen tote had come in yet.

I went inside the hotel and wound my way through the corridors on the first floor until I came to the shop I'd been in yesterday. The same clerk was there. When she spotted me, she ducked behind the counter.

I mean, *really*, was that any way to act when you saw a customer coming?

"Hello?" I said as I approached the counter.

A few seconds passed before she popped up.

"Oh, hello, Miss Randolph," she cooed. "I'm so sorry, but we haven't received a shipment yet today."

This didn't suit me, but I channeled my mom's I-can-be-nice-if-I-absolutely-have-to expression and said, "I'll check back with you later."

"Oh, no, don't come into the shop," she told me, then forced a fake I-didn't-mean-it-like-it-sounded smile.

"As soon as your bag arrives, I'll let you know. I'll call you immediately."

There was nothing more I could do but thank her—which I didn't really mean—and leave.

My Sea Vixen search hadn't boosted my day at all. In fact, it had made me cranky. So what could I do but take it out on somebody else? Like, maybe, a murderer.

Last night at the bar, Shane had told me about Jaslyn Gordon's boyfriend, a maintenance worker named Gabe Braxton. I decided I should take my I-don't-have-a-Sea-Vixen wrath out on him.

I didn't really know where to find this guy, but I knew where to locate the person who could tell me. I left the hotel and headed through the gardens and across the resort grounds in the direction of the docks and the employees' dorm.

The sun was warm in the cloudless sky; the trees, flowers, and shrubs swayed in the gentle breeze; and in the distance I could hear the pounding surf. And what better to do while in paradise than to review my mental list of murder suspects?

Gabe Braxton, the boyfriend, was at the top of my list because all the detectives on those TV crime shows said that if a woman was murdered, her killer was probably the husband or boyfriend. Who was I to differ? It had worked for twenty seasons, or something, for *Law & Order*.

Of course, I didn't have any motive or evidence to support that assumption. But I'd been told that Gabe tried to get Jaslyn to go up to the high cliffs on the back side of the island when he knew she was afraid of heights. Plus, her driver's license and cell phone had been found up there. At the bar last night Shane had also mentioned that Jaslyn was more interested in getting her degree than anything else. Maybe Gabe hadn't liked that he was in second place in her life?

Tabitha had seemed like a really nice person, but she'd been a little too anxious for details about Jaslyn's death when I'd talked to her in the hall outside my room yesterday. It made me wonder if she'd simply been concerned for her own safety, or if something else was going on, like maybe she'd murdered Jaslyn. If she had a motive, I hadn't discovered it yet.

I wasn't feeling all that great about Avery. She'd maneuvered me into talking to Walt Pemberton, the head of resort security, but I had a feeling there was something more behind her actions. Detective Shuman had thought Avery had gotten me in there for Pemberton to have a look at me as a murder suspect. Like Shuman, I could think of only one reason she'd want to throw suspicion on me, which was to keep suspicion off of herself.

As much as I didn't want to, I had a weird feeling about Sebastian. He seemed like a nice guy, and I wanted Sandy to meet somebody nice who would treat her decently. But all those things Sandy had reported to us at breakfast this morning that she'd learned about Sebastian during their walk on the beach didn't sit right with me. Plus, I couldn't ignore what Shane had told me at the bar last night. He'd said that Sebastian was golden. I wasn't sure exactly what that meant, but it probably wasn't something good. There was, of course, the possibility that Shane had said those things about Sebastian out of jealousy or envy, rather than something concrete.

My brain was crowded with suspects who weren't really suspects, who had no real motive or means of murdering Jaslyn that I'd discovered yet. There was only one thing to do—somehow today, I was going to have to find a Starbucks mocha Frappuccino if I was going to have any hope of solving this murder.

I followed the narrow, paved road past the dock and the helipad where we'd landed. No ship was tied up there; few people were out. I gazed toward the mainland but didn't see any ships headed this way so I figured my Sea Vixen wouldn't be here anytime soon.

The road curved sharply inland and disappeared behind a wall of swaying palms and thick, towering shrubbery that had been planted, I'm sure, so the sight of the resort's inner workings wouldn't offend the delicate sensibilities of its rich and famous guests. Up ahead was a dull yellow two-story building that looked kind of like the military barracks I'd seen in old movies, plain but functional. I spotted a tram waiting out front while employees climbed aboard; I figured they were on their way to the resort for their shifts.

I followed the road past the dorm and spotted a big metal building. Two men wearing gray Dickies work clothes stood near the rolled-up door. Inside, I saw workbenches, shelves full of all kinds of maintenance equipment, and a dozen or so lawn mowers.

One of the men did a double take when he saw me approach the building. He nudged the other guy, who

turned to stare. I figured they'd pegged me for a guest—
and why wouldn't they, thanks to the fabulous resort
wear I'd maxed out several credit cards to buy—and
were suspicious about why I was there.

"Hi," I said, using my there's-nothing-to-be-alarmed-
about voice.

They just stared.

I tried again with my I'm-really-a-nice-person voice
and said, "Can you tell me where to find Gabe Braxton?"

Neither of them said anything, making me think that
they were either too stunned by the sight of a resort
guest on their portion of the island to speak or that they
were afraid something major had gone down and they
were in some sort of trouble.

I knew the feeling.

"I need to talk to Gabe," I said. "I know he and
Jaslyn Gordon were seeing each other. I'm the one who
found her body, so I figured Gabe would want to hear
about what happened."

They both continued to stare, and finally one of
them said, "That was bad. Really bad."

"She was a nice girl," the other one said. He pulled a
radio from his belt and said, "I'll tell Gabe to meet you
near the docks."

"Thanks," I said, and left.

I walked back down the narrow road, past the dorm,
the helipad, and dock. When I entered the resort grounds,
I saw a maintenance worker dressed in gray work clothes
headed in my direction. He stopped in front of me, and
I saw the name GABE stitched on a label above his shirt
pocket.

He was huge, easily six five, with wide shoulders, a solid chest, and bulging arm muscles. I figured him for late twenties. The sun had given his skin a golden glow and streaked his dark hair with yellow highlights.

I thought he looked great.

I also thought he looked like he could have killed Jaslyn Gordon with little effort.

CHAPTER 10

"I'm Haley Randolph," I said.

Gabe Braxton stared down at me. Obviously, the maintenance team wasn't required to memorize photos of resort guests, as the hotel workers were, because he looked at me as if I were a bug he wanted to squash—which, from the size of him, I thought he could easily have done.

"I'm the one who found Jaslyn," I said.

Now he looked as if I'd squashed him like a bug. His big shoulders slumped and he turned away, shaking his head.

"I heard that you two were seeing each other," I said, "so I thought you'd want to know."

He whipped around, glaring at me. "Who told you that? Who told you about Jas and me?" he demanded.

I jumped, startled by his sudden anger.

No way was I throwing Shane out in front of this bus, so I just gave him an it's-no-big-deal shrug and said, "A lot of people mentioned it. I guess you two were a great couple."

Okay, that was a total lie but—thank goodness—it seemed to calm him down.

The hum of a tram's electric engine sounded behind me.

"Let's go back here," Gabe said, and led the way off of the road and behind a couple of big bushes.

"Jas was special. She was awesome. So smart," Gabe said. "And driven. I've never seen anybody as dedicated to something as Jas was."

He paused while the sound of the tram grew louder as it passed us. I glanced toward the road but couldn't see much through the bushes, just a broken glimpse of the tram and the uniformed employees onboard, heading for the resort. When the noise faded, Gabe spoke again.

"All Jas talked about was getting her degree. She was an art major. She wanted to go to Europe to visit the museums. She had a long list of places she wanted to go, lots of different cities where she could look at those paintings and statues," Gabe said. "She was crazy about that artsy stuff."

It sounded like a yawner to me, but who was I to shoot down someone's dream?

"Were you going with her?" I asked, to bring the conversation back around to the two of them.

"Sure. I'd have gone," Gabe said. He shook his head. "But she was so focused on that stuff I don't think she'd have wanted anybody with her, not even me. She was kind of in the zone when she talked about it, you know? Completely wired in."

"At least you two had your time here at the resort to-gether," I said. "Did she like working here?"

"Yeah, I guess. She liked that she could work here on her breaks from school. I guess a lot of students do that. Jas thought the work was easy and the pay was good—better than the last place she worked." Gabe said.

"Did something happen there?" I asked.

"Somebody was giving her a hard time. She didn't want to talk about it." He frowned. "But in the last week or so she seemed upset. You know, troubled about something."

My senses jumped to high alert, sure I was about to discover a major clue.

"What was wrong?" I asked, and managed to sound concerned and not merely anxious to dig up something that would help *me*. "Did she tell you?"

"No."

So much for a case-breaking clue. Still, I pushed on.

"Was she having a problem with a coworker?" I asked. "Her supervisor, maybe?"

Avery was Jaslyn's supervisor, and I'd wondered about her possible involvement in Jaslyn's death.

"She wanted to change teams," Gabe said.

Thank goodness—a clue I could actually use.

"Why?" I asked.

"She didn't say," Gabe told me. "But she and that supervisor of hers didn't get along."

"You mean Avery?" I asked, just to be sure.

"Jas said she was always riding her about some-thing," Gabe said. "Claiming she wasn't following re-sort policies, crap like that."

If that were true and Jaslyn wasn't keeping up with

the housekeeping schedule, it would reflect poorly on Avery, maybe even get her in trouble with the resort's upper management. I mean, jeez, the standards at the Rowan Resort were incredibly high, and they probably paid key employees very well to maintain those standards. No way would Avery want somebody on her team dragging her down.

But was that a reason to kill someone?

Maybe not a cold, calculated murder, but I could see it happening in the heat of the moment, in an argument that escalated.

"I don't think changing teams was really bothering Jas that much," Gabe said.

Damn. So much for that clue.

"Did you get the feeling she wanted to break up with you?" I asked.

Okay, that was a crappy thing to ask, because Gabe seemed genuinely upset about Jaslyn's death. But I wanted to get something from him that would allow me to take him off my mental suspect list—so it was for his own good. Really.

"No. No way." Gabe slammed his fist into the palm of his hand.

His anger spun up so quickly I stepped back. I realized I was totally alone with him behind the bushes, at the edge of the resort, out of sight of absolutely everybody.

Not a great feeling.

"Jaslyn and I were solid," Gabe told me. "And if I'd found out that somebody else was sniffing around her, they'd have been sorry."

Maybe coming out here to talk to him wasn't such a hot idea.

"Look, I've got to get back to work," Gabe said.

I didn't disagree.

His anger disappeared in a heartbeat—which was kind of scary, too. It made me wonder about how comfortable Jaslyn really had been in their relationship. If she'd wanted to break up with him, would she have dared tell him?

"So do you think she, you know, she . . . suffered?" Gabe asked.

It took a couple of seconds for me to realize that he was asking about Jaslyn's death—the reason I'd lured him to this meeting in the first place.

Really, I've got to get better about keeping up with things.

"No," I said, and I honestly believed it. "She looked peaceful. Like she was just sleeping."

Gabe nodded, then walked away.

I took off in the opposite direction and wound my way through the resort grounds, anxious to get back to the hotel, where someone could hear me scream if necessary. I'd learned some useful info from Gabe that I'd have to follow up on, but the thing that stuck with me was his volatile temper.

No way could I take him off of my suspect list.

That meant I needed more info on Gabe. I could think of only one way to get it.

I stopped near the bungalows, pulled out my cell phone, and called Detective Shuman. He answered on the second ring.

"How's the vacation?" he asked.

Shuman sounded relaxed—like he was the one on vacay.

"I need a favor," I said. "Can you do a background check on a guy for me?"

I guess Shuman picked up on the distress in my voice, because immediately he switched to cop mode.

"What's wrong?" he asked.

Shuman in cop mode was really hot—but I was too rattled at the moment to properly appreciate it.

"I'm just picking up a weird vibe from somebody here," I said.

"Are you involved in the murder investigation?" Shuman asked, and I could tell from his tone that he already knew the answer and wasn't happy about it.

"You don't understand," I said. "I don't exactly have a choice."

"Then explain it to me," Shuman said.

This didn't seem like the best time to get into the whole I'm-solving-a-murder-to-avoid-a-wedding thing, so I went with something easier.

"If anything bad turns up on this guy, I'll tell you everything," I promised.

Shuman was quiet for a while. I knew he wasn't happy about it, but I also knew he'd go along with it.

"Text me the info," Shuman said. "I'll get back to you."

"Thanks," I said. "I owe you."

He hung up.

I texted him the info I had on Gabe Braxton and then slid my phone into my pocket. This really wasn't the vacation I'd hoped for. I had to turn things around.

At breakfast, Marcie and Bella had said they were heading to the beach. This sounded like just the boost my day needed. I decided to put my murder investiga-

tion on ignore and forget about all my other problems—for a while, anyway.

"Haley?"

I knew by the way my knees started to tremble and
my heartbeat picked up that Luke Warner had called
my name.

I spun around and, oh my God, there he stood.

I got the feeling he'd been watching me for a while,
which caused my heart to beat even faster.

Luke walked over. "I saw you talking to a maintenance worker. Is everything all right?"

He sounded genuinely concerned—and, jeez, he
looked great—but I couldn't forget our history. I
forced myself to calm down.

"Are you stalking me?" I asked.

"I was just out for a walk," Luke said with an easy
grin.

Luke has a terrific grin.

He was also a terrific liar—all in the line of duty, of
course.

Luke was an FBI agent who'd been working undercover when we'd met a few months ago. He had extensive experience pretending to be someone other than
himself, so a lie could roll oh so smoothly off of his
tongue. When he'd finally revealed his true identity, I
wasn't happy about being deceived—or about some of
the other things that had happened. Luke tried to make
it up to me, but I was done with him.

Until now.

Maybe.

I wondered if he'd mention what had happened between us a few months ago when we'd both been

searching for a murder suspect in the Garment District and something had sparked between us—long story. I doubted he would—the whole thing wasn't exactly a shining moment for him—and that was okay with me. I didn't really want to think about it, either.

"I saw you yesterday inside the hotel talking to the detectives," Luke said. His brows drew together. "Are you all right?"

I couldn't be certain whether Luke knew what was going on with Jaslyn's murder.

"You don't know?" I asked.

"I'm just here for a wedding," he said, and gave me another grin.

I'd fallen for his cover story once before; I wasn't doing it again.

"A hotel maid was murdered," I said. "I'm sure you heard about it."

"I read it on the Internet," Luke said. "But I'm staying away from the news as much as possible, since I'm on vacation."

"You hadn't heard that I found her body?" I asked.

"Haley, that must have been awful for you," he said, and again sounded genuinely concerned.

This hardly seemed like the time to remind him that Jaslyn's was not the first dead body I'd ever discovered.

"Why did you come into the room where the police were interviewing me?" I asked.

Luke gave me an I'm-an-idiot-sometimes shrug, and said, "I made a wrong turn, went into the wrong room."

"Which room were you looking for?" I wanted to know.

He paused, and I saw in his expression that he knew I didn't trust what he was saying.

And it was true. The bottom line was that I didn't trust Luke. He'd claimed he was here for a wedding, and that may have been true—or he could have been here working undercover investigating Jaslyn's death, or something totally different.

Of course, working undercover was his job—and a pretty cool job, at that—so I guess he couldn't help that he had to lie about things. And even if he was working undercover, he couldn't tell me—which would be a repeat of what had happened between us before.

"The cigar room," Luke said. "I was looking for the cigar room."

Okay, now I felt kind of stupid. His reason made perfect sense because the hotel's first floor was a maze of hallways, alcoves, and dead ends, and was crammed with shops, restaurants, and a zillion other who-knows-what-they're-for rooms.

Maybe he really was telling the truth.

"The detectives just wanted to ask me some questions because I found Jaslyn's body," I said. "That's all."

Luke nodded—I could see he was in semi-FBI mode—toward the resort grounds. "And the maintenance worker?"

It irked me that Luke was grilling me as if I were a suspect or something. But maybe he really was concerned about my safety.

That's the thing about Luke—I never knew what the truth really was.

Was it a coincidence that I kept seeing him? Okay,

sure, this was an island, but it was a sizable one, so why would we *just happen to* keep running into each other?

Or were we?

Was Luke following me? Was he really here working undercover? Was something else going on that involved me and the investigation of Jaslyn's death—or some other totally unrelated crime?

"I asked the guy if he knew when the next supply ship was docking," I said. "I'm waiting for something."

Of course, that was a lie—which was the very reason I was unhappy with Luke, but still.

He grinned. It was an I-know-your-deepest-thoughts kind of grin that set my toes to curling again.

"A handbag," he said.

Jeez, he really was handsome.

"You're still crazy about purses," he said.

Why did he have to be a man I couldn't trust?

"Which one is it this time?" Luke asked, still grinning.

Why couldn't things be different between us?

"You're the FBI agent," I told him. "You figure it out."

I walked away.

CHAPTER 11

As I approached the hotel, I spotted Sandy and Sebastian standing near the entrance. He was doing some serious male, I'm-a-cool-dude posturing, and Sandy was responding with the female wow-you're-a-cool-dude giggle. Normal stuff. Yet there were things about Sebastian that bothered me.

Or maybe I was a little envious that Sandy had found a guy, despite our no-men-on-this-vacation pact.

Not a great feeling.

"Oh, Haley, you should have been at my art lesson," Sandy said as I walked up. Her eyes were round and her cheeks flushed. "Colby Rowan—she said I could call her Colby—she's fabulous. She's awesome. Oh my God, she really is a celebrity."

"And this one here?" Sebastian said, and laid his hand on Sandy's shoulder. "She's got real artistic talent."

Sandy blushed and made girl noises. "No, I don't."

"Yes, you do," he insisted.

"No, not really," Sandy said, and dipped her chin demurely.

"Yes, really," he told her, and leaned closer.

"No," she said.

"Yes," he said.

I had to break this up.

"You were at the lesson?" I asked Sebastian, noting that once again he wasn't dressed in a Rowan Resort uniform.

"He stopped by to make sure I was enjoying myself," Sandy explained, and gave Sebastian an endearing smile.

He returned her endearing smile with one of his own.

Okay, these two were starting to get on my nerves.

Sebastian must have picked up on my you-two-are-making-me-nauseated expression, because he stepped away and said, "You two girls enjoy your day. Sandy, I'll see you later."

He walked away, then glanced back and waved. Sandy gave him a little wave in return, and he disappeared behind a stand of palm trees.

Her gaze lingered on the palms for a few seconds, then said, "Sebastian invited me to have drinks with him later."

"That's nice," I said, and, really, I could have put a little more enthusiasm into it, which was bad of me, I know.

"Am I doing the wrong thing?" Sandy asked, sounding serious and more than a little troubled. "I mean, I have a boyfriend—a real boyfriend, and he's abandoned the work he loves to go on sabbatical so he can recharge his emotions and improve his art."

I had a feeling that Sandy's tattoo artist boyfriend's *sabbatical* was code for *Las Vegas*.

"Do you think I'm being a bad girlfriend?" Sandy asked.

I was convinced that if Sandy ever did something not quite right in her relationship with her boyfriend, it was nothing compared to some of the things he'd done to her—long story

"You're not being a bad girlfriend," I told Sandy. "You're just having a nice vacation, that's all."

She thought about it for a while, then sighed. "I guess you're right. And Sebastian is an employee here. He's probably just making sure I'm having a good time."

I thought there was a little more to Sebastian's interest in Sandy than even the astronomically high guest-relations standards the Rowan Resort required of its employees, but thinking otherwise seemed to help Sandy deal with her am-I-being-a-bad-girlfriend situation with that idiot boyfriend of hers. She deserved a guy who would treat her well, and Sebastian seemed to be doing that.

Still, I wished I didn't have a weird feeling about him.

"Haley, you absolutely have to take an art lesson from Colby," Sandy said. "She's so smart, and so gifted. You'll love her."

I didn't really see myself loving an art lesson, but hey, this was my vacation. Maybe I would give it a try.

"She's super nice," Sandy said, then frowned. "I don't think she liked Sebastian, though. She started acting kind of, I don't know, kind of strange when he showed up."

Okay, Colby could have acted strange around Sebastian for a lot of reasons, but since I was picking up a weird vibe from him too, I decided I needed to check it out. I knew just what to use for cover.

"Want to go to the beach with Marcie and Bella?" I asked

"Sounds great," Sandy agreed.

"I'll meet you there in a few minutes," I said. "I want to check with the shop and see if my Sea Vixen is in."

I knew my totally fabulous tote hadn't arrived yet, because I'd just been to the docks and there had been not even the slightest glimmer of a supply ship on the horizon. But it was the easiest way to check out Sebastian without Sandy knowing what I was doing.

We walked into the hotel together, and Sandy headed for the staircase in the lobby. I hung back, shifting into stealth mode.

I figured the resort had a business center, so I checked the directory posted near the snack bar and saw that it was located down the same hallway as the shops, restaurants, and other specialty rooms.

I headed that way, following the signs, changing directions a zillion times, going deeper and deeper into the hotel. The carpet was thick, muting my footsteps. The lighting was low. So far, I hadn't seen anyone.

My this-place-is-kind-of-creepy meter jumped up a few notches.

I heard the murmur of deep voices coming from a room up ahead, then saw as I passed that, according to the discreet sign beside the door, it was the cigar room.

Luke flew into my head. He told me that's where

he'd been headed when he wandered into my interview with the homicide detectives, so at least now I knew a cigar room actually existed—even though it was nowhere near my interview location.

Damn. Why did I keep thinking about him?

I forced Luke out of my head, turned right, then left, and finally—whew!—found the business center.

Inside were a half-dozen computer workstations, fax and copy machines, and shelves containing every office supply product on the market. It all looked out of place among the dark wood furniture and the black-and-white olden-days photos on the walls.

I had the room to myself, so I chose the computer farthest from the door and sat down, ready to do some serious research on Sebastian. I had only sketchy info on him—his full name, the type of business he owned, and the possibility that he came from a wealthy Connecticut family—but I figured it was enough.

I was wrong.

I Googled everything Sandy had mentioned about Sebastian and came up with nothing. Absolutely nothing. I got no hits on his name, his business, his family, or his home state. I typed every possible combination of info I could think of into the search engine, and still nothing popped. I couldn't even find a Facebook page for him.

I sat back in my chair, not feeling so great.

True, a great many people probably weren't accessible on the Internet. It could happen—even these days.

But a guy who claimed he owned a consulting firm? From a maybe-wealthy family? In Connecticut? With a distinctive name like Sebastian Cannon Lane? Not likely.

So that could only mean one thing—Sebastian had lied to Sandy.

And I'd encouraged Sandy to get involved with him. Oh, crap.

"Was that text from him?" I asked.

"No." Marcie huffed irritably and tossed her phone into the tote bag—a way cool Coach—next to her lounge chair.

We were on the beach enjoying the sun, the ocean breeze, the smell of fresh salt air—not to mention fruity umbrella-topped drinks. Bella was dozing in her lounge chair, and Sandy was listening to her iPod.

"I'm never going to hear from him," Marcie grumbled.

Her first-date guy from a few days ago still hadn't bothered to respond to her text message thanking him for a nice evening—which was really crappy of him, I thought.

"It's for the best, I suppose," Marcie said.

Marcie had a way of always looking on the bright side—which could be really annoying, at times. But I decided that if she could let it go, so should I. And I did—kind of.

Ty popped into my head.

Jeez, what was going on with me? I hadn't thought about him this much when we were dating.

"You're making that face," Marcie said. "The one you make when the handbag you're dying for is not available. Except, you're not thinking about a handbag, are you. It's something else."

CHAPTER 12

"What's wrong?" I asked when I reached Joy.

"I'll fill you in on the way," she said,

Joy took off down the road toward the hotel. Wow, she was really moving in those pumps. I had to hurry to keep up with her—and I have pageant legs.

"It's important that you keep calm when you talk to her," Joy said. "She's on the brink."

A vision of Yasmin standing on the ledge outside one of the hotel's tower rooms, threatening to jump, bloomed in my head.

"I've seen this before in brides," Joy warned.

My mental picture shifted, and I imagined Yasmin on the ledge holding an AK-47 assault rifle.

"We don't want this situation to turn into a full-blown crisis," Joy said.

Now, in my head, Yasmin was picking off loving couples strolling through the gardens. And Joy expected me to talk her down? *Me?*

Honestly, my people skills aren't the best.

"Where is her mother?" I demanded as I followed Joy through the hotel grounds.

Joy shook her head. "Yasmin asked for you. Only you."

Great.

We circled the hotel, and Joy stopped.

"She's inside," she said, pointing.

I hadn't seen this section of the hotel before, an area with numerous pergolas draped with white, billowy curtains set amid ferns, small palms, and flowering shrubs. I smelled scented candles and heard prerecorded rain forest sounds.

Hang on a minute.

"Is this the spa?" I asked.

Joy didn't answer, just darted between the pergolas and disappeared through a set of open French doors. I followed the sound of her clacking pumps on the tile floor and caught up with her in the pedicure salon.

"Call if you need backup," Joy said, and headed for the door. "Good luck."

I definitely heard a "you'll need it" undertone in her voice.

I spotted Yasmin seated in one of the pedicure chairs, both feet in the water. The pedicurist was cowering on a stool looking like a bomb disposal expert watching the timer tick toward zero.

What the heck was going on? And—more important—why was I here?

Yasmin spotted me and shrieked, "Haley! You came! Oh my God! You came!"

Three other women were having pedicures. They all turned and stared at me.

"You *have* to help me, Haley," Yasmin called, waving me over with both hands.

A zillion possibilities flashed in my head: Tate-Tate-Tate had called off the wedding—not that I blamed him—or her mother had a stroke—I could definitely see that happening—or maybe her only attending guest had cancelled—which I totally understood.

Whatever the crisis was, it seemed that I alone was needed to deal with it. I braced myself to hear awful news, shifted into I-can-be-supportive-if-I-absolutely-have-to mode, and walked over.

"I don't know what to do," Yasmin moaned, and threw herself back in the chair. "I just don't *know!*"

I glanced around the room trying to pick up on some tiny clue of what was going on. I got nothing.

"This is just—well, it's just too much," Yasmin said, and flung out both hands. "I can't do this. I can't!"

"Can't do what?" I asked.

Yasmin looked at me as if I'd just suggested she carry a knockoff Louis Vuitton clutch on her honeymoon.

"Decide!" she wailed, pointing at her feet. "White or pink? I can't *decide!*"

"White or pink what?" I asked.

Yasmin jerked her feet up, splashing water everywhere.

"Toenail polish!" she exclaimed in a why-doesn't-anyone-*get-it* voice.

Okay, now I *got it*—and I wasn't happy about it.

My worry bypassed annoyance in a heartbeat, and amped up to anger. I guess it showed on my face, because the pedicurist rolled her stool farther away and leaned forward, ready to make a break for the door.

I'd be right behind her.

Yasmin deflated like a week-old birthday balloon and sank back in her chair.

"Everything has to be perfect for my wedding," she said, tears pooling in her eyes.

Okay, now I felt kind of bad. Of course she wanted perfection on the biggest day of her life.

I drew in a big breath, forcing myself to calm down.

"I have really cute toes," Yasmin said, gazing at her feet, twisting them left, then right. "Tate says they're the most beautiful toes he's ever seen."

No way could I stand here and get mired down in another Tate-Tate-Tate story. I pushed through.

"Okay, so what color nail polish do you like best?" I asked.

Yasmin studied her feet for another long moment, then finally said, "I think I'll get white."

Wow, that was fast.

"Okay," I said, and turned to leave.

"No, pink. I think pink would look the best," Yasmin said.

Crap.

"What do you think?" Yasmin asked.

"Pink would look great," I told her.

"Do you think so?"

"Yes, I think so. I definitely think so," I said.

"White is more fitting for a bride," Yasmin pointed out, "more virginal."

I was positive that train had already left the station, but I rolled with it.

"Then get white," I said.

Yasmin tilted her head, studying her toes from different angles, and said, "I'll probably like pink better."

I huffed. "Do you want me to decide for you?"

She looked relieved. "Yes."

"Okay, get white."

Yasmin frowned and said, "Pink would be prettier."

"We're done here." I turned to the pedicurist. "Put on the white."

I left the salon, fuming, annoyed beyond belief with Yasmin but also with myself.

That's what I get for taking time off from my investigation. I should have stuck with it and found Jaslyn Gordon's killer, so I wouldn't have to deal with all this wedding crap—I'm on vacation.

As if I weren't already annoyed enough, I realized I'd taken a wrong turn somewhere and ended up inside the hotel. Good grief. How did Sidney Rowan's kids ever find their way to their bedrooms at night?

I turned a corner, then another, and oh my God, there was Sebastian ahead of me, walking into one of the rooms.

My anger flared again.

Perfect. Just the person I could take it out on.

I hurried down the corridor, questions of just who he was and what was up between him and Sandy filling my head. No way was I going to let him hurt my friend.

I charged into the room, ready to blast him, only— he wasn't there. Nobody was there.

I froze and looked around. It was a small lounge, with sofas and chairs, two tall bookcases, and a flat screen on the wall.

This was crazy. What the heck was going on?

I looked around the room, into every corner. I was absolutely positive this was the room I'd seen him duck into, but he wasn't here.

How could Sebastian have disappeared? Was I losing my mind?

I scanned the lounge for a couple more minutes—just to be sure my eyes weren't playing tricks on me—then darted into the corridor searching for Sebastian.

No sign of him.

I power-walked along the hallway, checking the shops, the restaurants, everything.

Nothing.

Sebastian had disappeared faster than Kate Spade handbags at an outlet store. How could that be? I'd recognized him—yes, okay, it was from the back—but I was positive it was him, and I'd definitely seen him duck into that lounge. Yet he wasn't there a few seconds later when I walked in? How had he simply vanished?

And why was I involved in this whole Sandy-and-Sebastian-thing, and why was I in the middle of Yasmin's—I hate her—wedding? None of this was supposed to be happening. I'm on vacation.

By the time I reached the hotel's main corridor I was completely rattled. I spotted the snack bar, rushed inside, and picked up three packages of M&M's. I dumped half a package into my mouth before I reached the cashier—she didn't blink an eye; obviously mine wasn't the first chocolate emergency she'd witnessed—and walked outside into the courtyard.

The day was beautiful. A mild breeze stirred, the flower blooms were fragrant, and the trickling fountains were soothing.

Yeah, okay, the place was beautiful, but the sights and sounds didn't help like the M&M's did. I was two whole bags in before I calmed down.

I collapsed onto a bench near a water feature that looked like a brook winding through a village of tiny fairy cottages.

The chocolate kicked in big-time, and Sebastian filled my head. Something was weird about him. Shane, the bartender at the beach bar, had called him golden and warned that he was trouble. Sandy had said that at her art lesson she'd gotten the impression that Colby Rowan hadn't liked him. I'd found nothing on the Internet— zero, nada, zilch—about him, his family, or the supposed consulting firm he owned.

Something wasn't right about Sebastian. But what, exactly?

Was he one of those scam artists who hung with the rich and famous, even though he was completely out of their league? A male gold digger who thought that, since Sandy was a guest at the I'm-so-rich-I-brush-my-teeth-with-gold-dust Rowan Resort, she was wealthy?

Or was something else going on?

I finished off the last package of M&M's, but my supercharged chocolate-coated brain cells didn't reach a higher level of consciousness. Sebastian was definitely up to something, but I couldn't figure out what it was.

I was tempted to head back to the snack bar for another round of brain-boosting chocolate—maybe I'd have better luck with a couple of Snickers bars—but my cell phone vibrated. I pulled it from my pocket and read a text from Marcie letting me know they were leaving the beach, hungry for lunch. I texted back that I'd meet them in our room, and headed upstairs for a quick shower.

At the top of the stairs I saw two housekeeping carts

at the opposite ends of the hallway and hoped they'd already finished with my room. There's something really nice about coming into a neat, freshly cleaned room—especially if someone else had done the work.

I opened my door and saw that the beds had been made, and I headed for the bathroom. A knock sounded on my door. I figured it was Marcie, so I opened it. Only it wasn't Marcie. It was Tabitha.

She darted into the room, forcing me to step back, then slammed the door and fell back against it.

"What are you—"

"Shh," Tabitha said. She whipped around, looked out the peephole, then turned to me again and said, "I'm not supposed to do this. It's against the rules. I could get into big trouble."

Her eyes were wide and I could see that she was trembling slightly. Obviously, Tabitha had no stealth-mode skills. Maybe I'd work with her on that later.

"I saw you come into your room," Tabitha said. "I've been watching all morning. I have to talk to you."

My this-could-benefit-*me* instinct took over.

"Sure," I said, using my tell-me-everything-so-I-can-use-it-for-my-own-good voice, something I'd picked up from my beauty queen mother at a very early age.

"I saw you talking to Gabe," Tabitha said, and for some reason she was whispering.

"When?" I asked, and for the same reason—whatever that was—I was whispering too.

"I was on the tram and I saw you two talking," Tabitha said. She drew back a little. "Are you two, you know, are you dating or something?"

I got a weird feeling. Was Tabitha interested in

Gabe? Had she come here to find out if I was trying to move in on him? To stake her claim? Tell me to back off?

Maybe she was stealthier than I thought.

Not a good feeling.

"Heck, no," I said.

Tabitha looked relieved—but not in a good way.

"He's kind of, you know, kind of crazy," Tabitha said. "He gets really mad, really quick. You should stay away from him."

My internal this-could-definitely-benefit-me alarm went off.

"Did Jaslyn know he was like that?" I asked, anxious to move the conversation toward a new clue. "Was she afraid of him?"

"She was acting, I don't know, kind of weird the last week or so before she . . . before she died," Tabitha said.

Gabe had told me the same thing, but he claimed he didn't know why. I wondered now if he himself had been the reason—an excellent clue I could use for solving the murder.

"Was she acting weird because of Gabe?" I asked. "Did she want to break up with him, maybe?"

"No. It wasn't because of Gabe," Tabitha said.

So much for that clue opportunity.

"There was something about Jaslyn," she went on. "Men liked her a lot. They kind of wanted to own her, you know? She had such a free spirit, it was like they wanted to put her in a glass jar or something. You know?"

I didn't recall any man wanting to be with me that badly, but I could understand what Tabitha was getting at. It reminded me of something Gabe had mentioned about trouble with someone at a previous job.

"Did Jaslyn ever mention any problems with someone at her last job?" I asked. "The one she worked before she started here at the resort?"

"Oh, yeah, that guy." Tabitha nodded. "He kept calling and texting her, but she wouldn't have anything to do with him. It was kind of crazy."

Or maybe the guy was kind of crazy.

"Did she ever tell you his name?" I asked.

Tabitha thought for a few seconds, then shook her head. "I don't think so. It was in L.A. Some magazine or something. She got hired there because she knew a lot about paintings and that kind of stuff. They wanted her to stay, become a permanent employee, but she wouldn't do it."

I figured that if Jaslyn, an art major, had left that sort of job she must have really wanted to get away from the guy who was psycho-interested in her.

"So why do you think Jaslyn was upset the week before she died?" I asked.

Tabitha shrugged. "I don't know. She just started acting weird. She got kind of quiet, you know? She didn't talk to me very much. She wanted to change teams. She volunteered for extra work."

Volunteering for extra work definitely sounded weird to me.

"I think she got into trouble," Tabitha said.

My major-clue antennas sprang up.

"I don't know," Tabitha said, shaking her head. "She didn't say, but I heard that Avery—she's our team leader—was mad at her."

Before I could ask anything else, Tabitha gasped softly, seeming to realize how long she'd been in my room, and said, "I've got to go."

She whirled around and opened my door slowly, glanced up and down the hallway, then disappeared.

I grabbed my robe, went into the bathroom, and turned on the shower. The water pulsed and steam rose quickly, but I didn't get in. Tabitha's words kept rattling around in my brain.

Jaslyn had worked at a magazine or something, she'd said. Both she and Gabe told me there'd been a problem with a guy who worked there. Apparently, Jaslyn wasn't interested, he didn't like it, and he had cyber-stalked her.

Had he followed her here to the Rowan Resort? Was that possible?

No way, I decided, unless he was wealthy and could afford this place. The only other way to get here was to secure a job, because absolutely nobody else could get onto the island without—

Wait a minute.

Oh my God.

Ben Oliver bloomed in my mind.

He'd refused to tell me the reason he was here. He'd claimed that he—a newspaper reporter—wasn't interested in Jaslyn's murder.

Tabitha had said that Jaslyn's previous job had been at a magazine or something. Maybe that *something* was a newspaper.

I got a weird feeling.

Had Jaslyn actually worked at the newspaper where Ben worked?

My weird feeling got weirder.

Had Ben been the guy who was crazy about Jaslyn? The guy who'd stalked her?

My weird feeling got crazy-weird.

Had Ben trumped up an idea for a story and convinced his editor at the newspaper to send him here so he could see Jaslyn?

Had Ben murdered her?

Oh, crap.

CHAPTER 13

I had to talk to Ben. I'd showered and dressed in way-cute yellow shorts and an even way-cuter sleeveless print blouse—which would have looked fabulous with a Sea Vixen—just as Marcie had returned to our room from the beach. I'd told her I'd meet her, Bella, and Sandy in the lobby and had taken off to find Ben. I'd made a sweep of the hotel grounds and had even tried his cell phone but hadn't located him. Finally, there was nothing left to do but eat.

"How about horseback riding this afternoon?" Sandy said as we all sat at a table on yet another of the Rowan Resort's outdoor dining patios, finishing lunch.

"I'm out," Bella said. "I'm going up to my room and take a nap. That's what vacay is all about."

She did look worn out, yet she'd managed to style her hair into the shape of a sail after returning from the beach. Definitely a high point in Bella's regatta of tropical hair designs.

"Riding sounds like fun," Marcie agreed.

"We're bound to see some celebrities on the riding trails," Sandy said. She gasped. "Maybe we'll see Channing Tatum. He's so hot. I'd love to see him."

Who wouldn't?

Since finding Ben was my most pressing matter and I hadn't been able to do that, I figured an hour or so of horseback riding wouldn't create a devastating delay in my murder investigation. This was an island, after all; Ben had to be here somewhere.

"Let's do it," I said, and we all rose from our chairs.

"I'll call Avery and ask her to make the arrangements," Marcie said, and pulled out her cell phone as we left the dining area.

"Don't fall off," Bella called as she headed toward the hotel.

I was just about to suggest that Sandy and I grab some snacks to take along on our ride when I spotted Joy and Yasmin headed our way. Yikes! No way was I ruining my afternoon because of those two.

"Let's go," I said in my get-moving-for-our-own-good voice.

Sandy, apparently, had no understanding of the get-moving urgency in my voice because she didn't get-moving. Instead, she said in a really loud voice, "Oh, look. There's Yasmin."

Sandy, apparently, also had no comprehension of my what-the-heck-are-you-doing eyebrow bob, because she waved both hands and called, "Yasmin! Hey, Yasmin!"

Yasmin's attention turned to us like one of those heat-seeking missiles homing in for the kill. She sped toward us, Joy hurrying along beside.

"Hi, Yasmin," Sandy said, smiling. "How are the plans for your wedding coming—"

"Haley, what is going on with my bachelorette party?" Yasmin demanded. "Joy said you haven't done one single thing."

I drew in a big breath, determined not to let her upset me.

"You're trying to ruin my special day, aren't you," Yasmin said. "You're jealous—you've always been jealous of me—and now you're doing everything possible to make my wedding miserable!"

"I really don't have time to get into this with you now," I said in the same tone my mom used when some hapless salesclerk offered to show her an off-the-rack gown. "I'm going horseback riding."

"Horseback riding?" Yasmin demanded. "Haley, how can you be so selfish? How can you even think about something like that when my wedding is coming up?"

I felt like I'd just walked into a screening of *Psycho Bride Part Two: Back With a Vengeance.*

"You hate me, don't you?" Yasmin wailed, then burst out crying.

I was about to assure Yasmin that I did, in fact, hate her when Sandy took Yasmin's arm and urged her toward a nearby bench, whispering comforting words.

Joy and I watched as Yasmin plopped down, then threw herself onto Sandy's shoulder, sobbing. Finally, Joy said, "We need to finalize the plans for the bachelorette party."

We? How did I get in the middle of this?

Joy seemed to read my mind—or maybe it was my I'm-screaming-on-the-inside expression—because she said, "Yasmin's maid of honor isn't coming, remember? The bachelorette party is your responsibility now. We talked about it yesterday."

I remembered talking about it, but I thought sure I'd dodged that bullet. Joy probably knew that but, obviously, she wasn't going to crash-and-burn on Yasmin's wedding prep alone, and wanted to drag me in so she'd have someone else to blame.

That's what I would have done.

Since there seemed to be only one way out of this, I shifted into event-planner mode.

"Okay, here's what we'll do," I said.

Joy whipped open her iPad and started pecking at the keys.

"Male strippers. Lots of booze. Hot waiters with no shirts," I said.

Joy stopped pecking and shook her head. "That's not what Yasmin wants. It's supposed to be a garden party theme."

"A garden party?" I might have said that kind of loud.

"It's the latest trend," Joy explained.

"For a bachelorette party?" I'm sure I shouted that.

"*Brides* magazine covered it in their last issue," Joy said.

Damn. Here was my chance to see some hot guys, drink a little too much for a really good reason, and party down, and now it was ruined—all because of Yasmin.

I hate her.

Still, no way could I argue with *Brides* magazine.

"We'll stage it outside at one of the dining areas," I said, the whole event blooming—in pink—in my head.

"White wicker furniture, pink table settings. Set up an arched arbor for guests to walk through when they arrive, and put white carpet beneath it. I want pink flowers everywhere."

"What about food?" Joy asked, typing frantically into her iPad.

"Petite samplers," I said. "Four kinds of meat, salads, and whatever vegetables the chef thinks are freshest."

Joy nodded. "Dessert will be a fabulous cake, pink icing, of course."

"Make it one small cake for each guest," I said. "Get a signature drink, something pink. And a hot-looking bartender with no shirt on."

Joy smiled, but I'm pretty sure she didn't write that down.

"I've got the music handled," she said. "Entertainment?"

What seemed entertaining to me would be watching Tate-Tate-Tate walk into the party and tell Yasmin exactly what he thought of her—which, surely, would be the same as I thought of her—and dumping her on the spot.

But, really, I was probably the only person who would find that entertaining.

"Grab Yasmin's cell phone and download all her pictures," I said, confident that all of the photos would be of her. "Get one of the resort's tech guys to set up a slideshow and we'll put them on a flat screen during the party. Have Yasmin show you all of the clothes she bought for her honeymoon, then duplicate each look, hire models, and put on a fashion show."

Joy paused. I was pretty sure I saw a this-will-cost-a-fortune frown wrinkle her forehead. I ignored it, of course. I figured that Yasmin's mom and dad would want Yasmin to love her wedding so they wouldn't have to listen to her whine, moan, and complain about it for years to come, and if Tate was paying for the wedding, well, better that he knew what the rest of his life would be like, married to Yasmin. So, really, I was doing all of them a favor.

"Can you put all of that together by tomorrow afternoon?" I asked.

"I'm juggling three weddings this week and this is the simplest by far," Joy said. "And it's nothing compared to the event coming up in a few weeks."

I figured it was for a major Hollywood star but didn't ask. I was sure Joy wouldn't tell me, anyway.

Even though I'd talked only to Joy about Yasmin's wedding plans, I knew she had a huge staff to help with every facet of each event, so I wasn't worried—and, thankfully, this would be the end of my involvement, except to show up at the wedding ceremony.

Joy consulted her iPad. "The florist is flying in with the flowers, and the Heart of Amour will arrive on schedule with the security team."

Okay, that was cool. I was definitely getting an expensive jeweled pendant for my bouquet so I could have a security team when I got married.

"If any problems arise, I'll let you know," Joy said.

"Please don't," I said.

Joy laughed as if that were the funniest thing she'd ever heard—I don't think she believed me—and whispered something to Yasmin. I couldn't hear what she said—nor did I care—but Yasmin immediately stopped crying, got up, and walked toward the hotel with Joy.

"Avery scheduled us for horseback riding," Marcie said, joining me. "Do you still want to go?"

I figured Marcie had been hiding out, waiting for Hurricane Yasmin to blow through and, honestly, I didn't blame her.

"Sure," I said, and my spirits lifted.

Riding would give me an opportunity to wear the fabulous Roberto Cavalli jeans I'd bought for this trip, along with the totally awesome Prada backpack I'd gotten.

We headed into the hotel to change, and just as I passed the snack bar I spotted Ben Oliver standing in front of a display of chips and cookies.

"I'll be up in a minute," I said, freezing in my tracks, my gaze glued to Ben.

Sandy and Marcie stopped, too.

"Hey, it's that guy," Sandy said. "I saw him in the store one time."

Wow, Sandy had a great memory.

"Who is he?" she asked.

No way was I going to give it away that Ben was a reporter—at least, not until I found out the info I needed from him.

"Just a friend," I said. "I'll meet you upstairs in a few minutes."

Marcie gave me a you'll-have-to-give-me-details-later look, then left with Sandy.

I walked to the entrance of the snack bar and watched as Ben studied the shelves of goodies. His back was to me, but I recognized the same khaki pants and blue polo shirt he'd had on yesterday.

Jeez, I really wish he'd let me put together a glam squad for him.

My next thought was to jump in front of him and accuse him of murdering Jaslyn—I'm all about the shock factor, at times—but I didn't want anyone to overhear and call security. I had to try a different tact.

For a few seconds I attempted the Vulcan mind meld, but all I got was the image of chocolate, which was way cool, of course. I considered for a moment that my mind meld was successful, then realized those chocolate-coated thoughts were probably mine, not Ben's.

Damn. I hate it when that happens.

Ben gave up on the snacks and headed out into the courtyard. I made my move. I followed, ready to dart around him and force him to stop.

Ben suddenly swung around and glared at me. "Stop following me."

He'd known I was behind him all along?

I was definitely going to have to work on my Jedi skills.

"I figured out why you're here," I told him. "You knew Jaslyn Gordon, didn't you."

Ben gave me a not-this-again eye roll.

I pushed on, undaunted—that's what all we great interrogators do.

"You two worked together at the newspaper," I said. "You were in love with her."

"You're wrong," Ben said. "As usual."

"You stalked her," I said.

"No."

"You followed her here to the island, but she wanted nothing to do with you," I said. "So you killed her."

Ben drew back a little.

I realized I was starting to sound like those homicide detectives who'd interviewed me and accused me of things I hadn't done.

Not a good feeling.

Still, I wasn't going to let Ben off the hook so easily. Not until I found out what was really going on with him.

Ben glared at me for another few seconds, then heaved a giant I-surrender sigh.

"Okay, look," he said. "I'll tell you why I'm here, but you can't tell anyone—*anyone*. Okay?"

This was so cool. Not only was Ben about to come clean about why he was at the resort but, apparently, I'd get to know a huge secret, too.

"Okay?" Ben demanded.

"Okay," I told him.

Ben glared at me for a few seconds, like he was trying to read my mind or something—which, thank goodness, he couldn't do—then glanced around and moved closer.

Just to show that I could be as stealthy as he was, I glanced around, too, and leaned in.

"I got tipped by someone on the security team of a Hollywood celebrity," Ben said quietly.

I didn't see how this could possibly be connected to Jaslyn's death, but it was obviously major stuff. I leaned closer.

"Which one?" I asked.

"I can't give up that info," Ben said, and glanced around again. "But it concerns criminal activity involving high-profile stars, and it's been linked to this resort."

Oh my God. This was good stuff.

Visions of stalkers, financial scams, and theft of intellectual property rights flashed in my head.

"What kind of criminal activity?" I asked.

Ben shook his head. "I can't get into specifics."

No, no, he couldn't stop. Not now. This was like finally locating the last fabulous Chanel bag in a department store only to realize it was promised to someone else.

"You have to give me *something*," I insisted.

"No way. Absolutely no way," Ben told me. "You're not going to blow this story for me."

I appreciated that he hadn't added, "Like all those other times."

Still, I wasn't giving up.

"And this story of yours that you're investigating here has nothing to do with Jaslyn Gordon's murder?" I asked.

"Absolutely not," he said, then went on before I could ask anything else. "And I didn't know that girl. I never worked with her. I didn't stalk her, and I didn't murder her."

I switched on my truth-inducing triple-stink-eye.

Ben didn't flinch.

"If I was going to stalk and kill anyone, it would be you," he said.

I couldn't argue with that.

"You can't tell anybody about this," Ben said, then gave me triple-stink-eye right back.

"I won't," I said.

"Swear," he told me. "Swear you won't tell."

"I swear," I said.

Ben kept glaring.

"I swear," I said. "Okay? I swear."

Yeah, I'd just sworn—twice—that I wouldn't tell, but come on, this was major gossip. It would be really hard not to tell someone.

I guess Ben didn't pick up on my I'd-love-to-tell vibe, because he walked away. I watched as he disappeared behind some shrubs and leafy palms, feeling a little jealous.

Wow, Ben was on a cool Hollywood celebrity story, working undercover. How come I couldn't do something awesome like that?

I definitely need to reassess my life.

I headed back into the hotel, more than a little disappointed that my great Ben-did-it theory hadn't worked out exactly as I'd hoped. While I wasn't so sure I believed every aspect of his celebrity-criminal-activity story, it sounded reasonable enough that I could shift him to my mental back burner of murder suspects.

So who did that leave?

As I walked past the room where homicide detectives Pearce and Vance had interviewed me, Luke Warner popped into my head. But instead of that toe-curling feeling I usually got when I thought of him, something totally different flashed in my head.

Luke was an FBI agent who worked undercover.

Had he been working undercover at the magazine—or whatever it was—with Jaslyn?

He'd told me that he was on the island for the wedding, but would he really have taken off time from his job for a college friend?

He'd walked into the interview room, and when I'd asked him about it later he'd claimed he was looking for the cigar room. But the cigar room was nowhere near the interview room. How could he have wandered into the interview room by mistake?

Had he gone into the interview room on purpose to try to get some info on the detectives' investigation? He'd seen me in that interview room. Had he *supposedly* run into me so often on the island to see if I'd learned anything new about Jaslyn's death?

Had Luke met her while working undercover? Had he fallen for her? Stalked her? Killed her?

Oh, crap.

CHAPTER 14

I needed more info on Jaslyn.

No way would my maybe-Luke-did-it theory fly without some evidence, and I knew that Luke, a trained FBI agent, wouldn't divulge any info, despite my I-saw-this-technique-on-a-Lifetime-channel-movie-and-it-worked-great interrogation method.

There was only one thing I could do: call Jack Bishop.

I got the I'm-a-total-girl triple whammy—curling toes, gooey stomach, pounding heart—at the mere thought of Jack. He was a private detective I'd met last fall when I worked for the Pike Warner law firm in Los Angeles. I'd worked in the accounts payable department and Jack had done security consulting for the firm. We'd become friends when he'd helped me out with that whole administrative-leave-investigating-pending thing I'd gone through at the firm—which was totally not my fault—and I'd helped him out with some of his cases—long story.

Jack was hot—way hot. Tall, rugged build, brown wavy hair, gorgeous blue eyes, just barely on the other side of thirty.

Something definitely could have gone on between us back then, but I'd had my official boyfriend Ty Cameron—and I'm a real stickler about that sort of thing—so Jack had respected my position. Really. Right up to the point where he came pounding on my door one night and—well, let's just say that, for once, Jack's timing was way off.

I pulled out my cell phone and called Jack; my palm instantly started to sweat. He answered right away.

"How's the vacation?" he asked.

Oh my God, how did he know I was on vacation? I hadn't told him. How had he found out?

Jack knows everything. It's way hot.

"I got dragged into a wedding," I said, "and I might actually murder the bride before she can walk down the aisle."

"That would be the always enchanting Yasmin," Jack said.

"Yeah," I said. "How did you know that?"

"Maybe we'll share secrets sometime," Jack said.

He used his Barry White voice. I'm totally helpless against the Barry White voice.

Then I recovered enough to remember that Jack worked security for lots of places including, probably, the law firm that Yasmin's dad owned, the same firm for which Tate-Tate-Tate was making the ultimate sacrifice in the hope of making partner sooner, rather than later. More than likely Jack had heard the office gossip about the wedding or, maybe, he'd been involved with it in some official capacity.

"I need info," I said, thinking it better to get on with the reason I'd called. "Have you heard about Jaslyn Gordon? She's the one who—"

"—was murdered at the resort." The playfulness left Jack's voice and he shifted into private investigator mode. "What are you doing? Why are you involved in that?"

He sounded a little angry now, which didn't suit me. Really, I had enough to deal with.

"It's a long story," I said.

"I've got plenty of time," Jack told me.

I huffed, just to make sure he knew I wasn't in the mood for this sort of thing, then said, "I need some info on Jaslyn so I can get out of going to Yasmin's wedding."

I got nothing from Jack, but I pictured him with that what-the-heck-is-she-talking-about-now expression on his face.

I've seen it a few times.

Okay, more than a few times.

"Look," I said. "I need info on one of Jaslyn's former employers. It was a magazine or something in L.A. somewhere. I think a guy she worked with might have been stalking her."

I wasn't sure if Jack had connected the dots with the whole wedding thing, but luckily he moved on.

"You think this guy might have killed her?" he asked.

I saw no need to mention that I suspected Jaslyn's stalker was an undercover FBI agent. Jack might be reluctant to get involved with the Feds—not that I blamed him, of course. But, jeez, I needed the info. I'd tell Jack later, if it was necessary.

"It's the strongest lead I've found," I said.

"Leave this alone, Haley," Jack said. "Let the police handle it."

He sounded stern and more than a little concerned—which was really hot, of course. But no way was I backing off.

"Are you going to help me or not?" I asked.

I heard heavy breathing from Jack—which was really, really hot—then he finally said, "I'll see what I can do."

"Thanks, Jack," I said. "I owe you."

I expected him to respond with his usual I'll-tell-you-what-I-want-when-I-want-it, but he didn't.

Instead, Jack said, "Be careful, Haley. There's a killer on that island."

He hung up.

The hotel lobby was crowded when Marcie, Sandy, and I came down dressed in our fabulous horseback riding attire, which was great because I had on my Roberto Cavalli jeans and carried my Prada backpack and, really, lots of people should have the opportunity to see me in them.

We'd just exited the hotel heading toward the stables when my cell phone vibrated in my pocket. My senses immediately jumped to high alert, thinking it was Jack calling back, or maybe Detective Shuman, who was checking into Gabe Braxton for me. But when I pulled out my phone and looked at the caller ID, I saw that it was Ada calling.

Ada? Ada was Ty's grandmother. She was a real hoot, and we'd spent some fabulous hours together shopping, but I hadn't talked to, or seen her, since Ty and I broke up. Why the heck would she be calling me?

Then it hit me—oh my God, something had happened to Ty.

I froze. My heart raced. My head filled with a couple dozen horrible things that could have happened to him—a plane crash, a heart attack, a zombie apocalypse—and I had a major flashback to a few weeks ago when I'd been at work and the hospital in Palmdale had called and told me Ty had been in an auto accident.

I'd never been so scared in my entire life. I'd rushed to the emergency room and discovered that he was fine, thank goodness, with just a few bumps and bruises.

The whole incident had been kind of odd, really. I'd learned later that Ty had cancelled all his afternoon appointments that day, ditched his totally hot Porsche for a rented car, and changed out of his suit into jeans and a polo shirt at a convenience store before becoming involved in the accident.

We'd broken up before Ty had explained what, exactly, he'd been up to that day.

Now, standing outside the hotel staring at Ada's name on my cell phone, all I could think was that Ty hadn't been so lucky this time and something awful had happened to him.

Marcie and Sandy saw the oh-my-God look in my eye and stopped, too. I hit the green button.

"Haley, dear, how are you?"

Ada sounded light and breezy, but maybe that was just her way of easing into bad news.

I hate being eased into bad news.

"What's wrong?" I might have said that too loud.

"Well, why would you ask that?" Ada said.

"Did something happen to Ty?" I'm sure I said that too loud.

Ada laughed gently. "If something had happened to Ty, you would have heard about it before I did."

My fear immediately deflated. Thank goodness nothing was wrong.

Then something else hit me—Ada thought Ty would call me in an emergency? Did she not know we'd broken up? Had Ty not told her?

Okay, this was weird.

"I wanted to thank you," Ada said, "for stepping in to help Yasmin with her wedding."

Okay, now I was confused.

"I spoke with her grandmother—we're old friends—and she told me how wonderful you'd been," Ada went on.

Okay, now I got it.

Yasmin's family and Ty's family were wealthy so, of course, they knew each other.

"I'm not going to make it to the wedding," Ada said. "This darn hip of mine is acting up again."

"Sorry to hear that," I said.

"No matter," Ada said. "I'll be up for a shopping trip with you again soon. We'll make a day of it."

I couldn't help but smile. I really liked Ty's grandmother.

"You bet," I said. "Take care of yourself."

"I will," Ada said, and hung up.

"Is everything okay?" Sandy asked as I slid my cell phone into the pocket of my jeans.

"That was Ty's grandmother," I said. "She wanted to thank me for helping with Yasmin's wedding."

"You looked totally panicked," Sandy said.

I nodded and said, "I thought maybe she was calling to tell me something had happened to Ty."

"Ty didn't tell her you two broke up?" Marcie asked.

"You broke up with somebody?" Sandy asked, looking concerned in a whole different way now.

I wasn't sure how much Sandy knew about my relationship with Ty. Because he owned the Holt's Department Store where I worked part-time with Sandy and Bella, we'd tried to keep our relationship quiet—unless it benefited *me*, of course.

"It was several weeks ago," I said.

"You don't look like you're over him yet," Sandy said. "I guess the breakup was his idea, huh?"

Sandy can be wise, at times.

It's kind of scary.

I drew in a deep breath and said, "Yeah, it was his idea, but I went along with it. It was for the best, I guess."

And that was true—or at least, that's what I'd told myself for the last several weeks. But I'd also asked myself why I hadn't fought for our relationship. Why had I let it go so easily?

"You must still have feelings for him," Sandy said.

Okay, her all-seeing probe into my heart and mind was starting to get on my nerves now.

Marcie sensed it—as a BFF would—and said, "Let's go. We don't want to miss our horseback ride."

"Oh my God, do you think Ty is coming to Yasmin's wedding?" Sandy said. Her eyes widened and her mouth fell open. "What if he does? What if he sees you? What if being surrounded by all that wedded bliss makes him realize he was wrong to break up with you? That he still cares about you? That he *loves* you, even? Oh my God, that would be so cool."

"I think you're getting ahead of yourself, Sandy," Marcie said.

"No, it could happen," Sandy insisted. "Yasmin said she has that special pendant for her bouquet. The Heart of Amour, remember? She said that the last four girls who caught the bouquet with that pendant attached got married. If Haley catches the bouquet, she could end up marrying Ty."

"I'm not catching the bouquet," I told Sandy.

Okay, I admit I'm somewhat competitive—I've raced the stranger beside me on the stationary bicycle at the gym, but doesn't everybody do that?—yet no way had I ever, or would I ever, make the slightest attempt to catch a bouquet at a wedding. In fact, I always run the other way. That's my policy, and I saw no need to change it.

That's how I roll.

"Still, it would be really romantic," Sandy pointed out.

"Right now, we have a date with three horses," Marcie said. "Let's go."

We all started walking toward the stables again.

I was glad Marcie had stepped in—not that I was actually caught up in the mental picture Sandy had conjured up of Ty seeing me at the wedding, realizing he'd made a mistake, and begging me to come back to him. Really.

Well, okay, maybe a little. Maybe I still had feelings for Ty. A little.

Maybe more than a little.

I'm not thinking about that now. I'm on vacation.

We followed the walkway that wound through the hotel gardens, past the bungalows until we reached the edge of the grounds. To our right, the path led to the docks, helipad, and the employee dorms. We turned left, toward the center of the island where the stables were located.

"Oh, look!" Sandy said. She hopped up and down and pointed. "There's Colby!"

I caught sight of a woman walking away from us, headed in the direction of the hotel. She was too far away for me to get much of a look at her, just an impression that she was short, thin, with dark hair.

"Colby!" Sandy shouted. She waved both hands in the air. "Colby! Hey, Colby!"

She kept walking.

"I guess she didn't hear me," Sandy said, her shoulders drooping. "I wanted you to meet her."

"She looked like she is in a hurry," Marcie said.

"I'm sure she is," Sandy said. "She's very busy taking care of all the art in the resort's collection. Plus, she creates her own paintings and sells them abroad. She's recognized internationally as one of the premiere artists. They love her work in Asia."

"Did you read that in *People* magazine?" Marcie asked.

"Colby told me herself when I was in her art class," Sandy said. "Wow, I really wish my boyfriend were here. I know the two of them would talk for hours about their art."

We started walking toward the stables again. I glanced back. Colby had disappeared.

But I couldn't help wondering what the daughter of multibillionaire Sidney Rowan, an internationally renowned artist and the curator of the resort's art collection, had been doing at the employees' dorm.

CHAPTER 15

"It's b.s.," Bella said. "You asks me, it's b.s."

Bella, Marcie, and I were seated at a table near the beach bar, watching as Sandy danced with Sebastian. We'd finished our horseback ride, taken a nap, had dinner, and were now having snacks and drinks by tiki torchlight to the sounds of reggae music and the pounding surf.

"I think they make a cute couple," Marcie said.

"Something's not right about that guy," Bella said, shaking her head. "All that talk about owning his own consulting firm? No way. It's b.s."

I was with Bella on this one, but I didn't want anyone to know I'd been suspicious enough to check out Sebastian on the Internet.

"Besides," Bella said, "this is supposed to be a no-men vacation. I guess we're changing that now—and me without my lucky panties."

"You never heard from the security people about your panties?" Marcie asked.

"Not a single word," Bella grumbled. "Some other woman is wearing my lucky panties—and probably getting lucky. Now *that's* b.s."

Marcie and I shared a glance. I knew we were both thinking that maybe the no-men aspect of our trip wasn't such a hot idea after all. I was pretty sure that Marcie was still thinking about that first-date guy who hadn't contacted her. And since Sandy had suggested it earlier today, the thought that Ty might show up at the resort for Yasmin's wedding kept creeping into my head.

My cell phone rang. My heart jumped, thinking it might be Ty calling. Then my thoughts flashed on Jack— that happens a lot. But when I looked at the caller ID screen I saw that Detective Shuman was calling, and my heart jumped in a totally different way.

"Having fun?" he asked, when I answered.

"Sure," I said, rising from my chair and stepping away from the table. "I'm on vacation."

I guess he picked up on something in my voice— he's a detective, after all—because he said, "Sounds like your trip needs a boost."

"I'm having a great time," I said. No way would I admit the truth.

"Sitting on the sidelines when you should be dancing?" Shuman asked.

Okay, that was weird.

"What makes you think I'm—"

"You and your friends should be on the dance floor," Shuman said.

"How the heck would you know—"

I gasped and whirled around. I spotted Shuman standing near the bar, holding his cell phone up to his ear, and grinning.

Oh my God, I couldn't believe he was here. And he looked great.

The last time I saw Shuman was when that whole thing with his girlfriend went down—long story—and he'd been a total wreck then. Now, his dark hair was blowing in the breeze. He had a definite island vibe going on with white trousers, a blue shirt with the sleeves rolled back, and flip-flops. He looked rested and rejuvenated.

I slid my phone into my pocket. Marcie and Bella both turned to see what had taken my attention so quickly.

"That's Shuman. What's he doing here?" Marcie said. "Wow, he looks awesome."

"Hey," Bella said, "I've seen that guy come into the store."

"I'll be back," I said.

"Ask him if he's got a brother," Bella called.

Shuman came forward and we met at the edge of the dance floor. Wow, these tiki torches, candles, and twinkle lights made for great lighting. I hoped it was doing as much for me as it was for Shuman.

"What the heck are you doing here?" I asked.

Shuman leaned closer.

Wow, he smelled great.

"I'm undercover," he whispered.

Shuman was undercover? Ben was undercover? Maybe Luke was undercover? How come I couldn't be undercover?

I'm definitely addressing that when this vacation is over.

"Let's take a walk," Shuman said, and nodded toward the beach.

We left the bar and dance floor—Sandy saw us and gave me a thumbs-up—and followed the path until it ended at the beach. The music faded and the surf grew louder. Tiny lights in the trees and shrubs twinkled.

"What's going on?" I asked. "Why are you here?"

"I was worried about you," Shuman said.

My breath caught. I hadn't expected to hear that, and I wasn't sure I wanted to—not after what Shuman had been through with his girlfriend getting murdered not so long ago. I figured he was emotionally vulnerable, and no way did I want to take a chance that he might want to get involved with me at a time like this—I'd already dodged that bullet once.

"This murder investigation of yours may be bigger than you think," Shuman said.

So he really was here just to talk about Jaslyn's death. I kind of felt like an idiot now.

"How so?" I asked, anxious to keep the conversation going.

"After you asked me to check into Jaslyn Gordon's boyfriend, Gabe Braxton," Shuman said, "I did some digging and learned that Colby Rowan lives here at the resort."

This was not exactly a brilliant piece of police work; it had been reported in *People* magazine. Still, I knew Shuman well enough to realize something more was coming.

"She was part of a robbery team that targeted up-scale shops in L.A.," Shuman said.

Again, *People* had covered it.

Maybe I should give him a subscription for Christmas.

"Colby was the advance person for the robberies,"

Shuman said. "She dressed as if she belonged in those stores, thanks to her daddy's billions, so she didn't raise suspicion. She went in, checked out the security, the employees' routines, delivery schedules, everything."

This, *People* hadn't reported—or if they had, Sandy hadn't mentioned it.

"They got away with millions in jewelry, watches, statues, paintings, all kinds of high-end merchandise," Shuman said.

"Was any of it recovered?" I asked.

"Some of it has surfaced overseas," Shuman said. "One member of the team was never caught."

Then it hit me. Oh my God, I might have solved two crimes.

"Was it Gabe Braxton?" I asked.

"Definitely not Braxton," Shuman said.

Damn. I hate when that happens.

"But with the murder of the hotel maid here at the resort," Shuman said, "I was able to convince the brass upstairs to let me come here and check things out, see what I could turn up on Colby's accomplice."

"LAPD is spending money for you to stay at this place?" Haley asked. "Those robberies happened years ago."

"There's always been considerable pressure on the department to close this case and recover the stolen goods," Shuman said. "Sidney Rowan carries a lot of weight. He, apparently, doesn't want that last gang member left at large, maybe causing problems for Colby in the future."

"What kinds of problems?" I asked.

Shuman shrugged. "Implicating her in other aspects of the crimes."

Then something occurred to me.

"Hey, isn't Sidney Rowan dead?" I asked.

Shuman grinned. "He's very much alive."

Jeez, somebody should let *People* know about this.

"Our police chief would like nothing better than to make Rowan happy by putting the last thief behind bars," Shuman said. "It never hurts to be in the good graces of a billionaire, especially if you have political aspirations."

"Do you think there's a connection between Jaslyn's death and those old robberies?" I asked.

Honestly, I didn't see it. But maybe Shuman knew something I didn't.

"Two people were killed during those robberies," Shuman said. "Witnesses claimed it was Colby, but their testimony never made it to trial."

"Do you think Sidney Rowan paid them off?" I asked.

Shuman didn't respond in the affirmative or negative, so I figured I had my answer.

I could see that happening. Like most dads, Rowan would have done anything to make things better for his daughter, so he sure as heck wouldn't want anyone testifying to worse crimes than the robberies she'd already been charged with.

We stood there for a few minutes looking at each other. I stopped thinking about Jaslyn, Gabe, and Colby. I think Shuman did, too.

We both seemed to realize it at the same second.

"I guess I'd better go," Shuman said.

"I guess," I said.

Another few seconds passed. Light from the moon

seemed to get softer, the ocean somehow sounded more intense, the breeze grew warmer.

Shuman drew closer, then stepped back.

"I'd really better go," he said.

"Yeah, me too," I said.

We walked back down the path to the bar. The dance floor was packed now, and all the tables were taken. A limbo game had started up in the sand nearby, and four guys were playing darts.

"Want to join us?" I asked, and nodded toward Sandy, Marcie, and Bella, all seated at our table.

Shuman hesitated a bit, then shook his head. "No, I've got things to take care of."

"Oh. Well, I guess I'll see you around," I said.

Shuman tried for a grin but couldn't quite pull it off.

"Sure," was all he managed.

He started to walk away when I remembered that he hadn't given me the info I'd asked him for.

"What about Gabe Braxton?" I asked.

All attempts at a grin disappeared from Shuman's face. He shifted into cop mode big-time.

"Stay away from Braxton," he said.

I got a weird feeling.

"He was picked up for assault and domestic violence," Shuman said.

Yikes! I hadn't expected to hear that, but given his explosive temper I'd witnessed, I guess I shouldn't have been surprised.

Then something else hit me.

"How did he get a job here?" I asked. "This place is super careful about everything that concerns the security of their guests. They're bound to do background checks on all their employees."

"Charges were dismissed," Shuman said.

His expression shifted from cop mode to something else that I'd never seen before. I didn't know what it meant.

"Stay away from Gabe Braxton, Haley. Do you hear me? Stay away," Shuman said. "Don't go near him. Don't talk to him. Don't even let him know you're alive. He's dangerous."

Now didn't seem like the best time to mention that I'd already questioned Gabe, so what could I say but "Okay."

Shuman turned on his lie-detecting, supercop-stink-eye glare—like he thought I wasn't telling the truth, which I wasn't, of course—then walked away.

I went back to our table. Sandy was on the dance floor with Sebastian again, and Bella was now talking to a guy I didn't know at the bar.

"What's Shuman doing here?" Marcie asked.

If anyone but Marcie had asked, I would have said he was simply there on vacation. But no way could I lie to my BFF. She'd see right through it.

That's what BFFs *do*.

"He's working a case," I said, and lowered my voice. "Undercover."

Marcie didn't seem as impressed as I'd been with the whole undercover thing. What was that all about?

"The murder of that hotel maid?" Marcie asked.

"Yes, that's it," I said.

Okay, I knew that was a total lie, but an acceptable one. I couldn't tell Marcie—not even my BFF—what Shuman was really up to.

BFFs *do* that, too.

"Where's that waiter?" Marcie asked, gazing around the bar. "Never mind. I'll get us fresh drinks."

She left the table, and I had a major Shuman flashback.

It creeped me out thinking that I'd hunted down Gabe Braxton, introduced myself, asked him about Jaslyn, then deliberately antagonized him so he'd divulge more info—probably not my smartest move, given what Shuman had told me about that whole assault-domestic-violence thing.

But too late for that now. I couldn't even promise myself that I'd steer clear of Gabe from now on, because his past troubles with the law made him a really great murder suspect.

For a few minutes I considered talking to security chief Walt Pemberton about Gabe's history. But I didn't know if the LAPD had looped in resort security on Shuman's investigation. If I told Pemberton about Gabe, he'd want to know how I'd found out, and no way did I want to explain my connection to Shuman. Plus, without some reasonable explanation of where I'd obtained the info, Pemberton might report it to those two homicide detectives who'd interviewed me; they'd probably think I was making it up to throw suspicion off of myself. And, really, I'd just as soon not remind them that I was still around.

Besides, there was always a chance that Pemberton already knew about Gabe's problems with the law—though why the resort would allow him to work here knowing that info, I had no clue—and I didn't want to look like an idiot by telling him something he already knew, so I decided to keep my mouth shut since that would benefit *me* the most.

Then something else hit me—was Colby, with her criminal past and jail time, somehow involved with Gabe Braxton's sort-of criminal past even though Shuman had said they weren't connected? Maybe it was something he hadn't discovered yet. Had Colby gotten the resort security staff to somehow forgo Gabe's background check and hire him at her request? Were Gabe and Colby both involved in Jaslyn Gordon's murder?

I thought about this for a few minutes, then realized that, while it made a great theory, there was no real evidence.

Damn. That whole I-need-evidence thing kept getting in the way.

Then something else hit me: why was I thinking about this now? I'm on vacation.

And why was I sitting here by myself? I knew three—count them, three—good-looking, single guys right here at the resort, and you'd think one of them would want to take me for a spin on the dance floor, or buy me a drink, or at least sit here and talk to me. Where was Luke? Ben? Why the heck had Shuman taken off?

My evening needed a boost.

I glanced around the bar and saw that Bella was talking to three guys now. I had no idea who they were, but I figured I should definitely find out.

I was just about to stand up, throw caution to the wind, and razzle-dazzle those guys with the magic that is uniquely me when Ben Oliver sat down next to me.

Jeez, where had he come from?

And why was he still wearing those same wrinkled khaki pants and that tired blue polo shirt?

Ben leaned close. "That guy you were just talking to, he was a cop. Don't deny it. I recognized him."

How did he manage to still smell so good when he kept wearing the same crappy clothes?

"Seriously, Ben," I said. "I'm assembling my glam squad first thing tomorrow and I'm giving you a make-over."

He ignored my comment and said, "What did he tell you?"

"Oh my God," I realized. "You were watching me?"

"Shh," Ben whispered. "I'm telling you, this place is crawling with undercover security."

He glanced around as if he expected to see plain-clothes investigators dart from bush to bush.

Then it hit me—Ben wasn't here investigating Jaslyn's murder, he was following the story of Colby's old crime spree and searching for the one gang member who'd never been apprehended. Why else would he recognize and ask me about Shuman?

Ben had claimed he was investigating a tip from a Hollywood insider about thefts involving A-list celebrities, so I figured some of the jewelry, watches, and other stuff stolen in Colby's robberies had been connected to high-profile stars. Those shops stored expensive pieces for the wealthy, rich, and famous, especially since celebrity home break-ins were a constant threat.

"His name is Shuman, right?" Ben said. "He's a detective with the LAPD, right? What did he tell you?"

No way was I going to admit to anything that might give away something major and betray Shuman's trust.

Ben didn't seem to notice.

"Look, Haley," he said. "You owe me."

I did, in fact, owe Ben on some level, and I was surprised he hadn't reminded me of that before now.

Still, I wasn't going to be bullied—or guilted—into
telling him anything.

Ben must have sensed that, because his expression
softened—which was kind of hot, given the fabulous
lighting—and said, "This story will put my career into
the stratosphere. I'm talking *Rolling Stone*, the *New
Yorker*, talk shows, morning news broadcasts. It will
put me on the A-list of reporters. I'll have my pick of
jobs anywhere."

Ben sounded really excited—and kind of desperate.
I didn't blame him, of course. His career had spiraled
downward lately and I'd been kind-of-sort-of to blame—
not that I'd intentionally done anything to make Ben look
bad. It was just a series of tough breaks that I'd, well,
really, I'd been responsible for.

Still, I wasn't going to give away anything big.

"You're right," I said, "he's here on a case. Undercover—so don't blow it for him."

"What did he tell you?" Ben asked.

"This is a two-way street," I said. "I'll share, if
you'll share."

Ben stewed for only a couple of seconds—guess he
was desperate for info—then said, "Fine, sure, okay,
whatever. What did he tell you?"

"He's definitely here investigating a case that in-
volves someone at the resort," I said.

"I *knew* it." Ben clinched his fist and kind of
growled—which was way hot, of course.

"It's very high profile," I said.

"Yes." Ben gave another fist pump.

"He's investigating, so he doesn't have anything definite yet," I said.

"LAPD wouldn't have sprung for this place if they didn't think there was something to it," Ben concluded.

He nodded, and I could see that he was spinning the story out in his head, mentally composing his headline and picturing himself chatting with the gals on *The View*.

I'll definitely have to help with his wardrobe.

"Great. This is great," Ben said. "What else?"

I glanced around and leaned closer, the universal this-is-the-coolest-part move, and whispered, "Sidney Rowan is actually alive."

Ben fell back in his chair. His mouth fell open and, for a second, I thought his eyes might actually pop out of his head.

Then he shot forward and drilled me with what I guess was his I'm-an-investigative-reporter-and-I'll-know-if-you're-lying look.

"Are you sure about this?" he demanded. "You swear it? You swear it's true?"

It miffed me a bit that Ben actually thought I wasn't being truthful, but given our history, I didn't blame him.

"I'm only telling you what Shuman told me," I said. "I haven't actually seen Sidney Rowan roaming the resort grounds or anything."

Ben fidgeted for a moment—mentally composing yet another Pulitzer Prize–winning headline, I suppose—then hopped out of his chair.

"Keep me up-to-speed," he said. "Okay?"

"You do the same," I said.

"I will, I will," he said, then gave me a half smile.

Ben had a nice half smile.

"Thanks, Haley," he said. "This means *everything* to me."

I got a warm, tingling feeling in my belly knowing that, this time, I'd done something that would actually help Ben with his story. Finally, he and I were on the same page with one of his investigations.

What could go wrong?

CHAPTER 16

It was almost lunchtime before we got downstairs. Last night at the beach bar had been fun—the kind of fun that's a bit hazy the next morning. We all seemed to be in the same I-can't-believe-I-did-that-even-if-I'm-on-vacation mode, except for Sandy.

"Wow, Bella, I didn't know you could limbo so well," she said.

Sandy seemed as perky and happy as always—not the kind of thing that usually goes over well with the what-the-heck-did-I-do morning-after crowd.

"Limbo?" Bella asked.

I had to hand it to Bella. Even though she looked like a returned-for-store-credit Dooney & Bourke bag on a clearance table—really, we all kind of looked that way—she'd still managed to style a perfect sea turtle atop her head this morning.

"Last night," Sandy said. "You were in the limbo contest."

Bella frowned. "I was?"

"You won," Sandy said.

"Damn. No wonder my back is killing me this morning," Bella muttered. "I won, huh? Did I get a trophy or something?"

"You won a free drink," Sandy said. "One of those big ones that comes in a commemorative Rowan Resort pineapple glass."

"That explains a lot," Bella said, massaging her temples.

"Yeah," Sandy said, "and after that, you—"

"Don't tell me," Bella said, waving her off with both hands. "Whatever happened, I don't want to know."

I was with Bella on this one.

"Who's up for the breakfast buffet?" Sandy asked, as if she actually thought we'd consider it a good idea.

Where was my all-time favorite mocha Frappuccino drink when I really needed it?

Bella made a grumbling sound, and Marcie shook her head.

"Just coffee," I said. "Maybe a—"

I stopped dead in my tracks as we crossed the lobby. My heart rate shot up, taking my blood pressure along with it, and I gasped so loud that Marcie, Bella, and Sandy stopped and stared. I tried to speak, but I couldn't seem to form any actual words. All I could do was point, like one of those hunting dogs that had tracked down its prey. Only it wasn't some poor dead pheasant I'd spotted, it was a Sea Vixen tote bag.

I watched as a woman walked across the lobby and disappeared out the front door, the Sea Vixen hung casually in the crook of her arm. All I could think was, Oh my God, where did she get it? Then, all I could think was, Why was I standing here wondering instead of asking her?

I was about to take off after her when I spotted yet another Sea Vixen, this one on the shoulder of a different woman who was walking toward the rear of the hotel. *Two* Sea Vixens in the lobby at the same time? Was I dreaming—or maybe hallucinating?

My head got light. I thought I might actually faint.

Then it hit me—if two women whom I'd never seen before were now carrying the totally fabulous, ultra cool Sea Vixen tote bag, it could only mean the resort shop had gotten in a new shipment.

Mentally, I did a full double twisting layout with a back-handspring.

I stuck the landing.

"I have to go," I said—at least that's what I tried to say. It might have come out as, "Blah, blah, blah, blah."

Luckily, Marcie grasped the situation and said, "We'll catch up later," although it really sounded to me like, "Blah, blah, blah, blah."

I took off through the lobby, down the hallway that led to the rear gardens, then turned right into that long corridor where the shops, cigar room, spa, and who-knows-what-else were located. I'm pretty certain my feet never actually touched the carpeted floor.

Yet no need to hurry, I reminded myself. The salesclerk I'd spoken with had put one on hold for me, so I knew my Sea Vixen was sitting there waiting for me to pick it up and give it a good home.

Still, I couldn't stop the yay-for-me scenario from playing out in my head. I imagined women coming into the shop, seeing my Sea Vixen, falling in love with it, asking—no begging—for it, but no way could they have it. The Sea Vixen was mine—all mine. I'd walk into the shop and pluck it away, right under their noses. They'd be totally jealous, of course, and even—

Okay, maybe I was getting a little carried away.

I forced myself to stop at the shop's entrance. I drew a calming breath—which wasn't easy because I don't really like being calm—then channeled my mom's I'm-better-than-you expression along with her pageant walk, and glided inside.

Only two other women were in the shop, and they were bogged down in a discussion of which bracelet to buy, the one with the coral seashells or the one with the turquoise sand dollars. Both were hideous, and if I'd felt more generous with my time I would have told them so, but really, I can't take care of absolutely every-one, can I?

I stepped up to the counter, smiled my I'm-getting-what-I-want-and-no-one-can-stop-me smile, and said, "Good morning."

The salesclerk, who'd waited on me before, was faced the other way, sorting out a tangle of necklaces. She turned and said, "Why, good morning—oh, it's you."

Huh. Not exactly the we-give-great-service-here Rowan Resort greeting I expected.

No matter. I was getting my Sea Vixen. Nothing could upset me right now.

"You got in a shipment of Sea Vixen totes, I see," I said, and couldn't help bouncing on my toes.

"Well, yes. Yes, we did," she said, and backed away slightly, looking as if she'd been swatted on the nose with a rolled-up newspaper.

"I'd like to pick mine up now," I said.

"Well, yes. Yes, you would," she said. "I'm sure you would."

I was just about out of patience now—I don't have much under normal circumstances. My long-awaited, totally fabulous beach tote was inside the stock room, just steps away, waiting for me to take it into my arms and give it a good cuddle. If this clerk didn't speed things up, I might have to jump the counter and get it myself.

The clerk forced a smile. "I'm just going to call our manager."

Oh, hey, this was something new. Apparently, there was some sort of presentation that went along with transferring custody of the Sea Vixen from the shop to me. Cool.

The clerk picked up the telephone and gave me a things-are-great smile, then turned her back and murmured into the receiver. After a few moments she turned to me again.

"Patricia will be here momentarily," she said. "I've alerted Avery."

Wow, I guess this would be one heck of a handbag purchase. I glanced around the shop wondering if a shower of balloons would float down, or maybe confetti would shoot out of a cannon to mark the occasion.

I definitely wanted my BFFs here for the festivities.

I was reaching for my cell phone to call Marcie when a woman with an I'm-in-charge look appeared next to me. I figured her for midforties, dressed in a Rowan Resort color-coordinated burgundy and white skirt and blouse, with an I-just-stepped-off-the-set-of-*Mad-Men* hairstyle.

The look was really working for her.

"Good morning, Miss Randolph," she said, smiling pleasantly. "I'm Patricia. I'm the executive director of all the shops here at the Rowan Resort. Please, come this way."

She walked through the curtained doorway behind the counter. I followed, glancing right and left, expecting to see a camera crew waiting to capture the moment.

I saw no one.

"In here, if you please," Patricia said, gesturing to a small room off to the right.

I stepped inside and saw that it was an office crowded with a desk; chairs; some file cabinets; and a credenza covered with all kinds of papers, folders, and binders.

No sign of a photographer or champagne—or my Sea Vixen beach tote bag.

I got a weird feeling.

"Please, Miss Randolph, sit down," Patricia said, and pointed to one of the chairs in front of the desk.

I didn't sit down.

Patricia—wisely—didn't push it.

"I'm extremely sorry to say that I have some disappointing news," Patricia said.

The other salesclerk suddenly appeared in the doorway and said, "I'm standing by."

I was not sure if she intended to call security or fetch a portable heart defibrillator—from the look on her face, it could have been either.

My weird feeling got weirder—but not in a good way.

Patricia drew herself up, squared her shoulders, and said, "We did, in fact, receive a shipment of Sea Vixen beach totes this morning. However, we didn't get as many as we'd expected—it's a very popular bag this season."

I didn't say anything.

"And, unfortunately," Patricia went on, "our 'hold' list wasn't properly posted, and the bag designated for you was sold to someone else."

What the heck was she so upset about? Immediately, I saw a solution to the situation—one that benefited me, of course.

"So give me one of the bags designated for someone else on the list," I said.

Patricia's smile curdled. "We received only two totes. Both were sold. We have no more. There isn't another bag to give you, at this time."

I saw her mouth move and heard her words, but I couldn't quite seem to understand them.

"I'm terribly embarrassed about this situation," Patricia said. "I assure you, this isn't the way we operate here at the Rowan Resort."

I just stared at her. Surely any minute now she'd say something I could comprehend.

"As soon as the next shipment arrives, I'll personally make certain you receive your bag," Patricia said, then added quickly, "at no cost to you, of course, in the hope of rectifying this error."

I still couldn't seem to make sense of anything she was saying.

"Miss Randolph?" Patricia said.

She looked a little concerned now.

"Miss Randolph, please allow me to apologize for—oh, look who's here," Patricia said. She waved frantically. "Come in, Avery, come in. Please, please, come in."

Avery stepped into the office. She didn't look all that happy about being there.

"Well, I'll leave you two alone," Patricia said, and dashed out of the office, the other salesclerk hot on her heels.

I felt numb, fuzzy-headed, still unable—unwilling, really—to grasp the situation.

"I—I don't understand," I said.

"They gave your bag away to someone else," Avery said.

Her I'm-not-bothering-to-sugarcoat-it version sank in.

"Crap," I said, and plopped down into the chair nearest the desk.

Avery just stood there for a minute, then pulled over another chair and sat down beside me.

I'd been through a lot of stuff on this vacation—a vacation at a place where guests paid big bucks to make sure they didn't have to go through a lot of stuff. I'd found a dead body; I'd been interrogated by the police; Bella's lucky panties had been stolen right out of her room—and I'd rolled with all of it.

But this was different. This was a handbag—*the* handbag. The hottest bag of the season.

I was too mad to be mad.

"I'm sorry," Avery said.

She sounded like she meant it—honestly meant it, not like she'd said it just because she was expected to, or because somebody in the Rowan Resort publicity office had composed it for her.

My anger deflated because, really, there was nothing I could do.

I hate it when there's nothing I can do.

"Things happen," I said, and shrugged.

We both just sat there for a few minutes, staring at nothing, saying nothing.

"Are you going to get in trouble with your boss because of this screw-up?" I asked.

Avery looked surprised that I'd asked. I suppose guests here weren't overly concerned about anything more than getting their way on everything—not that I blamed them, of course. So what could I do but turn the situation around and use it as a ploy to help myself?

"I figure you're on the ropes—employment-wise—because of the problems you had with Jaslyn," I said. "I heard she wasn't a very good employee, but you were kind of stuck with her on your team."

"Where did you hear that?" Avery asked.

"It's not true?" I asked.

"Jaslyn was a good worker," she said. "She even volunteered to help another team that was shorthanded clean some of the downstairs rooms. She had trouble following the resort rules. So, yes, in that respect she was a problem employee."

Jaslyn didn't follow the rules?

I could totally relate.

"So you wanted to have her change teams permanently?" I asked. "Not that I blame you, of course, if she caused you trouble."

"Jaslyn kept overstepping herself," Avery said. "She sneaked into the hotel after her shift, which is always off-limits to employees. I caught her in the library twice."

"Jaslyn risked her job over coming to the library? The *library?*" I asked.

How weird was that?

"There are rare first editions in the library," Avery said. "Many of the pieces of the Rowan art collection are displayed there, too. They're beautiful. You should make it a point to see them."

I was pretty sure I'd pass on that.

"Jaslyn kept asking questions about things that, frankly, were none of her business," Avery said.

"Like what?" I asked.

"Things like whether Mr. Rowan visited the resort often, whether he kept an eye on things here, how actively he was involved with running the place," Avery said.

I guess Jaslyn thought Sidney Rowan was alive—or maybe she hadn't read *People* magazine lately.

"Strange things for a college student and hotel maid to be concerned with," I said.

"Yes," Avery said. "And, really, I have enough to deal with every day without the staff adding to my workload."

I couldn't disagree with her on that—nor did I miss the fact that I was one of those things Avery had to deal with.

Not a great feeling—but not bad enough that I considered backing off from my quest for a Sea Vixen or my questions about Jaslyn's death.

I remembered that someone had told me that Jaslyn had requested a transfer off of Avery's team. I wondered now if that was true, or if Avery had pushed Jaslyn to make the transfer request in an effort to get rid of her because of the headaches she caused.

Either way, it was obvious Avery wasn't happy with Jaslyn. But unhappy enough to murder her?

We were quiet for another minute, then Avery sat up straight in her chair as if she'd just realized that she'd let her I'm-a-Rowan-Resort-employee shield slip a little.

"Again, I'm very sorry about the situation with your bag," Avery said, then drew in a sharp, fortifying breath. "I fully expect you to report this to Mr. Cameron."

Report it to Mr. Cameron? What the heck did Ty's dad have to do with anything?

Avery pressed on, saying, "He's one of our frequent guests, and we truly appreciate his business. If you'd like me to explain the situation to him, I'll be happy to do so. In fact, my supervisor will personally handle the conversation as soon as he arrives."

What the heck was she talking about?

"When who arrives?" I asked.

"Mr. Cameron," Avery said. "He's joining you, isn't he?"

Then it hit me.

"Ty?" I might have said that kind of loud.

"Yes, I know you'd initially said this was a girls-only vacation," Avery said. "But after he called, I assumed he'd be arriving shortly."

Ty had called the Rowan Resort? He'd talked to Avery? She thought he was coming here?

This made no sense and, really, I didn't want to try to understand it—I'm on vacation.

I got up and left.

CHAPTER 17

Having my look-at-me-and-be-jealous Sea Vixen tote bag slip through my fingers was a tough blow to deal with—especially so early in the day. But I'd survived other tragedies, so I knew I could survive this one. In fact, I was determined to. This vacation had sustained a number of maybe-I-should-just-pack-up-and-go-home incidents, but I intended to push through.

Of course, it would be easier if I had a mocha Frappuccino to sustain me.

I left the shop, walked down the endless no-man's-land corridor to the hotel's main hallway figuring that a nice meal—heavy on the desserts—with the three best BFFs in the entire world was just what I needed to give my day a boost. I was reaching for my cell phone to call Marcie when I noticed a commotion up ahead in the hotel lobby. A large party of about a dozen people was making its way inside, causing heads to turn.

Wow, maybe this was some big celebrity checking

into the hotel. It would be cool to see who it was and tell Sandy. She'd be so impressed.

I walked a little faster, pretending I wasn't staring or the least bit interested, of course—a trait passed on to me genetically by my more-than-slightly-snooty pageant queen mom—and got to the lobby just as a Rowan Resort hostess was motioning all of them up the stairs. I bobbed and weaved a little, trying to get a better look at the woman at the center of the group, whom everyone was fussing over, to see who she was— and find out what she was wearing and how she'd styled her hair, of course. My BFFs deserved all the details I could get.

I stepped in front of another guest—hey, I can't help it that I'm tall—and got a partial view.

Wow, she looked great, all right, maybe my age, blond, terrific figure. I didn't recognize her, but I knew that anybody who caused this much hubbub must be a famous celebrity. I skirted around a wingback chair and came just short of elbowing aside a couple of old ladies to get a better look at her face, and—

Oh my God. *Oh my God*.

It was *that girl*. The one who used to work at Holt's and stunk up the breakroom with those microwaveable diet meals of hers—the girl whose name I can never remember. She lost like a hundred pounds or something, ditched her glasses for contacts, quit Holt's, and headed for Hollywood. I'd seen her in print ads, then a shampoo commercial. And now she had an *entourage?*

One of the old ladies next to me must have read my expression, because she nodded wisely and said, "She's a soap star. She's fabulous. Absolutely fabulous."

Oh, crap. This was too much. Just too much.

I mean, I was happy for her, of course. But, jeez, why couldn't I have an entourage? Or a cool undercover job? Or at least an official boyfriend? I didn't even have a fabulous Sea Vixen beach tote.

I hate my life—and I'm on vacation.

I decided that no way could I face my BFFs and pretend to have a good time right now. At this point, there was nothing to do but go upstairs and take a nap.

Even *I* know when it's time to take a breather.

I waited a minute or two for what's-her-name's entourage to clear the stairs, then dashed up to the second floor, anxious for the solitude. Three housekeeping carts were in the hallway. I spotted Tabitha going into a room, three doors down from mine.

Avery flashed in my head—which didn't suit me because I really wanted to lie down—and I remembered what she'd told me about Jaslyn helping out a different team that was assigned to clean some of the downstairs rooms. Somebody had told me that Jaslyn had requested a transfer off of Avery's team, but I'd wondered if the idea had actually come from Avery.

I didn't know who to believe, but I knew that no matter who initiated the request—Avery or Jaslyn—it would look bad for Avery. It would indicate she couldn't keep her own team member in line, something that surely would come up at Avery's next employee performance review.

I'd wondered if this situation had somehow escalated to murder, and I could still see that happening— jobs at the Rowan Resort paid big bucks, plus if you could make it here, you could make it anywhere, so I could understand Avery's desire to be successful in her position.

But I needed the real story, and I didn't think I was getting it from Avery. I couldn't help feeling as if something else was going on, and I figured Tabitha could tell me.

I walked down the corridor to the room I'd seen her disappear into. The door was propped open, and a big housekeeping cart was parked just outside. I squeezed around it and went in.

The curtains were open, flooding the room with bright sunlight, brilliantly illuminating the complete disaster. Jeez, it looked like a fabric bomb had gone off in there. Dresses, skirts, shirts, shorts, capris, bathing suits, cover-ups, and jeans were scattered on the floor and across both beds, along with the sheets, pillows, and blankets. Food wrappers, soda cans, and beer bottles covered almost every flat surface. What a mess. What was wrong with people?

Tabitha was at the desk tossing out trash. I didn't envy her job.

Maybe I could find her another place to work.

She saw me and gasped. Her gaze darted around the room like a cornered mouse looking for a hole to scurry into.

"It's just me," I said. "I need to ask you something."

Now her gaze whipped to the door.

"You're not supposed to be in here," she said. "I could get in major trouble if you're in here."

"It won't take a second," I said.

She shook her head. "I can't get fired. I need this job. I lost my financial aid last semester because I was sick, and I don't qualify for any scholarships. I can't lose this job."

Tabitha sounded frantic and desperate, and honestly, I couldn't blame her. But I didn't know when I'd see her again, and I needed to put this thing with Jaslyn and Avery to rest, one way or the other.

"Just one quick question," I said, and pushed on before she could protest again. "Did Jaslyn request a transfer to the team that cleaned downstairs? Or did Avery request it?"

"Oh, God, not this again," Tabitha said, and started to tremble. "All I know is that Jaslyn told me that when she helped out the downstairs team, something weird was going on in the library."

"How could something weird go on in a library?" I asked.

"I don't know," Tabitha said. "I guess she thought it wasn't being properly cleaned or something, because she kept talking about the condition of the stuff in there. And she kept going back to check on it, even though she knew she wasn't supposed to, and even after Avery had talked to her about it."

"Jaslyn risked losing her job over dusty books?" I asked.

"She was like that," Tabitha said. "She'd get on some cause that she was passionate about, and it was like she was in some other crazy zone or something."

"So she requested the transfer?" I asked, bringing our conversation back to my original question.

"I guess. She said she wanted to keep watch on things," Tabitha said. She glanced at the door. "Please, Miss Randolph, please. I don't want to get in trouble."

"Sure, I understand. I won't bother you again," I said.

"Please don't. I can't lose this job," Tabitha said.

"I won't," I said. "I swear."

I headed for the door.

"Miss Randolph?" Tabitha called.

I turned around.

Tabitha took a deep breath, then said, "Jaslyn told me she was going to complain to upper management."

"Did she?" I asked.

Tabitha shook her head. "I don't think she had . . . time."

"When did she tell you that?" I asked.

Tabitha gulped hard. "The day before she was murdered."

Oh, crap.

"Miss Randolph? Miss Randolph?"

I heard my name, but no way was I stopping, because I knew it was Joy calling—I heard the unmistakable *clack, clack, clack* of her pumps on the concrete walkway behind me.

I'd managed to take an it's-okay-because-I'm-on-vacation nap and awakened refreshed and rejuvenated to find a text message from Marcie. She was playing tennis, and we were all getting together for an early dinner.

I'd put on yet another fabulous I-have-great-taste-in-almost-everything outfit, this one denim capris and a sparkling white T-shirt, with tropical yellow, orange, and green accessories.

I looked terrific.

Maybe I should date myself.

I felt terrific, too, so no way did I want to ruin my good mojo by talking to Joy about Yasmin and Tate-Tate-Tate's wedding.

"Haley?"

Joy appeared at my elbow. Wow, she could really move in those pumps. I was definitely going to have to up my game.

"What is it?" I asked, not even bothering to pretend I hadn't heard her calling my name over and over again.

Joy didn't seem to notice.

"I wanted you to know that everything has been arranged for Yasmin's bachelorette party," she said.

"I don't care," I said.

Joy didn't seem to notice that either, because she kept talking.

"Now, there are just a couple of other things we need to go over." She flipped open her iPad. "First, there's a situation with the—oh, here's our MOB now."

Joy stopped in front of two women who were standing near one of the resort's many fountains. I stopped too, not because I cared if I'd look rude in front of the mother of the bride if I kept walking but because I hoped that Yasmin's grandmother was nearby and would join us. Ty's grandmother had specifically called to thank me for helping with the wedding, and since I liked Ada and Ada liked Yasmin's grandmother, I figured I'd like her, too.

It would be nice to actually like someone in Yasmin's wedding party.

Joy took care of the formalities, introducing me to Yasmin's mother Deandra and her aunt Elnora. Both women—sisters, obviously—were approaching fifty, had perfectly coiffed brown hair and full-on makeup, and wore YSL dresses—like, somehow, nobody had told them the wedding was at an island resort.

"So you're the one who wanted to be part of Yasmin's wedding," Deandra said.

Or maybe it was Elnora. I'd already gotten their names mixed up.

Both of them gave my outfit the once-over; I felt like I was a beagle at that Westminster dog show, with both of them judging me.

"Are you married, Haley?" Elnora—I guess—asked.

"No," I said, and smiled.

"Oh." Elnora's nose and mouth pinched together, as if she'd just smelled something stinky. "Well, don't worry. I'm sure you'll find someone special very soon."

Did I have a scarlet "single" emblazoned on the front of my shirt?

"Yes, of course she will," Deandra said, nodding thoughtfully but giving my T-shirt a dubious glance. "No need to worry. You're not very old, are you, Haley? You're only, what, twenty-one?"

"I'll be twenty-five soon," I said.

"Oh, dear," Deandra murmured. "You're *that* old?"

"She still has some time left to find that special someone," Elnora said, as if she were throwing me a bone.

"Really, I'm in no hurry to get married," I said.

"Well, you want to have children, of course," Deandra said.

Okay, these two gals were starting to work my nerves big-time. Still, I managed to smile pleasantly and say, "I'm not in a hurry for that, either."

Elnora gave me another unattractive frown and said, "I have to admit that I'm concerned about you, Haley. You're twenty-four years old, already."

"In just a few more years you'll have an increased risk of birth defects, Down syndrome, miscarriage," Deandra said.

"And the older you are, the less likely it is that you'll be able to get pregnant. So I think that having a child soon is something you should definitely consider," Elnora said.

How did my reproduction system become a topic of conversation—with strangers?

They both stared at me waiting, I guess, for me to announce that I intended to shack up with the next guy who walked past and get moving on the whole baby thing.

I said nothing.

"We just want you to be happy," Deandra assured me.

Elnora nodded in agreement.

Both of them probably suffered severe neck strain from constantly turning up their noses at everyone and everything, and sticking them into other people's business.

I guess they were done with me then, because Deandra turned to Joy and said, "I've rethought the napkins for the reception."

Joy snapped to attention and rushed in with her iPad. I made my escape.

I hadn't gotten very far when I spotted Sandy sitting

alone on a bench that was shaped like a butterfly, surrounded by ferns and red flowers.

She looked up as I approached but said nothing.

I don't have great people skills, yet even *I* could see
that something was troubling her. Luckily, Sandy isn't
one to hold back.

"Sebastian wants us to see each other after vacation,"
she said, and sounded upset at the prospect.

I was upset, too—but for a totally different reason.

"But I have a boyfriend," she said.

And I had encouraged her to hang out with Sebastian who, after my Internet search, wasn't looking like
such a great guy to me.

"Dump him," I said.

Sandy gasped and drew back a little.

Okay, maybe my advice was a bit harsh.

I tried to soften it by saying, "And in the interest of
fairness, dump your tattoo artist boyfriend, too."

That didn't seem to help—though I thought it was a
fabulous idea.

Sandy sighed heavily and said, "I don't know what
to do. I really like Sebastian but, well, I just met him."

"You should go slow," I said, when what I really
wanted to do was repeat my dump-him suggestion. "And
if you're even thinking about him, maybe you should
take another look at your tattoo boyfriend and ask yourself if he's really the right guy for you."

That, I decided, was an idea worthy of a *Cosmo* article.

Maybe I should write a column for them.

Sandy thought for a minute. "Yeah, maybe you're
right."

"Just give it more time," I said, even though I'm not

a wait-and-see kind of gal. "Find out how you feel about Sebastian while you're here, then decide what to do after you go home."

Another minute passed while she considered my suggestion.

"Okay," Sandy said. "That's what I'll do. I'll wait and see how it goes."

She sounded relieved and, really, I was too because that would give me more time to check further into Sebastian's background and run him off if he turned out to be a complete fraud.

"Hey," Sandy said, "there's a luau on the beach. Marcie and Bella are there. Want to go?"

"Sure," I said, and nodded toward the hotel. "But I want to check with the shops for a Sea Vixen."

It was a total lie, but I didn't want to tell Sandy that I actually intended to go to the business center and scour the Internet again for info on Sebastian's background.

"I'll meet you at the luau," Sandy said. She waved and headed toward the beach.

I crossed the grounds, went into the rear entrance of the hotel, and turned down the corridor toward the business center.

But something caught my eye. Situated beside a set of ornately carved doors was a small brass sign that read LIBRARY.

Huh. I must have walked past it a dozen times but never noticed it.

Imagine that.

Jaslyn flew into my head, and I remembered what Avery and Tabitha had told me about some sort of situation in the library that kept Jaslyn so intrigued that she got into trouble over it. I decided I should check it out.

I looked up and down the corridor and saw no one, then pulled open the big door and walked into the library.

The room was absolutely huge. Dark wood shelves rose about twenty feet, almost to the ceiling, on four walls, all of them stuffed with thousands of books. A shelf displaying statues, vases, plates, and other pieces topped the bookshelves on three of the walls. More pieces were scattered among the books on the shelves. Seating areas were situated throughout the room, covered in burgundy leather and old-fashioned tapestry fabrics. Lamps burned softly.

No one was in the library—I figured most people were probably at dinner or off someplace having actual fun. I walked to the center of the room. It was deadly silent in here, thanks to extra insulation, I suppose, to keep out sounds so people could read. I turned in a slow circle trying to imagine what the heck could have piqued Jaslyn's interest in this place.

I saw nothing—except for the tall, vertical ladders on rollers that allowed access to the upper bookshelves. They looked like fun, if you got a running start, hopped on, scrambled up, and rode them to the end of the room. But I couldn't imagine Jaslyn doing that, since I'd been told that she was afraid of heights.

I wandered through the library glancing at the zillions of leather-bound volumes, the busts of old guys I didn't recognize, some small statues and sculptures of things only people who hung out in galleries would likely appreciate—or understand. Still, nothing job-risking jumped out at me.

I decided to get a different perspective—thanks to an old Indiana Jones movie I've seen on TV—so I climbed one of the ladders all the way to the top. I'm not afraid of heights—actually, I think it's kind of cool to be up high—so I turned and looked down at the library.

Everything looked a little smaller now—but no less dull. I didn't see a giant "X" on the carpet that *marked the spot*, or an ancient symbol pointing to a major, case-breaking clue.

So much for my Indiana Jones move.

Still, I kind of liked it up here, so I wasn't anxious to climb down again. I turned on the ladder and checked out a couple of vases that were displayed on the shelf. They were about eight inches tall, with handles on both sides, painted bright colors.

Yikes! It was hard to believe these things were considered art. They were slightly misshapen, the paint ran together, and they reminded me of the things my mom had brought home during her, thankfully, short-lived ceramics phase.

The only cool thing about the vases was the colors—they had the same blue, orange, yellow, and green shades of the soon-to-be-mine Sea Vixen beach tote.

I picked up one of the vases to have a closer look and stopped still—not because of the vase, but because of the dust circle left behind. I set the vase down in a different spot and ran my finger across the shelf. Damn, the place was filthy. It hadn't been dusted in forever. Whichever crew had been responsible for cleaning the library wasn't doing a good job, at all.

I hung there on the ladder thinking about Jaslyn. She was an art major. She'd volunteered to help the downstairs team. Had she come into the library and noticed that the pieces on display weren't being properly cared for? Was that what made her so upset that she'd risked getting fired by coming back again and again? Was that what she intended to report to upper management?

Could dusty library shelves have caused her murder?

Okay, this was totally weird.

I was about to push the ladder farther down the shelves and check out a statue of a—well, I didn't know exactly what the heck it was—when I heard a faint scratching sound below me. I looked down but saw nothing. Then I heard a *click*. A section of the bookshelves swung open and Sebastian walked out. He closed it behind him, crossed the library, and disappeared out the heavy doors into the hallway.

Oh, crap.

CHAPTER 18

I woke up with Jack Bishop—on the phone, not in person. I grabbed my cell phone off of the nightstand on the second ring, saw Jack's name on the screen, hit the green button, and glanced over to see that Marcie was still sleeping in the other bed, all in one quick motion.

Pretty good moves for so early in the morning.

"Just a minute," I whispered into the phone as I rolled out of bed and headed for the bathroom.

"Is somebody there with you?" Jack demanded.

"No," I told him.

"I'll be right over," he said.

I figured Jack had some pretty good moves for so early in the morning, too, which made my belly feel all warm and gooey.

I closed the bathroom door behind me and glimpsed myself in the mirror. Yikes! I had a serious case of bed head.

Images of Jack, an early morning, and just how my hair might end up in tangles flashed in my head—which was perfectly all right since I'm on vacation. Then, just as quickly, I decided it was better to keep things professional between us.

I hate it when I have to do the right thing.

"What's so important you have to wake me up this early on my vacation?" I asked.

"Info on the stalker," Jack said.

It took me a few seconds—okay, more than a few but, jeez, it was really early and, despite my best effort, that whole bed head thing was still rattling around in my brain—to remember that I'd asked Jack to uncover some info on the guy Jaslyn had worked with at the magazine in L.A., the one who'd stalked her and, hopefully, murdered her.

I mean that in the nicest way, of course.

"There was a guy who wanted to date Jaslyn," Jack said. "He continued to pursue her after she left the magazine and went to work at the resort. I talked to him. He insisted there was no stalking, that he genuinely liked her."

"Do you believe him?" I asked.

Jack gave it about two seconds, then said, "He seemed like a straight shooter to me."

"So what happened?" I asked.

"He was, shall we say, convinced to leave her alone," Jack said.

"Gabe Braxton?" I asked, though I was pretty sure I already knew.

"He paid a visit to the guy," Jack said, "convinced him to back off."

I could only imagine the tactics Gabe had used.

"That means I can mark the stalker off my list of suspects," I said, and sighed. "The hunt goes on."

"I'm not finished with you," Jack said.

He used his hot, male-cologne-TV-commercial voice. I tried to respond but couldn't seem to form any words.

"I'm checking into something else," Jack said.

I pulled myself together and asked, "Yeah? What?"

It came out sounding kind of squeaky.

"Jaslyn Gordon's brother," Jack said. "He's in jail."

This, I hadn't expected, and I instantly shifted back into private-investigator-wannabe mode.

"For what?" I asked.

"I don't know yet," Jack said. "I'll let you know when I find out."

"Thanks," I said.

"You be careful," Jack said. "An island isn't the best place to be when there's a murderer on the loose."

"I owe you," I said.

"We'll settle up," Jack said, in his toe-curling voice. "I'll see to it."

"That's b.s.," Bella said. "You ask me, it's b.s."

All three of my BFFs stared at me and, really, I couldn't blame them. Some of the other people in the lobby were staring too, but I think it was because of the hair-sculpted starfish atop Bella's head rather than what I'd just said.

"I'm going to the library," I said again. "I just want to, you know, check it out."

Jeez, did that sound lame or what?

"I thought we could all have a spa day. Doesn't that sound great?" Sandy said, pointing to the picture in the resort brochure. "The spa is gorgeous. Crystal chandeliers, four-foot-deep Roman tubs, hand-painted Dutch scenes with windmills."

I guess I'd missed all of that the day I'd been in there dealing with Yasmin's toenail polish crisis.

"You've got a hot date, don't you?" Bella said. "I've seen you talking to good-looking men since we got here, men you already know. I remember seeing them in the store. What are they doing here? Are you having them flown in?"

Yeah, okay, I could have come up with a better excuse to go check out the library—other than using the actual see-the-library reason—but I'm on vacation, plus I haven't had a mocha Frappuccino or anything else chocolate in ages, so perhaps my I-always-think-of-fantastic-excuses superpower was a little off.

But, one way or the other, I was definitely going to the library to investigate just how the heck Sebastian had walked out of a secret panel in the bookcase last night. After he left, I'd scurried down the ladder for a closer look, but two old geezers with stacks of we'll-need-hours-to-read-these newspapers came in, so I left. I hadn't had time to hunt around for the hidden latch that opened the door, but at least now I had a good idea about how Sebastian had disappeared so quickly when I'd followed him into the lounge.

The only thing that made sense to me was that Sebastian was actually part of the resort's undercover security team. How else could he know about secret passages and hidden doors? It would also explain why I hadn't discovered any info about his supposed consulting firm, or his maybe-they're-rich family in Connecticut on the Internet.

Of course, if Sebastian was working undercover, he wasn't acting all that covert. I'd seen him wearing an official Rowan Resort polo shirt, plus he was dating a guest, dancing at the bar—he'd even showed up at Sandy's art lesson with Colby.

Sebastian was either the worst undercover security guy in history or something else was going on. Either way, I intended to find out what it was, and the best place I knew to start with was the library.

"The spa sounds great," Marcie said.

"Oh, wait. I have a better idea," Sandy said. "Why don't we have an art lesson? Sometimes Colby takes her classes to the beach, or up to the cliffs, or someplace with a fantastic view to paint. Wouldn't that be cool?"

Bella leaned toward the hotel grounds. "I'm pretty sure I hear the hammock terrace calling my name."

"The spa sounds good to me," Marcie said. "I'm could definitely use a massage."

"Yeah, that does sound good," Sandy said, and pulled out the resort brochure. "All their massages have ultra hydrating, rich, warm coconut milk to bring balance to the body, and exotic oils for a sense of calm."

"See you later," Marcie called as they walked away.

"The library?" Bella gave me the kind of stink-eye only a BFF can pull off. "I still say it's b.s."

"Yeah, it is, kind of," I admitted.

She nodded and said, "Whoever you're meeting, find out if he's got a brother."

"I will," I promised.

I trekked through the hotel, down the hallway, and went into the library. The place was like a tomb, silent and dimly lit, with three old gray-haired guys seated in chairs who looked like they were mummified. Since it looked as if they would topple over at any moment, I figured I could still search for the secret door that Sebastian had walked out of last night.

Then something else hit me as I stood in front of the bookcases.

I thought back to the history of the Rowan mansion-turned-hotel that our hostess Millicent had shared with us upon our arrival at the welcome center on the mainland a few days ago. I couldn't remember much—honestly, I've got to do better about drifting off—but I did recall that Sidney Rowan had been a big deal back in the day. I figured that somebody, somewhere, must have included his island mansion—complete with info about its secret passageways—in a book, and surely that book was here in the library.

I leaned back and studied the shelves of books climbing nearly to the ceiling. Yeah, okay, this might take a while.

"Hello, Haley."

A mellow male voice whispered in my ear, and a warm body eased up behind me. I knew by the way my knees immediately started to tremble that it was Luke Warner.

He moved alongside me and smiled.

Luke has a killer smile.

"What are you doing in here?" he whispered.

Luke also had a super sexy voice.

Not super sexy enough, however, that I'd tell him why I was here or what I was looking for.

I gestured to the books on the shelf in front of me and said, "Just looking for something to read."

Luke eyed the books. "Shakespeare, huh? The entire ten-volume collection? Ambitious."

Okay, obviously he knew I was lying, which really didn't suit me, so what could I do but tell another lie to cover for the first one?

Really, anyone in my position would have done the same thing.

"Shakespeare sounds good," I said, nodding as if I was actually thinking it over.

"Maybe something lighter?" Luke suggested.

I had absolutely no idea what kind of book anyone would want to read, so I mustered my I'm-thinking-it-over expression. I've found that if I hold this look long enough, the other person will eventually say something.

Luke said nothing.

Crap.

"Sure," I said. "Something lighter."

"A biography?" Luke asked.

What the heck is he even doing in the library?

"History?" he asked.

And why won't he leave?

"Self-help?" Luke asked.

Obviously, I was going to have to tell him something to get him out of here. Then it hit me—I could tell him the truth, part of it anyway.

"Architecture," I said. "I'd like to read up on the history of the hotel and learn more about its design and construction."

"There's bound to be a book here," Luke said. "I'll find it."

He took off like a bloodhound on a fresh scent—men are, essentially, hunters—then homed in on an old-school card catalogue situated in the corner. Luke opened a drawer, fingered the cards, then blasted to a shelf nearby as if he'd been shot out of a cannon.

It was kind of hot.

He selected a big, coffee-table-sized book from a high shelf, then presented it to me as if he'd just brought down a T-Rex.

That was kind of hot, too.

"This should give you all the information you need," he said. "But check it out, just to be sure."

Since Luke gave no indication of leaving, I carried the book to a love seat and sat down. He sat next to me and leaned close as I flipped through the pages.

It was mostly black-and-white photos on glossy paper showing lots of huge mansions, some under construction, with brief descriptions of their location, as well as the names of the owners and architect. Most of the houses were in Los Angeles's older areas of West Adams District, Bunker Hill, and Hancock Park.

"Nice places," Luke said softly. "Too bad most of them are gone now."

"I guess you had to be rich to build one of these houses," I said.

"Rich and worried," Luke said. "There was—and still is—a concern among the wealthy that they'd be robbed."

Ben Oliver and his claim that he was following a tip about some sort of theft involving celebrities flashed in my mind.

"Or worse," Luke said.

"Worse than being robbed?" I asked.

"Kidnappings," Luke said, and tapped his finger against a photo of a huge house in the West Adams District that kind of looked like one of the plantation homes in *Gone With the Wind*. "After the Lindbergh baby was kidnapped in the early thirties, well-to-do families started building safe rooms in their houses where they could hide, if necessary."

I glanced at the spot on the bookcase that Sebastian had walked out of last night.

"You mean with secret passageways and hidden doors?" I asked.

"Sure," Luke said.

I didn't want to dwell on the whole secret-and-hidden thing because I didn't want Luke to get suspicious. He was an FBI agent, after all. He got suspicious for a living.

So what could I do but turn the conversation to yet another topic that would benefit me?

"Have you heard anything new about Jaslyn Gordon's murder?" I asked, flipping pages oh-so casually.

Luke stilled. "No."

Okay, now I was suspicious. Something about Luke's body language and tone made me think he wasn't being truthful.

Not a good feeling—especially after all the other times he'd lied to me.

I decided to push further.

"Any news about problems connected to the resort?" I asked.

"Nope," Luke said, and leaned away from me, checking his watch. "I've got a golf game. See you later, Haley."

He left the library and I sat on the love seat, thinking.

Luke had definitely cut and run when I'd mentioned Jaslyn's murder and asked about any other situations concerning the Rowan resort. Either he didn't want to talk about criminal activity while on vacation or maybe he knew something and wasn't telling me.

But what was it?

All kinds of things sprang into my head—Jaslyn's murder; her brother in jail; Colby, who'd been in jail, Gabe Braxton, who probably *should* be in jail; dusty books in the library that jeopardized Avery's job; the A-list celebrities targeted by thieves who Ben was pursuing.

Was there some giant conspiracy going on at the Rowan Resort?

I needed more info, and I knew who I could get it from.

CHAPTER 19

I found Ben seated at a table in the garden outside the hotel snack bar, working on his laptop. A wrapper from a package of peanut butter crackers and a plastic water bottle sat nearby. He had on the same pants and polo shirt I'd seen him in for days, which looked as rumpled as ever. His whiskers had thickened.

I sat down in the chair next to him.

"Go away," Ben said, not bothering to look up from the laptop screen.

"Are you growing a beard?" I asked.

His gaze darted to me, then returned to the laptop.

"Really, Ben, I mean this in the nicest way, but you look like crap," I said. "Honestly, the beard is not working for you. And those same clothes? Why the heck don't you change?"

He ignored me.

"Look, I'll go to your room with you," I offered. "Even *you* would have packed more than one outfit for

this assignment. I'll put together a great look for you
that will—"

Hang on a minute.

I looked again at the meager snacks, his scraggly
beard, his tired shirt and pants, and it hit me.

Oh, crap.

"You're not a guest here," I said.

Ben kept his gaze glued to his laptop.

"You're not on assignment," I said.

"Shh!" Ben glanced around frantically. "Be quiet."

"Oh my God. I'm right, aren't I," I said.

"Keep your voice down," he hissed, throwing sur-
reptitious glances around us. "You're going to get me
thrown out of this place."

I leaned in and said, "You're like a stowaway or
something."

"All right, all right," Ben said, slamming the lid down
on his laptop. He turned to me. "Yes. Yes, I sneaked
aboard the supply ship and slipped onto the resort
grounds after dark, and I've been hiding out ever since,
dodging security and the staff. Okay? Are you happy
now?"

"Where have you been sleeping?" I asked.

Ben fumed for a bit, then said, "The hammock terrace, the beach, the sun porch, wherever."

I glanced at the wrapper of peanut butter crackers.

"Have you had anything decent to eat?" I asked.

"I'm okay," he insisted. "Just drop it, will you?"

No way was I letting this go.

I got up from the table. Ben caught my wrist.

"You're not going to rat me out, are you?" he asked.

"Just stay here," I told him.

I went into the snack bar, ordered a double cheese-burger all the way, fries, and two chocolate milkshakes, then took them outside and put them on the table in front of Ben.

I kept one of the shakes for myself, of course.

Ben glared at me, then picked up the burger. He wolfed down the whole meal in just a few minutes.

"Thank you," he said softly, licking the tips of his fingers.

"You're welcome," I said, and passed him a napkin.

"I'm still not going to tell you about the story I'm working on," he said.

"I know."

We sat there for a while, sipping our shakes, not saying anything. Sitting quietly wasn't what I did best, but for some reason enjoying the silence with Ben was nice.

"Okay. Fine. I'll tell you about my story," Ben said. "But don't you breathe a single word about it to anyone."

"I won't," I said.

"Swear it," he told me.

"I swear it," I said. "I swear it on my Sea Vixen."

"Your what?"

Honestly, why couldn't men keep up with fashion trends?

"It's a fabulous beach tote," I said. "I'm absolutely dying for it, and the shop here is holding one for me from their next shipment."

"Whatever," Ben said, waving away my words.

He scooted his chair over until we were elbow to elbow.

"Like I told you before," he said quietly, "I got a tip about thefts from A-list celebrities."

Visions of mounds of jewelry, boxes of cash, designer clothing, artwork, and Bentleys filled my head.

"Their things have been showing up for sale on the Internet," Ben said. "It's caused all kinds of problems."

"Don't rich, famous people have insurance to cover that kind of thing?" I asked.

Ben shook his head and said, "Panties."

Jeez, had all that food sent Ben's thought waves off in a totally crazy direction? I know my chocolate shake had my brain cells hopping pretty good. Still, I wasn't following him.

He must have read the confusion in my face because he said, "Panties. Bras. Thongs. That's what's being stolen."

"Underwear?" I asked.

"It's an underground Internet site," Ben explained, gesturing at his laptop. "Celebrity-panty-raid-dot-com."

Okay, I couldn't help it. My mouth fell open.

"Somebody is actually stealing underwear from stars and selling it on the Internet?" I asked. I shook my head. "Who would want somebody else's used panties?"

"Lots of people, and they're paying thousands for it," Ben said. "It's an auction site. Winning bids for top A-list stars reach into the tens of thousands of dollars."

I didn't think my mouth could fall open any farther, but it did.

"It's an invasion of privacy of epic proportion," Ben said. "Plus, this kind of purchase can encourage overzealous fans, which is never good. These stars have husbands and wives, some of whom aren't stars themselves and can't deal with this sort of thing, and aren't happy they can't protect their spouse from such a personal theft. The whole thing is driving security teams crazy. People are getting fired over it."

Wow, I guess I'd never thought about that sort of thing happening—over, ugh, already-worn underwear.

I glanced around, seeing the people near us in a whole different way.

"No wonder there's so much undercover security at this place," I said.

"Yeah, and like I told you the other day, there's a possible connection to this resort," Ben said. "I haven't found anything definite yet, but I'm closing in on something. The site has been teasing a killer item from a megastar for a couple of days now. If it's who I think it is, I'm going to be all over it. The story will be a lock."

"If you find the culprit and break the story, it will be a huge deal," I said, remembering what he had told me earlier. "Those celebrity TV shows will be all over it—and you. You'll be on talk shows around the clock, no doubt about it. Bloggers will go crazy for the story."

Ben nodded. "And I'll have my pick of jobs."

Something else occurred to me.

"Does your editor know you're doing this?" I asked.

Ben glanced away. "I'm freelancing on this one."

I could see that he was really out on a limb with this story. If it went the way he expected, he'd be the golden boy of the media. But if the story turned out to be nothing—or worse, if he reported it and it was later proved wrong—well, I didn't want to think about how far he'd fall.

I didn't like thinking that Ben's entire future was at stake but, really, there was nothing I could do to help. I cared about Ben, but celebrities and their undergarment problems were way down on my priority list.

I'd hunted down Ben to ask him if he knew whether Sebastian was working undercover for resort security, as I suspected, hoping he could confirm my suspicion and I could feel better about encouraging Sandy to date Sebastian. Obviously, that question was pointless now. Ben was doing everything he could to avoid the hotel's security personnel so as not to get dumped onto the next outbound supply boat, and maybe prosecuted for trespassing.

I didn't see how Ben could be of any help but, for some reason, I couldn't walk away when he had so much on the line.

"If I see anything suspicious, I'll let you know," I said.

Ben didn't seem to hear me. He opened his laptop and started typing.

"Oh my God, you'll never guess who we saw when we left the spa," Sandy declared when we all met up again. She covered her mouth with both palms, then shook her hands as if she were doing a jazz routine. "You'll never—ever—guess."

Bella looked back and forth between Sandy and Marcie. "Was it Brad Pitt? Did I miss Brad Pitt? Damn."

Sandy shook her head, drew in a star-stuck breath and said, "Chris Hemsworth."

"Chris Hemsworth? You saw Chris Hemsworth?" Bella demanded, her gaze darting around the garden as if he might be lurking behind a fern plant.

"Really?" I asked Marcie.

She shrugged and threw an apologetic smile Sandy's way.

"I wasn't sure it was really him," she said.

"Of course it was him," Sandy insisted, then collapsed into a dreamy smile. "Wow, he looked fantastic."

We all just stood there for a minute, thinking about how fantastic-looking Chris Hemsworth was.

"I'm hungry," Bella said, breaking the spell. "How about we get something to eat?"

Sandy pulled the resort brochure from her pocket.

"Let's try the barbeque pavilion," she said. "It's one of the resort's original structures. It was built with imported oak inlaid with rosewood, featuring carvings that portray Dionysus, the Greek god of vegetation and wine."

Sandy pointed to the photo in the brochure. I thought the guy looked more like Clint Eastwood in his *Rawhide* days, but didn't say so.

We all agreed that barbeque sounded good, so Sandy led the way through the resort grounds to a big, round, open-air pavilion surrounded by tall shade trees. It kind of looked like a dining hall at summer camp— if you attended summer camp in Switzerland. The huge stone grills and ovens were manned by a dozen chefs. Tables were made of distressed wood and decorated with lanterns and red-checkered linens—which was, I figured, as close as Rowan Resort guests ever came to roughing it.

As we approached the hostess stand, Sandy flung out both arms and stopped dead in her tracks.

She swung around to us and whispered, "Oh my God. Look who's here. It's that really hot guy from that TV show. The one in Hawaii. He's taking out his cell phone, standing by that bench. "

Immediately, we all jumped to high alert, stretching up and craning our necks—but trying to look casual at the same time, a standard celebrity-sighting move—at the guy Sandy was trying hard not to nod toward.

Marcie gasped. "I see him."

"I see him, too," Bella agreed. "He's calling somebody."

"Maybe he's calling Chris Hemsworth," Sandy said.

"He's standing next to—hey, wait a minute," Bella said. "That's not him."

"Yes, it is," Sandy insisted.

"That's another guy Haley knows. I've seen him in the store," Bella declared.

I scooted around Marcie for a better look, and—oh my God, it was Jack Bishop. What was he doing here?

Bella gave me stink-eye. "Have you got *another* hot-looking man on this island?"

All my BFFs were mad-dogging me, so what could I say but, "No, absolutely not."

My cell phone rang.

I yanked it out of my pocket and saw Jack's name on the caller ID screen.

Crap.

"Okay, fine," I said. "I know him."

"He'd better have a brother," Bella told me.

I hit the green button on my phone, waved, and said, "Over here."

Somehow, Jack knew where *here* was, because he immediately hung up and started walking our way.

"Are you sure he's not a movie star?" Sandy asked.

"He should be," Bella said.

I couldn't disagree. Jack was super-hot. Today he had on khaki cargo pants, an olive green shirt, and CAT boots.

"Hello, ladies," Jack said when he joined us.

"Have you got a brother?" Bella asked.

"Get us a table," I said to my friends. "I'll catch up with you in a few minutes."

They all just stood there—not that I blamed them, of course.

I walked away. As I expected, Jack followed.

"What are you doing here?" I asked when we stopped beneath a shade tree.

"I could ask you the same thing," Jack said, and gave me a disapproving look. "You're not vacationing."

I wasn't in the mood to explain myself to Jack. What I did on my own time was none of his business. Yeah, okay, I'd called him, involved him in Jaslyn's murder, and asked for his help with my investigation, but still.

I guess Jack picked up on my don't-ask mood, because he said, "I'm here with the security team for Tate Manning's wedding."

It took me a second to realize he meant Yasmin and Tate-Tate-Tate, and remember what she'd told me.

"The Heart of Amour for her bouquet," I said. "You're guarding a necklace?"

Jack nodded. "Among other duties."

"Is she making a big deal out of the murder of Jaslyn Gordon?" I asked.

"There are safety concerns," he said.

The only danger Yasmin was in came from me, but I didn't think this was the best time to mention it.

I guess Jack didn't want to talk about Princess Yasmin any more than I did, because he changed the subject.

"I found more info on Jaslyn's brother," he said. "He's a druggie."

Talk of murder, drug addicts, and jail terms was more appealing to me than Yasmin's wedding, which says something about *her*, not *me*.

"Was he arrested for possession?" I asked.

Jack nodded. "And other things. One of which was selling stolen property to support his drug habit."

I got a maybe-I-solved-the-crime tingle in my belly.

"Any connection to the Colby Rowan robberies?" I asked.

Jack gave me a look like my question had come out of left field, bringing on the more familiar I-haven't-solved-the-crime anti-tingle.

"What about them?" he asked.

I filled him in on what I'd learned about Colby's criminal acquaintances, her crime spree, jail time, and missing accomplice. Jack listened, but I had the feeling he already knew about it.

I doubted he'd learned it from *People* magazine.

"Jaslyn and her brother were close," Jack said. "She visited him in prison."

Having a brother who was a criminal—and who had criminal friends in and out of prison—could have tied to her murder somehow. I just didn't know how.

"Did you find any connection between her brother and Jaslyn's job here at the resort?" I asked.

"Not yet," Jack said.

I was about to ask another question when movement off to my right caught my attention. I turned and saw Walt Pemberton, the head of Rowan Resort security, half hidden behind a palm tree. He was watching me.

CHAPTER 20

"What are you wearing this afternoon?" Sandy asked as we left the barbeque pavilion, stuffed with massive quantities of vacation calories.

"Something with an elastic waistband," Bella moaned.

"This afternoon?" Marcie asked. Then she gasped and said, "Oh, yes. I'd forgotten. Yasmin's bachelorette party."

For a couple of seconds, I feared I might see my lunch again, in reverse.

"Don't even think about it," Marcie told me. "You're going to that party. It's the right thing to do."

I hate it when I have to do the right thing.

"Okay," I grumbled.

"I told Sebastian I'd meet him in the sun room after lunch, but I think I should go look at my clothes. I don't know what to wear," Sandy said, and reached for her cell phone.

Despite the calorie-carb mega feast I'd just consumed, a brilliant idea flashed in my head—I'm pretty sure the calorie-carb mega desserts I'd had helped.

Since I'd had no luck finding Sebastian's hidden door in the library—I'd searched the shelves after Luke left but hadn't found anything—I figured I could do the next best thing—ask him.

"I'll stop by the sun room and let him know," I said, using my let-me-make-this-easy-for-you voice.

"I was hoping you'd help me decide what to wear," Sandy said. "I've never been to a bachelorette party in a garden before."

"Nobody has," I said.

But I suppose every bride-to-be would be doing it soon, thanks to the article in *Brides* magazine.

"I'll help you," Marcie said.

"I'll be up in a bit," I told her.

"I'm taking a nap," Bella said, stifling a yawn.

We all headed across the grounds, through the gardens, and into the rear entrance of the hotel. I turned down the corridor-of-no-return and everyone else went upstairs.

I followed the signs for the sun room—taking a moment to mad-dog the entrance of the shop where my Sea Vixen beach tote had been switched-at-point-of-sale—and finally found it, a large, glass-enclosed room with wicker furniture and enough plants to stock every Home Depot garden department on the West Coast.

I didn't see anyone in the room—really, why would somebody be in here when they could be in the actual sun—until I spotted Sebastian stretched out on a bench, fiddling with his cell phone. Even though he had on his official burgundy Rowan Resort polo shirt, I doubted he was working.

Lying around, playing with a phone while on company time. I mean, really, who would do such a thing?

All the questions I'd had about him flashed in my head. No way was I letting him get away without answering them.

I shifted into kind-of-private-detective interrogation mode.

Sebastian glanced up from his phone as I approached. "Hi, Haley. How's it going?"

I didn't respond.

He rose from the bench and looked past me.

"Where's Sandy?" he asked. "Is something wrong? She didn't get hurt or sick, did she?"

I ignored the concern in his voice.

"Yeah, something's wrong," I told him. "But not with Sandy. With you."

I got the expected who-me eyebrow bob. It's a sure sign that someone is lying—I know because I've used it many times myself.

Sebastian shrugged and gave me an I'm-completely-lost half grin. "Nothing's wrong with me," he said.

"You're a liar," I said.

I got the what-do-you-mean double eye blink—and, yes, I've used that one, also.

It's a personal favorite of mine.

He uttered a weak laugh. "I don't know what you're talking about, Haley. In fact—"

"You don't own your own consulting firm," I said.

Now I got the maybe-I-can-still-wiggle-my-way-out-of-this shoulder roll—I'm way better at this than Sebastian.

"I really can't discuss my job here at the resort," he said. "Honestly, I can't."

"Then maybe you can discuss how you walked out of a secret door in the library," I said.

"What are you talking about?" he asked, and managed to look totally confused. "I don't know anything about a secret door."

I had to hand it to him. He was clinging to his bogus story determined, apparently, to ride it straight into the ground.

"I saw you," I told him.

Sebastian opened his mouth but didn't say anything.

"I also know you disappeared in the lounge," I said.

He gave it another few seconds, then accepted the inevitable.

"Damn." He sank onto the bench again.

"What the heck is going on?" I demanded.

"Nothing," he said, and seemed a little panicked now. "Nothing's going on. Just forget it, okay. Forget you saw me."

"No way," I told him. "Look, you're hanging out with my friend. I'm not going to let you lead her on with these wild stories about you being some sort of consultant when none of it's true."

"It is true," Sebastian said, jumping off of the bench. "I got hired to work here on a very special project. It's strictly confidential. I can't tell anybody—anybody—about it."

"And this special, strictly confidential project you're assigned to includes going through secret doors and creeping around in hidden passageways behind the walls?" I asked.

He looked away. "No. I found out about those by accident."

"How?" I asked.

"I was up in the tower room—"

"Avery said those rooms were for family only," I remembered. "Are you related to Sidney Rowan?"

"No. No way," Sebastian said, and shook his head. "I'm a college student. I need to work to pay my tuition and expenses. I was offered a job here, so I took it."

"Doing what?" I asked.

He shook his head. "I can't tell you."

I turned my confess-all-now X-ray vision on him.

"I can't tell you. I can't. I really can't," Sebastian said again. "If word got out, all hell would break loose. I'd get fired—and that would be just the beginning of my problems."

He sounded desperate—and truthful.

"But the other stuff," Sebastian said, shaking his head. "Well, it just kind of . . . happened."

My brain jumped to high alert. Was *the other stuff* code for *I murdered Jaslyn*?

"What stuff?" I asked.

Okay, not my most clever interrogation tactic, but I was investigating on the fly here.

Sebastian stalled for a minute or two. I could see he was mentally debating whether to confess, which didn't suit me, of course. Finally he seemed to give up the struggle.

"Okay, you got me. You saw me using the hidden passages," he said, and shook his head. "I can't lie about it—not to you, anyway."

Sebastian collapsed onto the bench. I sat down beside him.

"Look," he said. "If you tell anybody about this, a lot of people are going to be hurt."

Oh my God. Had I just uncovered a massive conspiracy here at the ultra exclusive Rowan Resort?

Wow, that would be so cool.

"I was working in the office I'd been assigned to up in the tower," Sebastian said. "Everything is old up there. It wasn't refurbished when the mansion was converted into a hotel, I guess. I was trying to get the drawer open on a built-in storage cabinet and, somehow, I bumped something by mistake and a hidden door swung open."

"Just like that?" I asked.

Sebastian shrugged as if he didn't really understand it, either.

"So I thought, what the hell," he said.

I'd have done the same—depending on the cobweb situation, of course.

"I went inside. You won't believe what I discovered," Sebastian said.

I felt like I'd walked into a Nancy Drew novel—or maybe how Americans felt when they found out who shot J.R.

"The old part of the hotel that used to be the Rowan home is honeycombed with staircases and hidden entrances into the rooms," Sebastian said.

I remembered what Luke had told me about wealthy families building safe rooms into their homes, back in the day. The architect who'd done the original design of the Sidney Rowan mansion must have intended the secret passageways for use in the same manner.

"There are secret entrances to all the rooms?" I asked.

"Most of them," he said.

"That's really creepy," I said.

"And dangerous," he said. "It's pretty dark in there. Some of the steps and banisters are rotted."

"Bugs?" I asked.

He nodded.

"And spiders?"

"Yep," Sebastian said.

"Oh, crap."

"It's worth it, though," Sebastian said. "The site has made a ton of money."

I got a weird feeling

"What site?" I asked.

"I named it Celebrity Panty Raid," he said.

Oh my God.

"That's the site that auctions off the underwear of A-list stars," I said. "You came up with that?"

"Yes, it was my idea," he said, with a modest shrug.

"You're taking things that don't belong to you. You're stealing," I told him, "then selling those things for profit."

"It's no big deal," Sebastian insisted.

I gave him my are-you-listening-to-yourself look.

"These celebrities have millions and millions of dollars. They have closets full of things on multiple continents," Sebastian said. "One article of clothing means nothing to them. What do they care about a missing pair of panties? I'm not hurting anyone."

"You use secret passageways and hidden doors to sneak into the rooms of unsuspecting guests—guests who think they're safe here—steal their underwear, sell it for hundreds or thousands of dollars, and you think nothing is wrong with that?" I asked.

Sebastian shook his head. "Look, I'm not a bad guy. I just need money for college."

It flashed in my head that Sebastian probably wasn't the only person involved with this thing. And from what Ben had told me about the site, thousands of dollars were at stake. It made me wonder whether this had somehow led to Jaslyn's death.

"Do other employees know about this?" I asked.

He shook his head. "No."

Okay, so I was wrong about that.

But the tip Ben had received was right. The it's-really-icky Celebrity Panty Raid site was connected to the Rowan Resort. Obviously, Ben hadn't yet learned that Sebastian was behind it.

"You're not going to blow this for me, are you?" Sebastian asked.

I thought about it. I wasn't exactly seeing the whole thing as harmless, as Sebastian had insisted. But I wasn't convinced that ratting him out was the best option, either.

If I told Ben that Sebastian—an employee of Rowan Resort—had come up with the idea and ran the site, it would really pump up his story.

But if Sebastian thought I intended to tell, he'd probably shut down the site to save his own skin—he'd have no other choice, really—and Ben's story would disappear into virtual reality, taking what was left of his journalism career along with it.

No way was I doing that to Ben.

"Look, it's just for a little while longer," Sebastian said. "I've got a huge item coming up for auction. I've been teasing it for a while now and if the bids go the way I think they will, I'll have enough money to cover my college expenses and then some."

"Do you really expect me to believe you'd give up this lucrative Web site that easily?" I asked.

"My job here is ending in a few weeks," Sebastian said. "I'll leave the island. I won't have access to the hotel rooms."

Okay, that made me feel a little better. But I couldn't control what Sebastian did—not now, anyway. Not with Ben's I'll-be-famous story on the line.

"And about Sandy," Sebastian said. "Yes, I did lie to her about my job here, but I couldn't help it. It's confidential. I signed an agreement."

I couldn't really argue with that.

"I like Sandy. I really do," he said. "I want to keep seeing her, if I can. Please don't ruin things between us."

Jeez, how did I get in the middle of so many important decisions involving other people? I'm on vacation.

"You'd better not hurt her," I told him.

"I won't," he said. "I swear. I won't."

I fumed for a minute, then said, "Okay, I won't tell anybody—as long as nothing bad happens."

"Nothing bad is going to happen," Sebastian said. "How could it?"

Good question.

CHAPTER 21

Marcie, Bella, Sandy, and I chose to wear sundresses in a variety of colors—except pink, of course—and, really, we all looked great when we showed up for Yasmin's bachelorette garden party.

Guests were greeted at what the resort brochure had termed the summer house, which wasn't really a house but an outdoor covered area with a white roof held up with white pillars, and a flagstone floor, all surrounded by green plants and shrubs.

"Everything is handled," Joy said quietly as I walked past. "You don't have to worry about a thing."

Good to know—even though I wasn't worried about the event in the first place.

We walked through the vine-covered arbor, and I was pleased to see that my vision of the event had turned out well. Pink, white, and a touch of mint green abounded. The linens were crisp, and the china and crystal sparkled. A bartender and two waitresses, all dressed in Rowan Resort burgundy uniforms, were busy serving drinks.

Really, it's never too early to start drinking at a function such as this.

The stage and runway were set up for the fashion show, and a flat screen played a DVD of Yasmin's photos. About a dozen or so young women were clustered in a small group watching the DVD, squealing and giggling each time they saw themselves flash on the screen. I recognized most of them; others must have been Yasmin and Tate-Tate-Tate's family members

Nearby stood Yasmin's mother, Deandra, and her aunt Elnora, both dressed in pastel Gucci dresses, four-inch pumps, with full-on jewelry and makeup. From the looks on their faces, I doubted neither would have squealed or giggled if they'd see themselves on TV.

"Looks like there might be hope for this party after all," Bella murmured as she nodded toward the rear of the area.

Two dark-haired men dressed in gray suits, brilliant white shirts, conservative neckties, and sunglasses stood at each end of a small table. Wow, they looked great.

"I knew he had a brother," Bella whispered.

Then it hit me—one of the men was Jack Bishop. I didn't know the other guy.

I realized then that on the table between them, the Heart of Amour pendant rested on a pedestal.

"I'll get us a table—right by him," Bella said. She headed toward Jack and his fellow security guard, Marcie and Sandy close behind.

"Hey, where are all the young studs?" asked a woman beside me.

"With no shirts on," I added.

We looked at each other and, immediately, I knew we'd connected—though to see us you'd never think we had anything in common. She was a tiny woman—probably no more than ninety pounds on a rainy day—with silver hair, in a yellow dress trimmed with leopard print. I figured her for seventy-plus, easily.

She squinted up at me. "You're Haley."

I don't usually like to admit to anything, especially where strangers are concerned, but I had a good feeling about her.

"I'm Francine. Yasmin's grandmother," she said, before I could answer. "Ada showed me pictures of you two shopping in London not long ago."

"You're Ada's friend," I realized, and couldn't help smiling.

"And you're dating Ada's grandson," she said, and threw arms around me. "I am so glad to meet you. Thanks so much for jumping in and helping with the wedding."

"You're welcome," I said, but couldn't quite bring myself to add the expected glad-I-could-do-it.

"So this is what passes for a bachelorette party these days, huh?" Francine said, gazing around the summer house. She shook her head. "Looks like a real yawner to me."

"It's the latest thing," I said. "Yasmin wanted it."

Francine uttered a disgusted grunt. "Figures."

I was liking her more and more every minute.

"When's Ty getting here?" she asked.

Hearing Ty's name spoke aloud gave me a little jolt. I ignored it.

When I'd spoken with Ada the other day I'd wondered if Ty had told her we'd broken up. Apparently, he hadn't—or if he had, the news hadn't traveled far enough to reach Francine.

I could have kept my mouth shut and let Francine think Ty and I were still a couple, but I didn't see any sense in it.

"Actually, Ty and I broke up," I said.

"His idea or yours?" Francine asked.

Okay, I wasn't all that excited about rehashing our breakup, but Francine didn't sound judgmental, so I rolled with it.

"It was his idea," I said. "But I went along with it."

"He'll come back," she said.

She sounded sure of herself, as if she knew Ty well—and maybe she did, since she and Ada had been friends for so long.

"I doubt it," I told her.

Francine shook her head. "Those Cameron men. What a bunch of workaholic worrywarts. Always looking for perfection."

"Ty sure as heck never found perfection with me," I told her.

"Has he called you?" she asked.

"No," I said. "I heard he's busy with some big acquisition."

"Figures. Distracting himself with work," Francine said. "The Cameron men expect perfection in themselves. If something goes wrong, if they think they've made a mistake, they lock up. Ty will figure out what he's done. He'll get over it. He'll call you."

I shook my head. "I'm not sure I want to get back together with Ty."

"Ada told me all about you two," Francine said. "Ty can't be very attentive, and you don't want to be smothered. You're perfect for each other."

I just stared at her. I'd never thought of our relationship in quite that way. Was it really that simple?

Luckily, a commotion among the guests took our attention; I didn't want to think about Ty and me anymore.

"Oh, my word," Francine muttered, shaking her head.

Yasmin was making her grand entrance into the party through the arbor. She had on a pink floral print dress, pink shoes, pink accessories, and a wide-brimmed pink hat trimmed with huge flower blossoms.

She looked like she was going to the Kentucky Derby.

I figured this was a good time to find my friends. I spotted them seated at a table near the Heart of Amour and its security team.

Honestly, I was more than a little irked by the whole my-wedding-is-so-special-my-bouquet-pendant-needs-its-own-guards thing. I mean, really, how pretentious can you get? This was a lot—even for Yasmin.

I walked over and sidled up next to Jack. He was in private detective mode. His jaw was set, his shoulders squared, his expression unreadable behind the sunglasses.

It was a really hot look on him.

"Are you supposed to thwart a robbery attempt?" I asked.

"Grab it and take off," Jack said, then switched to his Barry White voice. "You'll be glad you did."

Oh my God.

I plopped down in a chair at the table with my friends.

"Damn, it's hot today," I said.

Bella glanced up at Jack. "You're telling me."

Another dozen guests arrived and the festivities got under way. The food was delicious and the signature drink—something pink—helped considerably, when Yasmin got up to address the gathering. I listened for about three seconds, then it all turned into blah, blah, blah.

I didn't know how I would get through the wedding ceremony and the reception. I had to get out of it somehow.

Just as I was considering whether I could actually get away with my Uncle-Bob-died excuse, or if the tried and true touch-of-the-stomach-flu might work better, I spotted a Sea Vixen beach tote on the arm of a woman crossing the hotel grounds. Immediately, my senses jumped to high alert. I leaned back in my chair to get a better look at her. I couldn't see her all that well from this distance—just the vague impression of a small, dark-haired woman—but she looked familiar. Still, I knew she was definitely not one of the two women who'd gotten the totes from the hotel shop's last shipment. That could only mean—

Oh my God. *Oh my God.*

Had the shop gotten in another shipment of Sea Vixen totes and not told me? Had they given my bag away to some other woman—*again?*

No way was I sitting still for another of their "hold list" screw-ups.

"I have to go," I said to Marcie, and managed not to scream the words.

At least, I don't think I screamed.

I bolted out of my chair, skirted the edge of the gathering, and rushed out of the summer house through the arbor. I followed the path through the hotel grounds, bobbing and weaving my way around fountains, benches, shrubs, and planters of flowers, keeping the woman in sight.

My first instinct, of course, was to grab the Sea Vixen off of her arm while screaming mine-mine-mine—anyone in my position would do the same—but I decided to take it slow. I didn't want to cause a huge scene and have resort security get involved. Somehow, I didn't think Walt Pemberton would be all that sympathetic to my situation.

I hung back, following the woman. I figured that when she stopped I would rush forward—without looking like I was rushing, of course—and oh-so casually ask her where and when she got her tote. It was possible, of course, that she'd had it for a while and the hotel shop had not, in fact, failed to notify me that my tote had arrived. I decided to play it cool.

I hate playing it cool.

I picked up my pace and was closing in on her when she left the path and headed down the narrow road that led to the employee dorm.

Okay, that was weird. Why would a hotel guest be headed there?

I slowed down, putting a little more distance between us, and watched as she kept going. But instead of veering left to the dorms, she turned right and walked up to the dock. A boat was tied off, swaying with the swell of the ocean waves. I didn't know much about watercraft, but I knew this wasn't the supply boat. It was small, with *Unexpected Opportunity* painted on its white hull. A man jumped off, spoke with the woman, then took a package she pulled out of her Sea Vixen tote.

What the heck was going on?

I scrambled behind a hedge and crouched down, peeking through the bushes as the woman headed back in my direction. She drew closer, and I realized why she'd looked slightly familiar when I'd first spotted her. It was Colby Rowan. Sandy had pointed her out on this very stretch of road.

Then it hit me that nothing illegal or immoral was going on—which was kind of disappointing—but, rather, something dull and boring.

Sandy had told me that Colby created works of art at her studio here on the island and sold them internationally. Colby was simply shipping something to a buyer, or a gallery, or whoever handled those kinds of transactions, and she was using a private courier service—she couldn't very well send something that valuable via the postal service.

I hung out behind the hedge until Colby walked past—I figured I might startle her if I suddenly jumped out in front of her—and followed her to the hotel grounds, through the gardens, to one of the bungalows. She went inside and closed the door.

I stood near several small palms, deciding what to do. I really wanted to ask Colby where and when she'd gotten her Sea Vixen, but I didn't want her to think I was stalking her, or anything, since she was, after all, a kind-of sort-of celebrity.

Besides, it was an excellent excuse not to go back to Yasmin's so-called bachelorette party.

My spirits lifted as I knocked on the door of Colby's bungalow, and I imagined her opening up, inviting me inside, and the two of us bonding over our love for the Sea Vixen tote. We could become lifelong friends. Really.

The door opened and Colby stared out at me. I'd heard somewhere that she was in her thirties, but she looked older and kind of hard—apparently, serious facial moisturizers aren't allowed in prison.

"I don't give lessons without an appointment," she said, and pushed the door closed in my face.

I caught it with my hand.

"I'm not here for a lesson," I said. "I saw you just now carrying a Sea Vixen beach tote, and I wanted to ask you where you got it."

"You're mistaken," Colby said.

Okay, now I was seriously confused.

"The polka dot tote," I said. "It's an awesome bag. I'm dying to get one."

"I don't own a polka dot tote," Colby said.

"But I saw you—"

"Good day," she said, and pushed the door shut.

I stood there staring at the door for a couple of minutes, then stepped back.

What the heck was going on? I knew—*knew*—I

hadn't lost sight of Colby since I spotted her earlier. I knew I'd seen her with a Sea Vixen, and I knew I'd seen her go into her bungalow.

Why would she deny the whole thing? Why would she lie?

I had no idea.

CHAPTER 22

For an ultraexclusive—which is code for ultraexpensive—resort that catered to Hollywood stars and international millionaires, there was a heck of a lot of crime associated with the Rowan Resort.

I left Colby's bungalow and wandered aimlessly through the gardens—though not aimlessly enough that I'd end up at Yasmin's idiotic bachelorette party—thinking about all the criminal activity I'd uncovered here. Yeah, okay, it was nothing hard-core—except for Jaslyn's murder—but still it seemed to me that this place had more than its share of wrongdoing.

The weird part was that all the crimes were, somehow, connected to Jaslyn Gordon.

Colby, who shared the love of art with Jaslyn, had been involved in robberies in Los Angeles, done jail time, and one of her accomplices was still on the lam. Gabe Braxton, Jaslyn's boyfriend, had been arrested for assault and domestic violence, though none of the charges stuck. Jaslyn Gordon had a brother who was currently serving time. Sebastian ran a Web site auctioning off stolen underwear that, conceivably, Jaslyn could have been involved with—even though Sebastian denied it—since she was a hotel maid and had access to celebrities' clothing while cleaning their rooms.

The even weirder part was that I'd uncovered absolutely nothing—no evidence, no rumors, no wild speculation—that Jaslyn herself had been involved in any of those criminal activities. So if she hadn't been a part of it, why had she been murdered? How could it be that the only person *not* involved was dead? It didn't make any sense.

I turned down a different path and walked onto a small, wooden arched bridge. A waterfall splashed down some rocks, then flowed under the bridge. It was quiet here, peaceful. Not a lot of hotel guests were around. I stood there looking at the water and thinking.

Of course, the people connected with Jaslyn who had been in trouble with the law weren't the only ones I had concerns about. I'd considered Avery's possible involvement with Jaslyn's murder. She'd been unhappy with Jaslyn's blatant disregard for employee policies and had, I'm sure, been called on the carpet because of it. Maybe upper management had threatened Avery with her job if she couldn't keep her team members in line—and out of the library—and Avery had let her anger with Jaslyn get the best of her.

Hang on a second.

Oh my God—the library.

According to what I'd been told, Jaslyn had become obsessed with the library. Had she discovered the hid-

den door in the bookcase, realized the secret passageways connected to guests' rooms, and threatened to go
public with the story?

If so, the media frenzy would be epic. Rowan Resort
would undoubtedly be hit with multibillion-dollar lawsuits from everyone who'd ever vacationed here. Walt
Pemberton, as chief of resort security, would have a
great deal of explaining to do; no doubt he'd be fired
and would never find a job working in security again.

Was that a reason to murder someone?

Yeah, I thought it was.

Really, I wouldn't mind finding Pemberton guilty
of most anything, since I'd seen him creeping around,
spying on me; he'd probably instructed his undercover
personnel to keep me under surveillance, too.

Then something else hit me. What if Jaslyn had seen
Sebastian come out of the hidden passageway in the library, as I had? What if she'd confronted him, demanded answers?

My thoughts skipped ahead, and I got a weird feeling thinking that maybe Sebastian had murdered
Jaslyn. He didn't really strike me as the type, but you
never knew about people. Like some of the other employees I'd met here, Sebastian was desperate for
money to pay his college tuition and expenses. Maybe
in an all-out panic, he'd killed Jaslyn.

I stood on the bridge for a few more minutes, running all the scenarios through my head—jeez, a hit of
chocolate would sure help right now—and finally decided that I needed more evidence, more info.

I knew one place to find it.

I trekked through the gardens, into the hotel, and up
the stairs to the second floor. Just as I'd figured, the

housekeeping staff was still busy cleaning the guest rooms. I walked the corridor stopping wherever I saw one of the big carts and finally spotted Tabitha inside a room, pulling sheets off of one of the beds.

"Tabitha?" I said as I walked in.

She squealed, spun around, clutching the sheet in front of her. Wow, was she skittish or what?

"Oh, Miss Randolph, it's you." She heaved a heavy, relieved sigh and plopped down on the bed.

"Sorry," I said.

I don't think my apology helped. Her hands trembled. She gulped big breaths. Her face went white, and it looked like she might pass out.

Jeez, I really hope she doesn't faint. I'm not great in a medical emergency.

I eased closer and sat down on the edge of the bed opposite her. This sent her into a worse panic.

"You're not supposed to be in here," she whispered, twisting the sheet in her fingers. "Nobody is supposed to come into the rooms when we're cleaning. I told you that before. You're going to get me into serious trouble."

"I just need to ask you something," I said.

Tabitha drew the sheet up and held it against her chest like a shield.

"I don't want to answer any more questions," she said.

Like any good investigator, I ignored her remark.

"Why did Jaslyn keep going to the library?" I asked.

"I already told you everything I know," Tabitha said.

"Are you certain?" I asked.

"Of course I'm certain," she told me.

I didn't want to come out and ask her if Jaslyn had confided in her that she'd discovered the hidden door in the library bookcase, just in case Jaslyn hadn't told her. I'd promised Sebastian I wouldn't divulge his secret, and I intended to keep my word—unless I found some solid evidence that he'd murdered Jaslyn, of course.

Tabitha glanced at the doorway and, for a few seconds, I thought she might make a break for it. I tried a new approach.

"Did Jaslyn talk to Walt Pemberton?" I asked.

She looked totally lost now, and asked, "Who's he?"

Huh. Not exactly the key piece of incriminating evidence I'd hoped for.

I pushed on.

"You told me Jaslyn said she was going to talk to upper management about something," I said. "Do you know who she intended to speak with?"

"She didn't tell me, and I didn't ask," Tabitha said. "The only person she ever talked to was Colby Rowan. They talked about art and stuff."

"What stuff?" I asked.

"I don't know. Jaslyn didn't tell me everything," Tabitha insisted.

"She must have told you something more," I said.

Tabitha rubbed her temples and stared at the floor. She looked like she might crack at any second.

No way would she make a good spy.

"She—she told me that Colby had showed her some books about art in her bungalow one day," Tabitha said. "She told me Colby promised to introduce her to some of her art friends at the galleries in New York. She told me she'd miss their talks after Colby left because nobody else on the island understood art like she did. She said that—"

"Hang on a second," I said. "Colby was leaving?"

Tabitha nodded. "Yes. In a few weeks."

"Where was she going?" I asked.

"I have no idea," she told me. "But Jaslyn didn't think she was coming back. Ever."

This whole in-a-few-weeks thing rang a bell. Joy had mentioned she was coordinating a huge event scheduled to take place in a few weeks. Sebastian had claimed that his supersecret-highly-confidential-you-can't-make-me-tell job was ending in a few weeks. And Colby was planning to leave the island in a few weeks?

"Do you—do you think that has anything to do with Jaslyn's murder?" Tabitha asked in a faint whisper, as if she were afraid to ask the question—or maybe more afraid of what the answer might be.

"I don't know," I said because, really, I didn't.

Tabitha's eyes grew round and her breathing became labored.

"Don't tell anybody that I talked to you," she said, latching onto my arm. "Please. Please, don't tell anybody what I said. I don't want to get into trouble. I don't want anything else bad to happen."

"It's okay. Really, it's okay," I said.

I tried for my you-can-trust-me smile, but I couldn't quite pull it off.

I always have trouble pulling that one off.

"I won't bother you with this again," I said.

"That's what you told me the last time," Tabitha said.

"This time, I swear."

"You swore last time, too."

Crap.

"Okay, well, this time I'm triple-swearing," I said.

I guess that sunk in, because she let go of my arm. I

figured it was a good time to leave before Tabitha found a personal injury lawyer and sued me for willful infliction of emotional distress or something.

I left the room, squeezed around the housekeeping cart parked outside, and—oh, crap—spotted Avery three doors down. She saw me, too, and knew I'd come out of a room that wasn't mine. Her spine stiffened and her jaw tightened in that universal oh-my-God-what-did-I-just-witness stunned expression that, believe it or not, I've had directed at me many times.

So what could I do but go on the offensive?

"There you are, Avery," I said in my mom's I'm-better-than-you voice, as I walked toward her. "I've been looking all over for you."

It was a total lie, of course, but that's what being on the offensive was all about, right? And, I hoped, it would keep Tabitha out of trouble.

"Just an hour ago I saw another woman with a Sea Vixen beach tote," I said, as if I'd just witnessed an invasion of California by the North Koreans. "Where is *my* bag? I was assured I would get one from the next shipment. What is going on?"

Avery immediately shifted into total back-down mode.

"I don't understand," she said, and reached for her cell phone. "But I'll find out. I'll call Patricia right now."

"I would like us to go see her in person," I told her.

Really, I didn't want to go to the shop in person, since the whole thing was a big, fat lie. But I figured that if I got Avery away from here, it would keep Tabitha from getting an earful about unauthorized guests in the rooms.

It was the best I could do, at the moment.

"Yes. Of course. Whatever you want," Avery said.

We walked through the corridor together and down the stairs. When we got to the lobby, I stopped.

"This is too upsetting," I announced, touching the tip of my little finger to the corner of my eye.

I detected a slight this-is-really-convenient eyebrow bob from Avery, but I pushed on.

"You go talk to Patricia and call me when you know something," I said.

Avery wouldn't dare refuse. She nodded and continued across the lobby. I ducked out the front entrance.

I did a quick mental calculation and decided that if I went back to Yasmin's bachelorette party now, it would almost be over. Perfect timing.

As I passed the fountain with the water shooting out of the sea horse's nose, I heard someone call my name. I stopped, then realized—oh my God, I'd actually stopped. What had happened to my Holt's avoid-the-customer-at-all-cost training I'd engrained in myself since starting work there?

This was not all right—even though I'm on vacation.

"Haley, look at this."

Ben bounded up beside me, his laptop tucked under his arm.

He looked more ragged than the last time I'd seen him. Sleeping wherever, eating whatever, and wearing the same clothes had taken its toll.

"You've got to give those khakis and that polo a rest," I told him, and even managed to say it nicely.

"You have to see this," he said, pulling me toward a nearby bench.

"Do you need something to eat?" I asked, sitting down.

"It's happening," Ben said, and dropped onto the bench. "Just like I thought."

He opened his laptop and started pecking at the keys.

"I'm taking you shopping," I told him.

He ignored me.

"Let's go get you some food," I said.

"Here." Ben pointed at the screen. "Look. Look at this. It's just like I told you."

Both hands clinched into fists, he looked at his laptop with such intensity it startled me.

"See?" he said. "That's the Web site I told you about."

I looked at the screen and saw "Celebrity Panty Raid" across the top of the page in black, lacy letters.

"Check this out." Ben clicked on a red thong icon, then typed into a search box.

I leaned closer and saw that panties were up for auction.

"This is the big item I told you about. They've been teasing it for a couple of days," Ben said. "It proves this site is tied to the Rowan Resort."

I looked again but didn't see anything spectacular, just a pair of purple panties trimmed with zebra print and some kind of weird-looking appliqué on the front.

"I don't understand," I said.

"These are Beyoncé's panties," Ben said.

Okay, so here I was sitting on a bench at an exclusive resort, on my vacation, with a reporter, looking at a photo of Beyoncé's panties.

What has my life become?

"These panties are going to make everything in my life good again," Ben declared.

"Is your blood sugar low?" I asked.

"This proves what I've been saying," Ben said.

"Are you on some medication that you, maybe, skipped for the last few days?" I asked.

"The tip I got was right," Ben said. "Finally, I can break a story that will get me noticed."

"I don't think you're properly hydrated," I said.

"Look at these panties," he insisted, pointing at the screen. "Beyoncé's panties. They're all the proof I need to show that the Rowan Resort is connected to Celebrity Panty Raid."

"This is a pair of panties, Ben," I said. "They don't prove anything."

"No, you don't understand," he said, and started hitting the keyboard again. "Look at this."

The screen changed, and I saw a photo of the ocean and a sandy beach. People were in the water, playing in the sand, and lying on chaises. A thatched-roofed bar was nearby.

"That's here," I realized.

I got a weird feeling.

"Yeah," Ben said, and pointed. "And look who's sitting right there in the lounge chair. It's Beyoncé."

My weird feeling got weirder.

"This photo was taken just a few days ago, on the same day Celebrity Panty Raid started teasing a big item," Ben said. "It was taken by a couple of girls who spotted Beyoncé on the beach. She gave them an autograph and they took her picture. The girls posted the whole story online."

My weird feeling got really weird.

"Look. Right here on the beach at the Rowan Resort," Ben said. "It's Beyoncé."

Oh my God.

It wasn't Beyoncé.

"And those are her panties up for auction," Ben said.

Those weren't Beyoncé's panties.

The girl in the photo was Bella, and the panties up for auction were Bella's lucky panties, stolen out of her room.

Oh, crap.

"I don't know what's going on with her hair, though," Ben said, pointing to the dolphin sculpted atop her head.

It took everything I had not to blast off of the bench and hunt down Sebastian.

He must have been surfing the social sites on celebrity watch and found the post highlighting the supposed photo of Beyoncé and the story that she was vacationing at the Rowan Resort. Whether he knew the picture was of Bella and not Beyoncé—or if he even cared—it wouldn't have mattered after Beyoncé's fans saw it, because everyone would believe the story was true. So he used the secret passageways to sneak into Bella's room, steal her panties, and put them up for auction.

Ben nudged me with his elbow.

"Look at the bids," he said. "They're over ten grand now."

"Ten thousand dollars? For *panties?*" I might have said that kind of loud.

"Beyoncé is super hot," Ben said.

"Yeah, but panties?" I'm sure I shouted that.

"Fans will pay big bucks for anything connected to

her. But intimate apparel like her panties? There's no telling how high the bids will go."

This had to be the item Sebastian had told me about, the one he was certain would bring in a small fortune, the last one he'd need to pay his college expenses before he left the resort for good.

Ben went on talking, but I wasn't listening.

I wanted to find Sebastian, give him an earful for invading the privacy of my friend's room and stealing her treasured panties, then rat him out to Walt Pemberton and resort security.

I'd agreed to keep my mouth shut when Sebastian told me about his scheme—but this was different. Now my friend was involved.

Another troubling idea zapped my brain, derailing my I'll-get-you train of thought.

If I told Pemberton and betrayed Sebastian, it would totally ruin his budding relationship with Sandy and probably land him in legal trouble. I might even wind up in trouble also, for not reporting the thefts when Sebastian confessed them to me. Walt might think I was involved, and I wasn't anxious to be targeted by him.

I was tempted to take my chances with Walt Pemberton, though, but what would that do to Ben?

His career-making, I'll-be-a-respected-journalist, everyone-will-know-my-name news story was wrong—all wrong. Somebody somewhere would report that Beyoncé wasn't at the Rowan Resort at the time the photo was taken—maybe even Beyoncé herself.

If I said nothing and let him break this story, he'd end up the laughingstock of the news media. He'd be fodder for late-night comedians—forever. His life would be ruined—again—because of me.

No way could I let that happen to Ben.

And no way did I want to end up in the middle of another situation with resort security.

"I'll have this story ready to go by tonight," Ben said, typing furiously, "and tomorrow I'll—"

"Wait. No, wait," I said, and covered his hands with mine.

"I'm not waiting," Ben said, and pulled away from me.

"You really need to wait," I said.

Ben shook his head. He opened his mouth to speak, then stopped. His eyes narrowed and his jaw tightened.

"You know something," he said, breathing hard. "You've done something. You're going to ruin my story, aren't you."

"No, it's nothing like that," I said.

It was a complete lie, of course, but what else could I say? I knew I couldn't possibly convince him to abandon the story, but I had to get him to delay it.

"What you have here is gossip," I said, gesturing to his laptop. "I mean, I'm no journalist, but don't you need facts? Interviews with a spokesperson from the resort? Maybe a comment from Beyoncé's rep? Some investigation into who, exactly, is behind Celebrity Panty Raid? More info so you can present a balanced story?"

Ben's shoulders sagged and he seemed to deflate.

"Yeah, yeah, you're right," he mumbled, rubbing his eyes with the heels of his hands. "I don't know what I was thinking. I just . . ."

"You're exhausted. You're not thinking clearly," I said.

He heaved a heavy sigh. "Maybe you're right."

I pulled my resort card from my pocket and said, "Go up to my room. It's two-twelve. Order something to eat from room service. I'm sure things will look different after you get some rest."

Ben looked at my card.

"It's the only way you can get a real meal at this place," I said. I was sure he'd been pilfering chips and crackers, and whatever else he could slip away with, from the snack bars.

"Thanks, Haley," he whispered, and took my card.

He tucked his laptop under his arm and walked away.

I had to hand it to Ben, he'd definitely figured out that Rowan Resort was involved with the Celebrity Panty Raid Web site, but he'd done it with a connection that would be easily—and vehemently—denied, tanking his story, his reputation, and his career.

I couldn't bring myself to crush his future by telling him that it was actually Bella in the photo, not Beyoncé. I'd do it, though, as soon as I could figure how.

I slumped back on the bench, exhausted.

I need a vacation from my vacation.

CHAPTER 23

I cut through the hotel headed for the summer house and the very few minutes, I hoped, that remained of Yasmin's bachelorette party. I spotted Avery headed my way, cell phone in hand.

"I was just about to call you," she said, stopping in front of me. "Patricia assures me the resort has received no new shipment."

It took me a minute to realize she was reporting back on the wild-goose chase I'd sent her on to inquire about my Sea Vixen beach tote.

"That's a relief," I said.

It wasn't, of course, but what else could I say?

It seemed like a good time to change the subject.

"My resort card is missing," I said. "I'll need another one, please."

Avery gave a little not-another-problem shudder and started texting on her cell phone.

"It will be ready in just a moment," she said. "Shall I have it delivered to you?"

She sounded kind of anxious to get rid of me—not that I blamed her, of course.

"I don't mind waiting," I said.

I'm not big on waiting, but I figured this was a good chance to try to get some info on the big event coming up in a few weeks, which several people had mentioned. Even if it turned out to be completely unrelated to Jaslyn's murder, or anything, it might be some good gossip I could pass on to my BFFs.

That's what BFFs *do*.

"Everyone on staff must be gearing up for the big event in a few weeks," I said, in my oh-so casual voice.

I saw a quick oh-crap expression on Avery's face, but her I'm-great-at-dealing-with-difficult-guests training must have kicked in, because she pushed past it.

"All of our events are big," she said, a standard reply composed by the resort's publicity staff, no doubt.

"Not as big as this one, from what I hear," I said.

I'd totally embellished what I'd heard, of course, but how else was I going to get any info from her? Really, I owed it to my BFFs to get as much gossip as possible, and if I learned something that might help me solve Jaslyn's murder, all the better.

"There are always rumors," Avery said, stiffening her spine. "In fact—oh, look, here's your resort pass."

The door to the security office opened and Walt Pemberton walked out.

Oh, crap.

"Hello, Miss Randolph," he said. "Enjoying your stay?"

He said it nicely enough, but he was definitely mad-dogging me, like he knew I was up to something, or withholding information—which I was, of course, but still.

"Yes, I am," I said, "despite all the problems I've had."

I didn't think it would hurt to put him on the defensive.

He didn't get defensive. Actually, he looked kind of smug. Like he knew I'd been lying about things.

I hate it when that happens.

"If anything else comes up, please let me know immediately," he said, and handed me my resort pass.

"I'll do that," I told him.

I headed out of the hotel into the gardens. I didn't look back, but I knew Walt Pemberton was still watching me.

I knew, too, that Avery had lied about not knowing what the resort's upcoming big event was all about.

I strolled through the gardens—okay, I could have walked faster but I wasn't exactly in a hurry to get back to Yasmin's I-love-me bachelorette party—thinking about Jaslyn. I still hadn't come up with a reason for her to have been murdered. I'd found absolutely no motive. Everyone I'd spoken with had said she was a really nice person, a bright, intelligent college student obsessed with art who, aside from a run-in with Avery over visiting the library, hadn't caused anybody any trouble.

Jeez, *somebody* had to dislike her. Supernice people didn't get murdered for no reason.

Maybe I needed to talk to more people.

Colby popped into my head.

Tabitha had told me that Jaslyn was upset about Colby leaving the resort in a few weeks. I figured that was because Jaslyn would miss their conversations about art—which sounded kind of dull to me—but maybe something more was going on.

I wondered, also, where Colby was headed off to. She'd been a bit secretive about the whole thing, from what I'd gathered. Was she just trying to avoid publicity?

Possibly, I decided. After all, she was a convicted felon who's served time in prison. Maybe she didn't want her new neighbors, whomever they were, to learn that she was moving in and somehow block her attempt to join their community, a story that would surely find its way to the tabloids, bloggers, celebrity Web sites, and magazines.

Honestly, I couldn't really blame the new neighbors for not wanting Colby to live among them. The one time we'd met, I hadn't really liked her. Plus, she'd lied about being at the dock and about owning a Sea Vixen beach tote. Why would she do that?

My thoughts rushed ahead.

Obviously, Colby had attempted to cover up her visit to the dock, and by claiming she didn't own a Sea Vixen tote she could also deny passing a package along to the guy she'd met at the boat. It made me wonder if Colby was part of Sebastian's auction site. After all, Colby had lived in the mansion as a child, so she surely knew about the hidden passageways and secret entrances into the rooms.

I stewed on that for a couple of minutes, then decided that, honestly, I couldn't see Colby involving herself with a panty auction site. She wouldn't want the publicity if the scheme were exposed, plus she didn't need the money—she was Sidney Rowan's heir. She lived on an exclusive resort in a luxury private bungalow, where she could watch over the art collection and paint to her heart's content.

Good grief. I was getting nowhere, I realized.

I definitely needed a brain boost. The dessert at Yasmin's party loomed large in my head. I started walking faster.

The very thought of chocolate seemed to give my brain a jolt. I pulled out my cell phone and called Shuman.

"Have you had any luck finding Colby's old accomplice?" I asked when he answered.

"Maybe," Shuman said. "I got a lead on a man seen hanging around the resort's supply boat in Long Beach a few days ago."

Oh, crap. That must have been Ben they saw before he managed to slip aboard the boat bound for the island.

"Was it Colby's accomplice?" I asked.

Really, what else could I say?

"We're working the lead," Shuman said.

I decided this was an excellent time to bring the conversation back to a subject that would benefit *me*.

"Have you turned up anything concerning artwork?" I asked.

"Stolen artwork?" Shuman asked.

He sounded surprised and I couldn't blame him, since that question had come out of nowhere.

"Jaslyn and Colby both loved art," I said, "so I thought maybe there was some sort of connection."

"Still trying to solve that murder you're not supposed to be involved with?" Shuman asked.

He used his cop voice—which was kind of hot—but no way was I backing off.

Really, Shuman had known me for a long time. You'd think he'd know better than to ask.

"Of course," I said. "So have you heard anything about artwork?"

Shuman was quiet for a few seconds. I pictured him frowning his cop frown, running the whole scenario through his cop brain, shifting his weight, breathing a little heavier.

Always hot.

"I haven't heard anything, but LAPD wouldn't handle it," Shuman said. "The Feds would."

"The FBI?" I asked.

"The FBI has a rapid deployment Art Crime team that investigates the illicit trade in art and cultural artifacts," Shuman said.

Luke Warner flashed in my head.

I forced his image away.

"Look," I said, "if I hear anything, I'll let you know."

"Stay out of it, Haley," he said.

"I can't do that," I said.

"I know," Shuman said. "But it makes me feel better to say it."

His tone lightened, and I imagined him with a little grin on his face. It made me grin, too.

"Call me if you run into trouble," Shuman said.

"I will," I promised, and we hung up.

By the time I reached the summer house, the party was breaking up. Everyone was out of their chairs, clustered in small groups, chatting and laughing. Marcie, Bella, and Sandy had melted into one of the gatherings and seemed to be having a good time.

I made a dash for the dessert table.

Jack Bishop stepped in front of me, cutting me off.

"I need you," he said.

Dessert or Jack?

I looked back and forth between the yummy confections and Jack—a yummy confection in a whole different way.

Jeez, why are there so many difficult choices in life?

"We're headed to a photo shoot," Jack said.

I noticed then that a photography crew waited nearby. A guy was snapping pictures of Yasmin and some of her guests.

"A magazine is doing a story about engaged couples, traditional weddings, that sort of thing," Jack said.

Leave it to Yasmin to get her face and her kill-me-now wedding plastered all over a magazine.

"The Heart of Amour is in the shoot?" I asked.

Jack nodded. "Something about the pendant predicting who the next bride will be?"

"So I heard," I said. "Seems that whoever catches the bouquet with the pendant attached will be the next to get married. Supposedly, it's worked in the last four weddings."

"I need you to come to the shoot with me," Jack said.

I pinched my lips together to hold in a squeal.

Jack wanted me to work with him? Wow, this was way cool. Finally, something great would come out of Yasmin's wedding ordeal.

"Sure," I said, and managed to sound calm and composed—at least, that's how I hope I sounded. "What can I do?"

"You know Yasmin's friends," Jack said. "I need you to keep an eye on everyone at the shoot and let me know if someone shows up who shouldn't be there."

"You're thinking somebody might attempt to steal the Heart of Amour pendant?" I asked.

"Resort security was alerted to an incident at the Long Beach harbor," Jack said. "There's a possibility a man sneaked onto the island and is at large at the resort."

Oh, crap.

That had to be Ben Oliver.

"Do you think they'll find him?" I asked.

Jeez, I really hope they won't find him—considering that he's upstairs in my room right now.

Jack shook his head. "Resort security personnel aren't going to challenge their guests and ask for identification. If he makes a mistake, they'll catch him."

"Seems doubtful somebody would sneak onto the resort to steal the Heart of Amour," I said.

"I'm not taking any chances," Jack said. "You never know in this sort of situation. He could be a criminal, or just some nut case."

It hit me then that, really, I didn't know Ben all that well.

Jeez, I hope he's not in my room trying on my bras or something.

"Will you come to the shoot with me and keep an eye out for strangers?"

Wow, I was working a covert op with Jack. Cool.

"Sure," I said.

Joy squeezed between us.

"We have a problem," she said.

We? I don't think so.

"Yasmin has changed her mind about the location of the photo shoot," Joy said.

This hardly seemed like a problem to me.

"So we'll move it," I said.

"She found a new location a few days ago that she liked," Joy said.

Somehow, I knew it couldn't be that simple.

"But now she can't remember where it was," Joy said.

Visions of search parties combing the island and helicopters flying a grid pattern over the resort flashed in my head.

There had to be an easier way, and I thought I knew what it was.

I hurried over to where my friends were chatting with some of the other party guests.

"Do you have your resort brochure?" I asked Sandy.

I figured she did, since she'd been our unofficial tour guide since we arrived and hadn't been without it.

"Sure," she said, and pulled it from her pocket.

It was wrinkled, folded, and dog-eared, but it would do. I took it with me to the spot where Yasmin was huddled with the photographer.

"Haley, I'm so glad you're here," Yasmin wailed when I walked up. "You won't believe where they want to photograph me. At the beach, Haley, the beach."

I just looked at her.

"The beach is so *this morning*," Yasmin declared, with a truly unattractive pout. "What is Tate going to think? What is Tate's family going to think? How can I have Tate pose for photos at the beach? He won't like this. The beach? I mean, seriously, the *beach?*"

"You found another place you liked, right?" I asked, trying to move things along.

"I can't remember what it's called!" Yasmin sniffed hard and big tears pooled in her eyes. "How does anyone expect me to remember the name of every place on this island? I can't. I can't do it!"

I opened the resort brochure.

"Was it the sun porch? The morning room? The trophy room?" I asked, reading from the list of the property's amenities.

"No, none of that sounds right," Yasmin said.

"The organ chamber? The billiard room? The card room?" I asked. "How about the tap room?"

The tap room sounded great to me—it would certainly help everyone get through the shoot easier.

"No," Yasmin said, shaking her head.

I went back to the brochure. "The rotunda entrance hall? The stair hall? The great banquet hall—"

"That's it," Yasmin said, and gasped. "The one with the stairs. That's it. That's the one."

"The stair hall with the flying circular stairway?" I asked, showing her the picture.

"Yes, yes, that's it," Yasmin said. "The stair hall will be perfect. I'll look fabulous in the photos, don't you think?"

I had no idea what the stair hall was, so what could I say but, "Sure."

"Tate is going to be so happy." Yasmin clapped her hands. "Oh, Haley. Thank you. You've saved the day for me again—and I won't forget everything you've done."

"No, really, it's fine. Forget me," I said. *"Please."*

She didn't hear me.

While Yasmin, Joy, Jack, and the photographer discussed the new shooting location, I took the resort brochure back to Sandy. She was still talking with Marcie, Bella, and some of the other party guests.

"Do you need this one, too?" Sandy asked, holding out another brochure.

"No, the problem is—"

I stopped, realizing that Sandy was offering me one I hadn't seen before.

"What is this?" I asked, taking it from her.

"It's the resort's art collection," she said. "Avery gave it to me before my art lesson with Colby, remember?"

The art catalogue had slick, glossy, color photographs and descriptions of each piece in the collection. I flipped through the pages, and my gaze instantly homed in on the photo of the two vases I'd seen on the high shelf in the library, the ones that were painted the same bright colors as the Sea Vixen beach tote I was dying to own.

Only these vases looked different. The handles weren't quite the same shape as I remembered, and the colors were a couple of shades lighter.

Huh. That was weird.

"Haley, we've got a few details to work out for a new shoot location," Joy said, appearing next to me. "Yasmin is going to change her outfit while we go to the stair hall and set up. I'll have the florist, set dresser, and stylist meet us there. The hair and makeup people will come with Yasmin after she changes clothes and will be on standby."

It sounded as if Joy had everything handled—which suited me, since I hadn't wanted to be involved in the first place.

Jack and his partner were discussing transporting the pendant, Joy was on her phone while typing on her iPad, and the photographer and his crew were talking about lighting. I didn't really have anything to add to any of those conversations—which was just as well, because I couldn't stop thinking about the vases. Sure, the color might have been a bit off in the photos, but the shape of the handles? No way.

"Haley?" Marcie jarred me back to reality. "I need to talk to you."

Something in her tone kind of scared me. I knew something bad had happened.

"It's all over the Internet," Marcie said, holding up her cell phone. "Another maid from the resort has gone missing."

"Who?" I asked, but I was afraid I already knew.

"Tabitha Donahue," Marcie said.

Oh, crap.

CHAPTER 24

I'd tossed and turned all night, worried about Tabitha. She'd gone missing yesterday afternoon, according to reports posted on the Internet. Of course, celebrity blogs and Web sites were having a field day with the story—the second maid to disappear from the Rowan Resort.

I hoped she wouldn't be the second maid to turn up dead.

In typical fashion, nobody at the resort was talking. Everyone we'd asked had given the same story—the search was continuing, no foul play was suspected, and the staff was cooperating with law enforcement.

I figured the resort's publicity department must be working around the clock these days.

"This is a cool room, huh?" Sandy said as we sat down to breakfast. "It's the Renaissance room."

"Looks more like Dracula's castle to me," Bella said.

I was with Bella on this one. The room was gloomy,

thanks to the dark wood paneling, the open-beam ceiling, flickering wall sconces, and the huge stone fireplace.

The ambience, such as it was, didn't help my mood. I was worried about Tabitha's disappearance, of course, but now it looked as if there was no way I could get out of attending Yasmin's wedding today. If any of her guests had decided that maybe it was safe to come after all, no way would they show up after learning about another employee's disappearance.

Still, I clung to the tiny thread of hope that somehow Tabitha would be located—alive and well—and that I could find out who'd murdered Jaslyn in time for Yasmin's guests to get to the resort this afternoon.

Yeah, okay, it was a very small possibility it could happen, but I was still holding on to it.

That's how much I didn't want to go to Yasmin's wedding.

"The stained glass windows were designed in Europe by a famous artist and constructed just for this house," Sandy said as she consulted the resort brochure and gestured around the room. "They all depict Vikings at their evening prayers."

"We're going to need a prayer or two to survive this vacation," Bella said.

"Nothing new to report," Marcie said, glancing at her phone. She'd kept us updated on the search for Tabitha since yesterday afternoon when the news had broken.

The waiter appeared at our table, poured coffee and juice, and left a basket of fresh muffins before taking our orders.

I grabbed a chocolate chip—in the hopes of lightening my mood, of course.

"I know we're all bummed about this thing with Tabitha," Marcie said, and selected a blueberry muffin from the basket. "But we need to do something fun today. We're on vacation, and this is a fabulous place. We owe it to ourselves to make the most of it."

Marcie was right—Marcie was almost always right about things. Still, none of us jumped in with a suggestion.

"Well," Sandy finally said, "the wedding is today. That will be fun."

Nobody said anything.

"I'll check the brochure," she said, and whipped it open again. "How about a hula lesson? Or we could learn to play the ukulele. There's badminton and croquet."

We all just looked at her.

"Okay, then what about a yoga class?" Sandy said. "A meditation group meets on the cliffs. We haven't done the wildlife tour."

"I could use some relaxation," Marcie said. "Maybe a quiet day on the beach?"

"Now you're talking," Bella said, helping herself to a muffin.

"Sounds good to me," I agreed. "Are you in, Sandy?"

She thought for a few seconds then said, "I think I'll schedule another art lesson."

"And see Sebastian while you're at it?" Marcie asked, smiling.

Sandy blushed. "Maybe."

The mention of Sebastian's name darkened my mood further. I was tempted to tell Sandy everything I knew about him, but this hardly seemed the time or the place. Besides, this day would be difficult enough for me to get through, thanks to Yasmin's wedding, without adding to my problems.

We had breakfast and I felt a little better—thanks mostly to the tray of pastries we ordered. Sandy left for Colby's art studio, and the rest of us headed through the hotel to get ready for our morning at the beach. Avery was coming down the stairs just as we started up.

"Haley, I'm glad I caught you," she said. "Could I speak with you for a moment?"

"Sure," I said, and told Bella and Marcie I'd catch up with them in a few minutes.

"Good news. Patricia told me the shop is expecting a large shipment of Sea Vixen beach totes today, and she is personally unpacking them and putting yours aside," Avery said, looking pleased with herself. "So don't become upset if you see more of them on our grounds, like yesterday."

Yesterday I'd used the somebody-bought-my-bag-again story as cover after Avery had seen me coming out of the hotel room where Tabitha was working, in violation of the resort's policy. Now, with Tabitha missing—and maybe dead—I didn't feel so great about insisting Tabitha talk to me, even if I'd managed to distract Avery and send her on that trumped-up mission to find out what happened to my Sea Vixen.

Then it hit me—maybe I hadn't done such a good job covering for Tabitha after all. Maybe Avery had gone back upstairs, into that room, seen Tabitha, and figured out that I'd been in there with her.

I got a weird feeling that morphed into anger.

For a while I'd wondered if Avery was responsible

for Jaslyn's death. She certainly had the motive, and could have easily found an opportunity. And now Tabitha had gone missing—just like Jaslyn—not long after I suspected Avery had discovered her violating the resort rules—just as Jaslyn had.

"Did you know that I was in that room yesterday talking to Tabitha?" I asked.

Avery drew back, a little confused, no doubt, by my question—or maybe it was the I-know-you-did-it tone in my voice.

"Of course," she said. "It's my job to know."

"And now she's missing? Just like Jaslyn?" I demanded.

Color drained from Avery's face. "You think that I had something to do with Jaslyn's death and Tabitha's disappearance?"

"Yes, actually, I do," I told her.

"No, of course not," Avery said.

She glanced around at the hotel guests moving past us, then walked to a quiet corner of the lobby. I followed.

"How can you even suggest something like that?" Avery asked.

She looked totally confused, which made me think she was, in fact, innocent. But I wasn't going to let up.

"Do you expect me to believe this is just some crazy coincidence?" I asked.

Avery drew in a long breath, then let it out slowly.

"Jaslyn was a difficult employee. I've told you that," Avery said.

"And she created a lot of problems for you," I said, "so you got rid of her."

"Yes, she created problems," Avery agreed. "But nothing that would cause me to murder her."

"She kept going into the library when she wasn't supposed to," I said. "I'm sure your supervisors were on your case about her all the time."

"Oh, Jaslyn and that library." Avery huffed. "Always with questions about the art pieces."

"Hang on a second," I said. "I thought Jaslyn was unhappy about the library not being cleaned properly."

"If only that had been the limit of her interference," Avery said, shaking her head. "She kept asking where the art came from, when it arrived, how long it had been here. She asked about the provenance of each piece. Really, it was none of her business."

"She was an art major," I said. "She was interested in the history."

"Which was fine," Avery said. "But it wasn't her concern, and it was disruptive. We have a highly qualified curator at the resort who oversees every aspect of the collection."

"Colby Rowan," I said.

"I told Jaslyn that Colby had all that information," Avery said, "and that if she had questions, she should speak with Colby."

We just stood there for a minute looking at each other. Finally Avery spoke.

"Do you still think I was involved in Jaslyn's murder?" she asked.

"No," I said.

"Or Tabitha's disappearance?" Avery asked.

"When was the last time you saw her?" I asked.

"As I told Walt Pemberton, I spoke with her in the

hallway about not allowing guests into the rooms of other guests," Avery said, and gave me a partial stink-eye.

"And after that?" I asked.

"I didn't see her again. Nobody saw her after she left the hotel when her shift ended," Avery said. "Now, if you'll excuse me, I have work to do."

She left, and I stood there thinking about what she'd told me, how it might connect with Jaslyn's murder and Tabitha's disappearance. Both of them seemed like nice, sweet college students. Hard to believe that something awful had befallen both of them.

If only I could piece together just what the heck the two of them had gotten involved with.

I thought back to what Tabitha had told me yesterday and, really, it wasn't much, just that Jaslyn was upset that Colby was leaving in a few weeks. The whole conversation had spooked Tabitha, and she'd made me swear I wouldn't tell anyone what she'd told me.

I got a yucky feeling.

Had that simple conversation with me somehow led to Tabitha's disappearance? I didn't see how, but maybe something else was going on.

I needed to talk to Colby

The beach that yesterday had been too *this morning* for the photo shoot made a perfect location for Yasmin and Tate-Tate-Tate's wedding ceremony. The guests sat in rows of white chairs facing the reverend, who stood under an arbor, and beyond were the blue waters of the Pacific. Everything was festooned with pink floral arrangements and scattered with pink rose petals. Tate-

Tate-Tate looked handsome in his black tuxedo, flanked by his groomsmen.

Luke was one of them. My heart skipped a beat when I saw him.

Guess he was telling the truth about being at the resort for a friend's wedding, which meant that he wasn't working undercover, as I'd suspected, and that he really had no inside info about Jaslyn's murder, as he'd claimed.

Luke had told me the truth—but I wasn't sure that changed the way I felt about him.

Jack Bishop and his security partner stood a discrete distance away—looking fabulous in their suits—keeping watch over the Heart of Amour pendant that would come down the aisle shortly with Yasmin's bouquet.

I was seated with Marcie, Bella, and Sandy near the back on the bride's side. The turnout had been good, though not the hundreds of guests Yasmin had probably wanted.

I sat a little taller in my chair and looked over the crowd.

Marcie leaned in and whispered, "Do you see him?"

Leave it to my BFF to know what I was doing.

Francine had told me that Ty—my former official boyfriend—would be here today, and Avery had mentioned that Ty had called the resort—I still didn't know what that was all about—causing her to assume he'd be here.

I shook my head. "I don't see him."

"You know he's late for everything," Marcie pointed out.

We shared an as-long-as-he-doesn't-show-up-with-a-date look, as only BFFs can.

The string quartet struck up "Here Comes the Bride,"

and two little flower girls in pink dresses, the ring bearer in a white suit, and the attendants came down the aisle, followed by Yasmin. Her dress was gorgeous.

Sandy sniffed. I glanced over and saw that Marcie and Bella were teary-eyed, too.

While getting married was way off my radar, I couldn't help but think about Ty and all the time we'd spent together, and where it might have led. I tried not to, but those thoughts kept popping into my head.

Part of me hoped he wouldn't show up today, but another part of me—

I'm not thinking about that now. I'm on vacation.

The ceremony was lovely, and Yasmin and Tate-Tate-Tate made a beautiful couple. They gazed into each other's eyes, totally in love, totally enamored with each other, totally lost in the moment. I decided that all the upset, headaches, and aggravation involved with putting together a wedding were worth it.

The reverend pronounced them husband and wife, they kissed, the string quartet struck up again, and the newly wedded couple walked back down the aisle arm in arm, followed by the families.

"The reception should be really awesome," Sandy said as we rose from our chairs. "It's in the grand banquet hall."

"I hope they've got some good food," Bella said.

"They'll be a while with the wedding photos," Marcie said. "Let's head over."

Some of the guests were already headed to the reception, so we walked along with them. Everybody was in a great mood, smiling and chatting about the ceremony.

I glanced back and saw that Jack was still shadowing Yasmin and her bouquet. Luke was talking with the other groomsmen.

No sign of Ty.

"We missed you at the beach this morning, Sandy," Marcie said. "Didn't we, Haley?"

I knew she was trying to distract me from thinking about Ty—best friends are great that way—which was, really, a good idea.

"Yeah," I said. "How was your art lesson?"

"No lesson," Sandy said. "Colby wasn't available."

"Maybe you can try again later today," Marcie said.

"She's leaving," Sandy said.

"Where's she going?" Marcie asked.

"She can't be going on vacay," Bella declared. "Living at this place is a vacation."

Sandy shrugged. "She didn't say where she was going."

My senses jumped to high alert.

I'd heard that Colby was planning to leave the island in a few weeks, but she was leaving today? The day after Tabitha went missing?

A coincidence? Maybe. But I wasn't big on coincidences.

"I'm going to check with Joy and see if everything is set for the reception," I said.

It was the quickest excuse I could think of, and luckily no one questioned me.

"I'll catch up with you in the grand banquet hall," I promised.

Marcie, Bella, and Sandy waved as I hung back. When they disappeared into the gardens, I headed for Colby's bungalow. When I got there, the front door stood open a few inches.

Tabitha flashed in my head—and not in a good way. I knocked. "Hello? Colby?"

No answer.

I looked around but didn't see anyone on the paths nearby.

"Damn," I muttered. I must have missed her.

I knocked on the door once more—harder this time—and it swung open. I stepped inside.

The place looked like a cottage straight out of fairyland, with a miniature living room filled with pastel floral prints, pie-crust tables, and tufted footstools. White eyelet curtains covered the windows.

The tiny kitchenette had a can't-get-enough-of-the-seventies poppy orange refrigerator and stove, and earth-toned Corelle ware in glass-front cupboards. The avocado green countertops were cluttered with a museum-worthy coffeepot and toaster, and a wire utensil caddy held a few mismatched items.

I checked out the bedroom and found it's-so-old-it-must-be-antique furniture, and a twin-size canopy bed you'd imagine one of Cinderella's stepsisters slept in.

I peered into the closet and opened the drawers in the it-could-disintegrate-into-dust-at-any-moment bureau. They were empty.

The adjoining bathroom had those tiny octagonal tiles from the twenties, in a yellow and green checkerboard pattern, and a huge claw-footed tub. I saw no personal belongings.

Not exactly my taste in home décor, but I guess Colby liked it. Maybe she felt like Sidney Rowan's little princess in here. I was sure all the other bungalows had been upgraded for guests' use.

Everything in here was old and the place smelled

kind of musty, but I didn't see signs of a struggle or any indication that a crime had been committed here. Still, I couldn't get Tabitha out of my head.

A second bedroom was off the kitchen. I walked inside and saw that it was Colby's art studio. It was crowded with easels, one of those pottery wheels, a workbench, stacks of bare canvases, tubes of paint and boxes of brushes, and a jumble of every other imaginable art supply covering every flat space in the room. It smelled like paint and turpentine.

Colby sure as heck wouldn't go off and leave all this stuff behind. Maybe I hadn't missed her, after all.

Or maybe I had, I realized, since with the Rowan billions Colby could easily replace everything here.

Jaslyn popped into my head, and I pictured her coming to Colby's cottage after her shift, sitting in the living room, or maybe coming into the studio to discuss the world of art. She must have been thrilled thinking Colby would introduce her to gallery people and famous artists.

I didn't know if Colby had already left the island, but I had to find out. Maybe I could catch her at the helipad and ask what—if anything—she knew about Tabitha's disappearance.

I headed out of the room, and a flash of familiar colors caught my eye. On the workbench partially hidden under a drop cloth, I spotted the bright blue, orange, yellow, and greens of a Sea Vixen tote.

My heart jumped.

I *knew* she owned one. She'd lied about it—and this proved it.

I lifted the drop cloth and—hang on a second. This wasn't a Sea Vixen beach tote. It was a vase.

It was painted the same colors as the Sea Vixen and had handles on both sides, just like the one I'd seen pictured in the resort's art catalog and displayed on the top shelf in the library. But on this vase, both of the handles were cracked.

I threw back the drop cloth and—oh my God—three more vases. One was missing a handle, and the other two were chipped.

What the heck was going on? It looked as if Colby was attempting to re-create a priceless work of art in the Rowan collection. But why?

For a second it flashed in my head that these had been made by students in one of her art classes, but I remembered Sandy had told me that Colby only gave painting lessons, not ceramics, even though she owned a kiln.

Colby was an artist with an international reputation, supposedly. Why would she spend her time and talent making fake vases? They had no value, served no purpose. They were completely useless. What the heck could she possibly do with them? Nobody would want a copy of a—

Then it hit me.

Oh my God, could Colby have been making duplicates so she could sell off the original pieces?

But why would she involve herself with that kind of scheme when she was heiress to the Rowan billions?

I didn't know the answer—but it was the only thing that made sense.

The vases I'd seen in the library had looked a little sloppy compared to the ones pictured in the art catalog because they were phony, I realized. Colby, after numerous attempts, obviously, had created similar vases, switched them with the originals, and sold the genuine art.

Oh my God. She must have been handing them off to the guy I'd seen at the boat—her accomplice aboard the *Unexpected Opportunity*—when I'd spotted her carrying the Sea Vixen tote. That's why she'd denied the whole thing when I'd asked her about it.

Then something else hit me. Could this have been a one-time deal? Was it possible that other works of art from the Rowan collection had been copied by Colby and sold?

I knew how I could find out.

I pulled my cell phone from my pocket and called Luke.

"You're saving a dance for me, aren't you?" he asked.

I heard music playing in the background and knew he was at the reception.

"I need some info, right away," I said.

Luke must have picked up on the urgency in my voice because, after a few seconds, I heard the music fade and knew he'd left the reception.

"What's up, Haley?" he asked. "Are you okay?"

"The FBI has an art crime division, doesn't it?" I asked, and went on before he could respond. "I need you to find out if pieces of the Rowan art collection have turned up for sale anywhere in the world."

"Haley, what's this all about?" Luke asked. "Where are you?"

"Just make the call," I said, and hung up.

I stood there for a few seconds and something else hit me—something awful. I phoned Shuman.

"You need to stop Colby from leaving the island," I said, before he could say anything.

"What?" he asked. "Say again."

We didn't have a great connection. It sounded as if Shuman was at the beach and the wind was muffling our words.

"Go to the helipad," I said, louder this time. "Don't let Colby leave."

"What's wrong?" he asked.

"She murdered Jaslyn Gordon," I said.

"What?"

"Colby murdered—"

A totally creepy feeling swept over me. I turned and saw Colby standing in the doorway.

CHAPTER 25

"Well, aren't you the clever one," Colby said.
        I didn't feel so clever at the moment, only a little scared.

Colby stood in the doorway, blocking my escape. Both hands were behind her back. I couldn't see what she was holding, but I had a feeling it wasn't something that would benefit *me*.

"So, it's true?" I asked. "You murdered Jaslyn?"

"It was a shame, really. She was such a bright girl." Colby's expression darkened. "Too bright for her own good."

"Jaslyn was assigned to clean the library. She realized the artworks on display were fakes," I said.

Tabitha had told me that Jaslyn was upset about something she'd seen in the library and intended to speak to upper management about it. She'd questioned Avery about the provenance of the pieces in the collection and had been told, pretty much, to mind her own business because Colby was the resort collection's curator, the expert, and she was handling things.

"Jaslyn reported the fake vases to you," I said. "But you already knew about them, didn't you?"

If Jaslyn had told Avery exactly what she suspected, I'm sure Avery would have handled it differently. Instead, Avery had unknowingly sent Jaslyn to her death.

"The poor girl. So upset. So sure she'd stumbled upon the greatest art theft since Boston's Isabella Stewart Gardner heist." A sly smile crept over Colby's face. "And she was right."

I gestured to the damaged vases on the worktable.

"So these weren't the only pieces you made here in your studio, then substituted for the genuine ones," I said.

"Oh, heavens, no," Colby said. She smiled, pleased with herself. "This little project of mine has been rolling along quite nicely for some time now."

"The man I saw you with at the boat dock is your accomplice," I said. "You pass the genuine pieces to him, and he sells them. You must really trust him."

"He's an old friend," Colby said. "Very well connected in the international art market."

I figured he was the guy who'd been on the lam since Colby and the rest of her robbery gang had been captured, the one Shuman had come to the island to look for.

"Did you have other help here on the island?" I asked.

Colby dismissed the thought with a toss of her head. "Why on earth would I need help from anyone at this dreadful place?"

So much for my idea that Gabe Braxton was involved.

"Did Jaslyn suspect what you were doing?" I asked.

"Good gracious, no," Colby said, and rolled her eyes.

I figured that meant Jaslyn's brother hadn't been involved, either.

"Jaslyn had no idea I was behind it," Colby said. "I acted quite surprised when she told me, of course. Really, I gave a memorable performance."

Something told me she was really good at that sort of performance; she'd probably been pulling them off all her life.

"Her brilliant plan was for the two of us to report the whole thing to Walt Pemberton," Colby said. Her eyes lit up. "Another inspired performance on my part was necessary. It came to me in a snap. I convinced Jaslyn that, as chief of security, Walt was in on the thefts."

"And she believed you?" I asked.

"Why wouldn't she?" Colby said. "I told her to spend the night here in my bungalow, and the following day we would secretly take the supply boat to the mainland and call the authorities."

That explained why the search teams hadn't been able to find Jaslyn when they'd initially combed the island. She'd been in Colby's bungalow.

"Jaslyn went along with that?" I asked.

"Poor little thing was frightened," Colby said. "She didn't know who else to trust."

"So she trusted you," I said.

A really ugly image filled my head: Colby leading Jaslyn to the docks via the island's most remote beach—

her trumped-up excuse to avoid being seen by resort security, no doubt—then smashing Jaslyn over the head
with a rock.

I didn't like that picture. I pushed it out.

"You took Jaslyn's driver's license and cell phone up
to the cliffs to try to make her disappearance look like
a suicide," I realized.

"It was worth a try," Colby said with a shrug.

"How many pieces of the collection have you sold?"
I asked.

I didn't really care, but I wanted to keep her talking.

"Almost all of them," she said. Her expression
soured. "And I would have gotten every one of them if
it hadn't been for that other girl."

Tabitha flashed in my head. Oh my God, had she
suffered the same fate as Jaslyn at Colby's hand?

"What about Tabitha?" I asked.

"Suddenly disappearing the way she did created a
problem." Colby huffed irritably. "More media attention, more security personnel on the island, more people asking questions."

"You had to change your plans," I said.

"I did," Colby said.

I really hoped that meant Tabitha was alive and well.
But where? Did this fairyland cottage have a dungeon
beneath it where she was imprisoned?

"What happened to Tabitha?" I asked.

Colby lapsed into thought, as if she was considering
making yet another change in her plan, taking care of
one last problem before leaving.

I had a sick feeling that it was me.

No way would Colby have been so forthcoming if

she intended to let me live to share the info with law enforcement.

Colby snapped back to reality and said, "Now you know everything, which means I can't let you leave."

I remembered that Shuman had told me two innocent people had been killed during the holdups in L.A. and that Colby had been implicated.

Not a great feeling.

She drew her arm from behind her back, and I saw a big knife clinched in her hand, probably one from the utensil caddie I'd seen on the kitchen counter.

Oh, crap.

The studio was cluttered with art supplies, leaving only a narrow path to the door, which Colby was blocking. Not much room to maneuver. The only window was fronted by the workbench. No way could I scramble out quickly.

This seemed like a really good moment to stall for time.

"I don't know everything," I insisted. "I don't know why you did this. You're Sidney Rowan's daughter. You have billions of dollars. You live in a luxury resort—"

"Where I'm a prisoner!" Colby shrieked. "I'm held captive by my own father!"

She transformed before my eyes. No way did she look like a princess living in a fairyland cottage, or an heiress to one of the world's largest fortunes. Now she looked like a hardened criminal who'd done prison time, murdered an innocent college student—maybe two— and would think nothing of murdering again.

Colby's eyes narrowed. She took a step toward me.

I backed up a step.

"Look where he makes me live!" she screamed, gesturing wildly with the knife.

I'd sent Shuman to the island helipad.

"Here! In this tiny, wretched shack," Colby said.

I hadn't told Luke where I was.

"Where I'm forced to kowtow to pampered, egotistical nobodies so they can play at creating art," Colby said.

I hadn't told anyone where I was going.

Colby took another step toward me. I backed up again and bumped into the workbench.

If Shuman got to the helipad and saw Colby wasn't there, would he come to her bungalow?

Jeez, I really hope he comes to her bungalow.

"Where I'm watched by security forces every minute of every day." Colby's breath quickened. "That supposed loving father of mine doesn't think I know—but I know. That sneaky little Sebastian Lane isn't the first person he's sent to spy on me."

So that was the confidential job Sebastian had gotten here at the resort? Working for Sidney Rowan himself? To keep tabs on his daughter?

"The great Sidney wants everyone to believe how loving he is," Colby said. "But it's a lie. It's all a show he puts on for the world. He never cared about me! Never cared about what happened to me! He could have used his influence to keep me out of prison—but he didn't! He insisted it would teach me a lesson!"

Her face was flushed, and her eyes were wide. Each word she spoke sounded more and more hysterical.

"But you showed him," I said, hoping it would calm her down. "You sold most of his art collection."

"I had to," Colby declared, coming closer. "He cut me off completely after I was released. Forced me to live as a prisoner on this island. I needed money, and selling off his collection was the only way I could get it—the only way I could escape before he forgot I existed and left me marooned here forever."

Okay, now she sounded as if she'd lost her mind completely. I took a step to the side, thinking maybe I could push past her and dash out of the room.

"Why would your dad do that?" I asked, hoping to cover for my shift toward the door.

"He's getting married—for the seventh time," Colby said. "It's supposed to be a huge secret. But I found out about it. It's been in the works for months."

"The ceremony will be here at the resort," I said, and realized this must be the special event coming up in a few weeks that Joy was planning for, and the reason Sebastian's job would end at the same time.

Sidney Rowan had probably put Sebastian in place to keep an eye on Colby and report on any of her plans to disrupt the ceremony—not that I blamed him, of course. Sebastian probably wasn't the only undercover security personnel given the task.

Yet Colby had managed to outsmart them all. On the surface, she seemed like a totally reformed, artistic, gentle soul, so it was no wonder security personnel hadn't been watching her all that closely when she'd been selling off the art collection under the guise of shipping her own creations to buyers and galleries.

"Another wife to shower with attention," Colby said. "Another wife who'll be just the excuse he needs to ignore his children—to ignore *me*."

If I'd been in a more generous mood, I might have felt sorry for her that she'd been ignored and hurt by her father all her life. But I couldn't bring myself to muster any sympathy, not after what she'd done—and what, I felt sure, she still intended to do.

Colby lunged at me with the knife. I jumped sideways.

Where the heck was my hot FBI agent?

She swiped at me, the blade barely missing my shoulder.

Why hadn't LAPD's finest figured out what was going on?

Colby swung the knife upward. I jerked back and fell against the worktable.

Why was Jack Bishop guarding Yasmin's stupid necklace when I was about to get knifed to death?

At least Ben might get a Pulitzer Prize–winning story out of it.

I picked up a canvas and swung it at Colby, striking her on the arm. The knife flew out of her hand and clattered to the floor between us. She made a move for it but grabbed a drop cloth instead and heaved it at me. I threw out both hands and batted it away just as Colby bolted from the studio.

I raced after her, hot on her heels as she ran through the living room and out the front door. I knew she was headed for the helipad. No way was I letting her get there.

Colby disappeared around the corner of the bungalow. I followed, then jerked to a stop as two men appeared out of nowhere and grabbed Colby.

Oh my God, it was Luke and Shuman.

Another man stepped forward. It took me a second to realize it was Walt Pemberton.

Colby screamed and fought as they wrestled her to the ground and Walt snapped handcuffs on her.

Colby was still blabbing her confession—people on the mainland, no doubt, heard it—when several hot-looking guys from the resort security team showed up to take her away.

"Make her tell you what she did with Tabitha," I insisted.

Walt Pemberton gave me triple-stink-eye, ignored what I'd said, and kept talking to his security team.

I was in no mood.

"It's okay, Haley," Shuman said, and moved to stand next to me.

Something about the way he said it made me believe everything really was okay.

Luke eased up beside me.

"We got word just a few minutes ago. Tabitha's fine. She's at her mom's place," he said. "She was frightened about everything that had gone on here, so she left without telling anyone."

"I was afraid something awful had happened to her," I said.

Shuman touched my shoulder. Nice. Some of the tension went out of me.

"Are you okay?" he asked.

"Do you need anything?" Luke asked.

It was really great standing between the two of them— I almost wished something was wrong with me.

"I'm okay. Just a little shaken up," I said. "So how did the two of you end up at Colby's bungalow?"

"I went to the helipad, but she wasn't there," Shuman said. "I called Pemberton, told him what was going down, and headed here."

"I ran into the two of them," Luke said. "You were right, Haley. Pieces from the Rowan art collection are suspected of being sold to private bidders in Europe and Asia. The Art Crime Theft division will be all over it now."

"I saw Colby's accomplice," I remembered. "He came to the island aboard the *Unexpected Opportunity*. I saw the two of them exchange a package at the dock."

"Awesome," Shuman said, and gave me a wink.

Pemberton ambled over. Colby and the security team had disappeared.

"Miss Randolph, I'd like you to come with me," he said. "There're a few loose ends I need to tie up."

"Are you up to it, Haley?" Luke asked.

"You've been through a lot," Shuman said.

How cool to have two totally fabulous men fussing over me. Still, I was really okay, plus I was anxious to tie up whatever loose ends he was talking about and be finished with this whole thing.

"You need to call LAPD with the new lead," I said to Shuman. I turned to Luke. "And you should get back to the reception."

Neither of them looked as if they wanted to leave— which was way hot, of course.

"I'll meet you both at the banquet hall," I promised.

"After you," Pemberton said, and gestured me ahead of him.

He was quiet as we walked back to the hotel, but I saw a little smile on his lips, like he knew something I didn't—and could barely contain his joy.

Wow, he must have been really pleased with me. What else could it be?

CHAPTER 26

Obviously, I was going to get a reward of some sort.
I mean, really, why wouldn't I? I'd solved Jaslyn's
murder, identified the accomplice in Shuman's cold
case, broken up an international art theft ring—and
solved a couple of other crimes Walt Pemberton didn't
even know about—all without a single mocha Frappuccino. Was that reward-worthy or what?

I was feeling pretty darn good about things as we
crossed the hotel lobby and went inside the security office.

No one was there. No balloons fell from the ceiling.
No confetti cannon fired. Huh. What kind of celebra-
tion was this?

Pemberton didn't sit down. He didn't invite me to
sit, either.

I got a weird feeling.

"Your resort pass was recovered," he said.

My weird feeling got weirder.

He handed me the card, then opened the door to another office. It was an interview room furnished with a metal desk and four really uncomfortabe-looking metal chairs. The lighting was harsh, the air warm. Slumped in one of the chairs was—oh my God, Ben Oliver.

His shoulders drooped, his eyes were dull. His elbows resting on the table seemed to be the only thing holding him up. He looked worn out and disheveled in the same khaki pants and blue polo shirt he'd had on for days.

"Ben, are you okay?" I asked.

"He's uninjured," Pemberton barked. "This man was found using your resort pass. Do you want to explain how that happened, Miss Randolph?"

Oh, crap.

"Mr. Oliver here is not a guest of the Rowan Resort," he went on. "He'll be sent back to the mainland where he'll be arrested and prosecuted to the fullest extent of the law."

Ben covered his face with his hands.

"Arrested and prosecuted? Seriously?" I demanded. "Why would you do that?"

"Because I don't like reporters sneaking around my resort, spying on guests, and sticking their noses into things that aren't their business," Pemberton said. "Nor do I like guests doing that, Miss Randolph."

I'm pretty sure he meant me.

But there was little he could do, except maybe ban me from the resort for life—which, after this vacation, would be okay with me.

Still, no way was I going to stand there and let Ben get arrested and prosecuted for anything.

Immediately, I switched to I'm-better-than-you mode.

"Then maybe you should pay closer attention to what's going on here," I said. "Ben is an investigative reporter and he's ready to break a story about theft at your resort, perpetrated by your own employee against the very guests who come here expecting world-class security."

"He already knows," Ben moaned.

Pemberton gave me a smug smile. "Oh, yes, we discovered the Celebrity Panty Raid site. It's shut down. Gone. Out of business."

Okay, so that hadn't worked out as I'd planned. I pushed on.

"Then Ben will report on the hidden passageways and secret door in the hotel," I told him, using my you-can't-top-this-one voice.

"Carpenter crews have already closed them off. Walls have been painted and papered. There's absolutely no sign they ever existed, so no proof for a news story," Pemberton said. "Besides, Sidney Rowan owns, or influences, almost every media outlet in the country. I can guarantee the story will never see the light of day."

Damn. I hadn't thought of that. Still, I kept going.

"Sidney Rowan can't squash a story that's public record," I insisted. "Ben will cover the case against Sebastian Lane, the mastermind behind the whole scheme. The press will be all over it. Ben will make sure of it."

Pemberton shook his head. "Sebastian isn't being prosecuted. Actually, Mr. Rowan was impressed with his resourcefulness and innovative thinking. So impressed, in fact, that he's paying Sebastian's way through college and has already offered him a job after graduation."

Ben collapsed onto the table.

Oh my God, Pemberton was determined to destroy Ben's story, which would destroy Ben's career. I couldn't let that happen. I had to do something.

Jeez, a mocha Frappuccino sure would come in handy right about now for a brain boost.

Then it hit me.

"Fine," I said. "Go ahead and arrest him."

Pemberton's I'm-winning smile dimmed.

Ben banged his head against the table.

"Arrest him. Prosecute him. Bring out a battalion of lawyers," I said, waving my hand. "It's just the proof Ben will need to confirm that he succeeded in compromising the security of what is supposed to be the world's most carefully guarded vacation resort."

Pemberton stopped smiling.

Ben lifted his head.

"Every morning talk show and every celebrity TV show will be clamoring to have him on," I said. "Web sites, bloggers, newspapers, tabloids, magazines will carry the story of how Ben stowed away on your own supply boat, then sneaked onto the resort without even raising an eyebrow from security personnel and lived out in the open for days until your team stumbled over him for his unauthorized use of a resort pass."

Pemberton's expression soured.

Ben sat up straight in his chair.

"Yeah," he said. "Yeah, I did that."

"And when those reporters ask Ben why he came here in the first place, what do you think he'll tell them?" I asked.

"Everything!" Ben sprang to his feet. "I'll tell them about the secret entrances into the rooms, the hidden passageways that were never blocked off, and Celebrity Panty Raid."

"Everyone will believe him, and the resort will be buried under an avalanche of lawsuits from guests," I said. "And you'll be lucky to get a job as a Walmart greeter."

"All right!" Pemberton shouted.

He gave Ben and me serious quadruple stink-eye and fumed for a few minutes more, then said, "All right. Fine. No prosecution."

Ben smiled and headed for the door, but I wasn't ready to give up.

"What about my friend's lucky panties?" I said. "She wants them back. They better not have been sold."

"They weren't," Pemberton said. "I'll see to it they're returned immediately."

"And she should be compensated for the distress she suffered," I said. "Sebastian had a bid for ten grand for them. I think that should cover it."

Pemberton huffed. "I'll take care of it."

"Let's get out of here, Haley," Ben said.

I still wasn't ready to leave.

"Ben needs a job," I said.

Ben froze.

Pemberton's eyes narrowed and I'm pretty sure he was wishing I'd drop dead.

"If Mr. Rowan liked Sebastian's resourcefulness and innovation, I'm sure he'll appreciate the same in Ben," I said. "He needs a job as a reporter at Southern California's biggest newspaper."

"I'll talk to him about it," Pemberton grumbled.

I gave him my own version of mad-dog-stink-eye.

"I'll make it happen," he declared.

"Good," I said. "I think we're done here."

I put my nose in the air and left the interview room. Ben hurried out behind me.

"That was really cool," Ben said when we reached the hallway outside the security office.

"It was pretty darn cool, wasn't it?" I said, smiling.

I love being me.

We stopped and just looked at each other for a few seconds.

"I'd better get off this island before Pemberton changes his mind," Ben finally said.

"Don't go yet. You should enjoy some of your time here." I handed him the resort pass Pemberton had returned to me. "Go to the shop and get some new clothes."

Ben shook his head. "No, I can't do that."

"Look, after the miracle I just pulled off for you, don't you think I deserve to see you dressed in something decent?" I asked.

He grinned. "Yes, you definitely do. And I'll pay you back for the clothes, I swear."

"Meet me at the wedding reception at the grand banquet hall," I said, then added, "and don't argue with me about it."

Ben raised both hands in surrender.

"I'll be there soon," he said, and headed down the hallway toward the shops.

I hadn't solved Jaslyn's murder in time to avoid attending Yasmin's wedding, but at least I'd missed out on most of the reception. I decided some dancing, a glass of wine or two, and hanging out with my BFFs was just what I needed right now.

I took the stairs up to my room—no way could I show up at the reception unless I freshened up first—

and took my time reapplying my makeup and styling my hair. Standing in front of the mirror I was debating whether to change my dress when a knock sounded on my door. I opened it and saw Patricia smiling at me.

"The Sea Vixen tote bags just arrived," she announced. "I brought yours personally."

My spirits lifted. Wow, this was just what I needed to get me through the rest of my day.

"Great," I said, and noted she had a cart with her that was loaded with identical Rowan Resort gift bags. "You must have had lots of guests who wanted a Sea Vixen."

"It's a gorgeous bag," she said.

With great care—though falling balloons and a confetti cannon would have been nice—Patricia presented me with one of the gift bags. My heart soared as I moved the brilliant white tissue paper aside and pulled out my very own Sea Vixen, in all its polka dot glory.

It was gorgeous—absolutely fabulous—and it felt great to finally hold it in my arms. I'd had a heck of a time getting it, but I thought I should say something gracious, anyway.

"I really appreciate the resort giving me this," I said.

"It's the least we could do," she said.

"Thank you," I said, and stepped back, ready for some alone time with my new bag.

"Wait," Patricia said, and presented me with another bag. "This is for you, too."

Another gift? I couldn't imagine who would have sent it.

I took the bag, moved the tissue paper aside, and saw another Sea Vixen. Oh my God. Now I had two of them. A gift card stuck out of the top. I opened it and saw that it was from Ben.

I couldn't help smiling. He'd gone to the shop to get decent clothes for himself, yet he'd remembered I'd mentioned to him that I wanted the Sea Vixen. Yeah, okay, he'd charged it to my room, but since Holt's Department Store was footing the bill for my vacation, what did I care? I doubted Ben knew that, so I figured he'd attempt to repay me as soon as he started working that terrific job at Sidney Rowan's newspaper. I'd set him straight then. For now, this was totally cool.

"There's something else for you," Patricia said.

"Another gift?" I asked.

Wow, was this awesome or what?

I juggled the two Sea Vixen totes in their gift bags as I accepted the next one from Patricia. I opened it and—yikes! Another Sea Vixen. I fished out the card and saw that it was from Shuman.

"And another," Patricia said, and kept smiling.

I opened the next gift bag and—oh my God, yet another Sea Vixen. I dug out the card. This one was from Jack Bishop.

"And one more," Patricia said.

I couldn't believe it. She pressed another gift bag into my arms

Jeez, had I told absolutely *everybody* I knew that I wanted one of these totes?

I reached into the bag for the gift card, but Patricia said, "There's no card with this one. It was a phone order from someone who wished to remain anonymous."

A secret admirer had given me a Sea Vixen? Who

could it be? Every man I knew had already given me one.

Ty flashed in my head.

Oh my God, was this from Ty? It was just the sort of thing he'd do. But how would I ever know for sure?

"Enjoy your bags," Patricia said. She smiled and waved as she wheeled the cart away.

I ducked back into my room and placed the Sea Vixen tote bags on the bed. For a moment I considered lying down and rolling around with them—I mean, really, who wouldn't.

I was thrilled to have them but, jeez, five of the same bag?

Well, at least I knew what I could give everyone for Christmas this year.

I left my room and headed for the grand banquet hall. No way did I want to deal with Yasmin and all the wedding reception chaos after what I'd been through today. But hanging out with my friends for a while sounded perfect—along with a glass or two of wine.

Then it hit me.

While I adored my three BFFs—and a glass or two of wine, occasionally—what I really wanted was my life back. I was tired of being on vacation.

Yeah, vacations were great and I'd had some fun and relaxing times here at the resort, but what I craved now was my usual routine. My own apartment with my own bed to sleep in. My car. The drive-through at Starbucks and a mocha Frappuccino whenever I wanted it. I missed my friends at L.A. Affairs, and weird as it sounded, I kind of missed my crappy salesclerk job at Holt's.

The sameness of my life rated high on my own personal I-love-life meter right now. I wanted things the way they always were. I wanted to look into the coming weeks and months and know that nothing would change. Everything would be the same.

All I had to do was get through Yasmin's wedding reception. Tomorrow I could leave the resort and get back to my usual routine.

I went downstairs and followed the hallway to the grand banquet hall. The double doors stood open. Inside, hundreds of candles blazed gently illuminating the sparkling crystal and china and the zillions of pink flowers.

My life at home flashed in my head. First thing I'd do after leaving the Rowan Resort welcome center, of course, was head for the nearest Starbucks.

Most of the guests were seated at the tables, and a few were on the dance floor, even though the band wasn't playing.

Next, I'd hit the mall—and take my totally hot Sea Vixen tote with me, of course—and do a little shopping.

I skirted the edge of the tables and headed for the bar.

I'd look for a new dress, I decided, or maybe some capris and—

Something flew through the air at me. I grabbed it.

What the heck was going on?

A dozen people headed toward me and the whole place erupted in applause.

"You got it!" Yasmin squealed, pushing her way through the crowd. "I told you I'd throw it to you, and I did!"

Oh my God—I'd caught the bouquet.

Yasmin clapped her hands and hopped up and down. "This means you'll be the next to get married! You caught the bouquet with the Heart of Amour pendant! It's tradition! You'll be the next bride!"

Bella appeared next to me. "Yeah, but who's going to be the groom?"

She nodded to the crowd around us. Among the guests I spotted Shuman and Luke. Then I saw Ben and Jack. And then—oh my God, *oh my God*—Ty walked in.

Oh, crap.

Haley Randolph's 25th birthday is just around the corner, and the full-time fashionista knows it might be time to edge into being an "adult." All she has to do is ace the upcoming performance review for her hot L.A. event-planning gig, and she can finally quit her credit card-paying job at Holt's Department Store. She just has to make sure absolutely nothing goes wrong with the party she's planning for a Hollywood retirement home . . .

It really should be a fun bash—Hollywood Haven is home to a spunky group of retired actors, screenwriters, musicians, dancers, and other entertainers who have been in the biz for their whole lives. But when Haley finds Derrick Ellery, the home's assistant director, sprawled on his bloody office floor, she sees her hope of keeping her job—not to mention the dream of owning a Sassy, the season's hottest handbag—vanishing before her eyes.

Quietly finding the killer is Haley's only hope . . . but it turns out the list of suspects is longer than her last credit card statement. It seems Derrick made a lot of enemies and had somehow become wealthy far beyond what was possible with his salary—but how?

To make matters worse, Haley's kind-of-ex-boyfriend Ty is now a suspect in a different murder, and she just *knows* he couldn't have done it. Solving two murders while planning the perfect party—and always keeping her sights on a Sassy—won't be easy . . . especially now that there's more then one killer ready to select Haley's final outfit!

Please turn the page for an exciting sneak peek of the next Haley Randolph mystery SWAG BAGS AND SWINDLERS coming next month wherever print and e-books are sold!

CHAPTER 1

With age comes great wisdom.
Or was it power?

Or was it great responsibility that came with power?

But maybe that only applied to Spider-Man.

Anyway, I was staring head-on at birthday number twenty-five and was feeling pretty darn responsible. Truthfully, this wasn't a trait I'd ever noticed in myself—nor was it something my friends or family had commented on—but there it was.

I, Haley Randolph, with my tall-enough-to-model-but-I-don't five-foot-nine height, my *Vogue*-cover-worthy dark hair, and my too-bad-they-weren't-more-dominant beauty-queen genes, had fully embraced this new phase of my life because, really, it totally benefited me to do so in the best way possible.

This unexpected turn was unfolding courtesy of my job as an assistant event planner with L.A. Affairs. While the name of the company made it sound like a call girl service, it wasn't.

L.A. Affairs was an event-planning company that catered to the elite of Los Angeles, the stars of Hollywood, the well connected, the power players, and the industry insiders. I'd come aboard on the heels of a couple of other jobs that hadn't worked out as well as I'd have liked—long story.

If I do say so myself, things have gone great for me at L.A. Affairs. Well, okay, there've been a few unfortunate situations—none of which were my fault—but every job has an occasional hiccup, right?

The up side to all of this was that my probation period would come to an end in mere weeks, which meant I'd then be given a job performance review. Once I had the HR seal of approval, I would be deemed worthy of permanent, full-time employee status.

Since I'd done such a great job—except for a glitch or two here and there—I wasn't sweating it.

I pulled into the parking garage that adjoined the building that housed L.A. Affairs. It was a beautiful early November morning. Really, the only way to know the seasons changed in most of Southern California was to look at a calendar. Our weather was always mild, the breeze calm, the sun shining, and today was no exception.

I swung my Honda into a spot near the elevators. Our location was on the prestigious corner of Sepulveda and Ventura boulevards in Sherman Oaks, one of L.A.'s many upscale areas. Nearby were other high-rise office buildings, banks, apartment complexes, plus the terrific shops and restaurants across the street at the Galleria.

I grabbed my handbag—a classic black-and-white Chanel that perfectly complemented my black business suit—and took the elevator up to the third floor. The hallway was quiet as I headed for the entrance to L.A. Affairs, but that was because I was running a bit late this morning—which had absolutely nothing to do with any sort of responsibility issue that might impact my entire future.

Okay, maybe it did.

And, really, I was sweating my job performance review—big time. I had a lot—*a lot*—riding on it.

Permanent full-time status meant that I would be eligible for L.A. Affairs' benefit package, which included medical coverage—thus my new look-at-me-I'm-responsible mode. That, in turn, meant I could cancel the medical coverage I presently had through my crappy part-time salesclerk job at the seriously crappy Holt's Department Store. And beyond that, it meant *I could quit my job at Holt's*.

I did a mental backflip just thinking about it.

"Are you ready to party?" Mindy, our receptionist, shouted as I walked into the L.A. Affairs office.

Mindy was pushing fifty, a little on the full-figured side, with blond hair that resembled one of those glass balls people decorated their gardens with. I was unclear on how she'd gotten this job, and even more unclear on why she was allowed to keep it.

She giggled and fluttered her lashes. "They make me say that."

Nor was I clear on why L.A. Affairs insisted she chant that ridiculous slogan.

"I know," I said. "It's me. Haley."

"Oh, so it is," Mindy said, chuckling. "It's just so busy around here this morning."

No one was seated in the reception area. None of the lights on her telephone console were lit.

"Oh, have you heard?" Mindy asked, doing her own version of jazz hands. "Big news today—"

Her phone rang. Mindy recoiled, twisting her fingers together.

"Oh, would you just look?" she said, shaking her head. "Another call already today."

Mindy lifted the received and pushed a button on the telephone. "Are you ready to party . . . hello? Hello? Oh, dear." She punched another button. "Are you ready—? Hello?"

No way could I wait around for Mindy to answer the right line before I heard the big news of the day. I left, walking past the cube farm, the interview rooms, and turned down the hallway.

I'd taken the Holt's job about a year ago when I'd been desperate for some Christmas cash and my credit card balances had crept to troubling levels—plus Gucci had a fabulous new tote that I absolutely had to have. As things in life often do, Christmas had come and gone, my credit card balances had gone up and down like a bathroom scale before and after bathing suit season, and while I'd gotten myself that Gucci tote, it had soon after been relegated to the cool-a-month-ago-but-now-I-need-the-newest-style handbag repository in the closet of my second bedroom.

But I'd kept the job at Holt's, and not only because they provided medical coverage.

Anyway, a new, more responsible phase of life was

upon me. All I had to do was ace my upcoming job performance review. And in the meantime, I had to make sure that all the events I planned came off flawlessly, without a single hiccup or glitch—or, at least, no hiccup or glitch that L.A. Affairs found out about.

Even though I'd just arrived at work, there was, of course, no way I was going straight to my office. Instead, I went into the breakroom where several employees were lingering over coffee before starting the day.

For me, one of the best things about working for L.A. Affairs was that absolutely nothing mattered more than outward appearances. Everybody dressed in fabulous business suits and awesome shoes and carried designer handbags. L.A. Affairs had a reputation to uphold, and we employees were expected to project a certain image at all times—which I was totally on board with.

I spotted Kayla, one of my L.A. Affairs BFFs, helping herself to coffee. She was about my age, tall, curvy, with dark hair. She'd worked here longer than I had and knew the inside scoop on almost everything that went down.

"Big news," Kayla said as I walked up. "Suzie went into labor."

This came as no surprise. L.A. Affairs was staffed by women, dozens of women, most of us in our prime life-is-going-to-change-big-time years. That meant somebody was always going into labor, or announcing a pregnancy, or getting engaged, getting married, dating some hot guy, or dumping some jackass.

Still, if Kayla deemed today's news *big*, something was definitely going on.

She glanced over her shoulder and leaned in a little. "Suzie's baby wasn't due for another two weeks," she said. "That means her events are up for grabs."

Even though I had yet to pour my first cup of coffee, I knew where this was going—someplace great for *me*.

"I'm calling dibs," I said, "on everything."

Wow, this was just what I needed to prove to HR that I was worthy of permanent, full-time employee status. I could swoop in, take over Suzie's events, and save management the headache of trying to divide up the work. What better way to demonstrate my commitment to the company and cement my I'm-the-greatest rating on my job performance review so *I could quit my job at Holt's*.

"Dibs on everything?" Kayla asked.

"Heck yeah," I said.

"Well, okay, if you're sure," Kayla said. She lowered her voice. "You'd better jump on it. One of Suzie's parties is being eyed by you-know-who, if you get my meaning."

"Damn," I muttered.

I knew full well who you-know-who was. Vanessa Lord, senior planner and captain of the Raging Bitch squad.

When I'd first come on board at L.A. Affairs I'd been assigned to work under Vanessa as her assistant planner. We hadn't exactly hit it off—long story. Since then, I'd been handling my own events and she'd farmed out her events to several other assistants, thereby spreading her venom among many employees. No way would L.A Affairs get rid of her, though. Vanessa brought in the biggest clients—which made her the biggest bitch—so we were stuck with her.

"I'm going to talk to Priscilla right now," I said.

"Let me know how it goes," Kayla said, and left.

I filled my coffee cup, then dumped in a few sugar packets and topped it all off with a generous splash of French vanilla creamer. I was facing a make-it-or-break-it moment. I needed all the help I could get.

I left the breakroom, then circled back and grabbed a bag of M&M's from the snack cabinet, dumped the whole thing in my mouth, and headed out again.

Priscilla, the office manager, had an office down the hall. As I passed I saw that she was elbow deep in file folders—already. So what could I do but dash into my office, drop my handbag in my desk drawer, and hurry back?

"Hi, Priscilla," I said, as I paused in her doorway. "Can I get you another coffee? I'm on my third cup. Wow, this morning is flying by."

"I know what you mean," Priscilla said, looking up at me.

Priscilla was midthirties, tall, thin, with blond hair she wore in a blunt cut, and as office managers went, she was a good one.

She gestured to the mountain of file folders surrounding her and said, "I was behind before I walked in."

"Been there," I agreed, and we both laughed.

Immediately upon entering the workforce right out of high school—what I referred to as my parade of jeez-I-thought-that-would-have-worked-out-better jobs—I'd forged a credo, of sorts, the first tenet of which was my strict don't-volunteer-for-anything policy. I knew I was going against everything I believed in—and everything that had served me so well—by taking over Suzie's events, but I had my eye on a big prize: *I could quit my job at Holt's.*

I decided to come right to the point. I mean, jeez, I didn't have all day to stand around. Precious time was slipping past and I hadn't even updated my Facebook page or made lunch plans yet.

"I want to take over for Suzie," I said.

Priscilla sat back in her chair, stunned. "You what?"

"I want to take over for Suzie," I said again.

"Everything?" Priscilla asked.

"Yes."

"Everything?" she asked again as her eyes bugged out.

Wow, I'd really made her day.

"*All* of her duties?" Priscilla asked.

I'd totally overwhelmed her with my generous offer, obviously.

"Of course," I told her.

"Oh, Haley." Priscilla slumped onto her desk. "You're a lifesaver."

I smiled my yes-I-know-I'm-great smile, confident that now Priscilla knew I was great, too.

"Suzie's leaving two weeks early created a real problem for me," she said, and heaved a big sigh. "This is wonderful."

"I'm glad I can help," I told her, still smiling.

"No, really, it's fantastic." Priscilla plastered her palms over her eyes for a few seconds, then shook herself. "I didn't know how I was going to handle everything."

She's totally impressed with me now, I thought.

"I knew it would be a nightmare," Priscilla went on.

I'm her favorite employee—*ever*, no doubt, I told myself.

"You've saved the day," she said. "Thank you, Haley. Thank you so much."

My yes-I-know-I'm-great smile was starting to wilt, so I left and headed back to my office.

Yes, this was a fantastic way to start my day and my campaign to secure permanent, full-time employment status. And surely it wouldn't be difficult. I mean, really, how many events could Suzie—almost nine months pregnant—be handling?

My future flashed in front of my eyes. After I proved myself with the flawless and exceptional execution of not only my events but Suzie's, too, I'd be a shoe-in for permanent, full-time employee status.

And I could quit my job at Holt's.